PRAISE FOR

Dreamland Burning

★ "Latham presents a fast-paced historical novel brimming with **unsparing detail and unshakeable truths** about a shameful chapter in American history.... An **unflinching, superbly written story** about family, friendship, and integrity, set during one of America's deadliest race riots."
—*Kirkus Reviews*, starred review

★ "Latham **masterfully** weaves together the story of two well-off, mixed-race teenagers—Rowan, in the present, and Will, who lived in Tulsa in 1921—in this **fast-paced, tension-filled look at race, privilege, and violence in America**.... This **timely story** gives readers an unflinching look at the problem of racism, both past and present, while simultaneously offering the hope of overcoming that hatred." —*Booklist*, starred review

★ "**Enthralling**, expertly paced."
—*SLJ*, starred review

DREAMLAND BURNING

JENNIFER LATHAM

LITTLE, BROWN AND COMPANY
NEW YORK BOSTON

Little, Brown and Company
Hachette Book Group
1290 Avenue of the Americas, New York, NY 10104
Visit us at LBYR.com

Originally published in hardcover and ebook by Little, Brown and Company
in February 2017
First Trade Paperback Edition: February 2018

Little, Brown and Company is a division of Hachette Book Group, Inc.
The Little, Brown name and logo are trademarks of Hachette Book Group, Inc.

The publisher is not responsible for websites (or their content) that are not owned
by the publisher.

The Library of Congress has cataloged the hardcover edition as follows:
Names: Latham, Jennifer, author.
Title: Dreamland burning / by Jennifer Latham.
Description: First edition. | New York ; Boston : Little, Brown and Company,
2017. | Summary: "When Rowan finds a skeleton on her family's property,
investigating the brutal, century-old murder leads to painful discoveries about the
past. Alternating chapters tell the story of William, another teen grappling with
the racial firestorm leading up to the 1921 Tulsa race riot, providing some clues to
the mystery." —Provided by publisher.
Identifiers: LCCN 2015049682| ISBN 9780316384933 (hardcover) | ISBN
9780316384940 (ebook) | ISBN 9780316384926 (library edition ebook)
Subjects: | CYAC: Mystery and detective stories. | Murder—Fiction. | African
Americans—Fiction. | Race relations—Fiction. | Riots—Fiction. | Tulsa
(Okla.)—Race relations—Fiction.
Classification: LCC PZ7.L3483 Dre 2017 | DDC [Fic]—dc23
LC record available at https://lccn.loc.gov/2015049682

ISBNs: 978-0-316-38490-2 (pbk.), 978-0-316-38494-0 (ebook)

Printed in the United States of America

LSC-C

Printing 10, 2021

For Sean, Sophie, and Zoë

And for all the Tulsans whose stories
were never heard

Part I

By Repeated Blows the Oak is Felled.
(Multis Ictibus Dejicitur Quercus.)

Class of 1921 motto
Booker T. Washington High School

Rowan

Nobody walks in Tulsa. At least not to get anywhere. Oil built our houses, paved our streets, and turned us from a cow town stop on the Frisco Railroad into the heart of Route 66. My ninth-grade Oklahoma History teacher joked that around these parts, walking is sacrilege. Real Tulsans drive.

But today my car is totaled and I have an eleven-thirty appointment with the district attorney at the county courthouse. So I walked.

Mom and Dad wanted to come home and pick me up after their morning meetings. I convinced them the walk would help me clear my head, and it did. Especially when I got to the place where he died.

Honestly, I'd been a little worried that being there again would mess me up. So to keep myself calm, I imagined how things must have looked the night Will and

Joseph and Ruby tried to survive. There's this old map of Tulsa online, and the streets I walked along to get here are on it. In 1921, the Arkansas River cut them off to the south, just like it does today. But back then they ran north into trees and fields and farms. There aren't any farms now, only highways and concrete.

It was probably quieter a hundred years ago, but that doesn't necessarily mean better. I understand now that history only moves forward in a straight line when we learn from it. Otherwise it loops past the same mistakes over and over again.

That's why I'm here, wearing one of Mom's knee-length business skirts, sitting on a bench near the courthouse, waiting to tell the DA what happened. I want to stop just one of those loops. Because it's like Geneva says: The dead always have stories to tell. They just need the living to listen.

———

Everything started the first Monday of summer vacation. It was my only chance at a real day off, because the next morning I was supposed to start the internship Mom had arranged. It was the kind of thing that would look good on college applications and get me recommendation letters from people with MD after their names. I didn't especially want to be locked up in a sterilized research lab all summer, but I never bothered to look for something better. The way things stood, I had one day all my own to sleep late, eat Nutella with a spoon, and send James a thousand texts about nothing.

Only I didn't get to do any of that.

At 7 AM on the dot, a construction crew pulled into the driveway and started slamming truck doors and banging tools around. Hundred-year-old windows do a crap job of keeping things out, so even though the men spoke quietly, I could hear their murmurs and smell the smoke from their cigarettes.

After a while, the side gate squeaked open and the guys carried their tools to the servants' quarters behind our house. Just so you don't get the wrong idea, that sounds a lot more impressive than it is. I mean, yes, we have money, but no one in my family has had live-in servants since my great-great-grandparents. After they died, my great-uncle Chotch moved into the back house. Years earlier, when Chotch was two, he'd wandered out of the kitchen and fallen into the pool. By the time the gardener found him and got him breathing again, he was blue and brain-damaged. He'd lived, though, and was good at cutting hair. Dad says he gave free trims to all the workers at the oil company my great-great-grandfather founded, right up until the day he died. That was in 1959.

The only things living in the back house since then have been holiday decorations, old furniture, Uncle Chotch's Victrola, and termites. Then, last Christmas, Mom decided that even though there are three unused bedrooms in the main house, we needed a guest cottage, too.

Dad fought her on it, I think because he's a nice liberal white guy weirded out by the idea that the back house was built for black servants. If it had been up to him, he would have let it rot.

Mom was not okay with that.

Her great-grandfather had been the son of a maid, raised in the back house of a mansion two blocks over. He'd gone on to graduate first in his class from Morehouse College and become one of Tulsa's best-known black attorneys. Mom went to law school to carry on the family legal tradition and ended up *owning* a back house. For her, it mattered.

"I won't stand by and let a perfectly good building crumble to dust," she'd argued. There had been some closed-door negotiations between her and Dad after that, then a few days where they didn't talk to each other at all. In the end, Dad started referring to the back house as his "man cave," and while he shopped for gaming systems and a pool table, Mom interviewed contractors.

That was six months ago. The renovations started in May.

I lay there listening to the workmen's saw, figuring I had maybe three minutes before our grumpy neighbor, Mr. Metzidakis, started banging on the front door to complain about the noise.

Only he didn't have to.

The saw stopped on its own. The gate creaked open.

Equipment clunked against the truck bed. And the men talked so fast and low that I could only catch four words.

Huesos viejos. Policía. Asesinato.

Which, yes, I understood—thank you, Señora Markowitz and tres años de español. And which, yes, was enough to get me out of bed and over to the window in time to see their truck back out onto the street and drive away.

Something strange was going on, and I wanted to know what. So I snagged a pair of flip-flops and headed for the back house.

It was a disaster inside. A week before, the workmen had demolished the ceiling and pulled all the toxic asbestos insulation. After that, they'd hacked out big chunks of termite-tunneled plaster from the walls and ripped the old Formica countertops off the cabinets. A gritty layer of construction dust coated everything, including Uncle Chotch's old Victrola in the corner. *At least they covered it with plastic*, I thought, stepping around boxes of tile and grout on my way to the fresh-cut hole in the floor at the back of the room.

Only once I got there, I forgot about the Victrola completely and understood exactly what had sent the workmen running.

Huesos viejos. Policía. Asesinato.

Old bones.

Police.

Murder.

WILLIAM

I wasn't good when the trouble started. Wasn't particularly bad, either, but I had potential. See, Tulsa in 1921 was a town where boys like me roamed wild. Prohibition made Choctaw beer and corn whiskey more tempting than ever, and booze wasn't near the worst vice available.

My friend Cletus Hayes grew up in a house two doors down from mine. His father was a bank executive muckety-muck with a brand-new Cadillac automobile and friends on the city council. For that reason alone, Mama and Pop generally let Clete's knack for mischief slide. He and I got along fine eighty percent of the time, and kept each other's company accordingly.

One thing we always did agree on was that misbehaving was best done in pairs. Plenty of the roustabout gangs running Tulsa's streets would have taken us in, but I always figured the two of us were spoiled enough and maybe even smart enough to know the difference between hell-raising and causing real harm. Those gangs were chock-full of unemployed young men back from the Great War who'd come to Oklahoma looking for oilfield work down at the Glenn Pool strike. They'd seen bad things, done a few themselves, and liked showing off for locals. Problem was, the locals would try to one-up 'em, the roustabouts would take things a step further, and in the end, someone always spent the night in jail. That's why Clete and me kept to ourselves. We weren't angels, but we weren't hardened or hollow, either. Of course, even fair-to-middling boys like us veered off the righteous path from time to time. Some worse than others.

I was only seventeen, but had the shoulders and five-o'clock shadow of a full-grown man. More than one girl at Tulsa Central High School had her eye on me, and that's the truth. None of them stood a chance, though; Adeline Dobbs had stolen my heart way back in second grade, and the fact that she was a year older and the prettiest girl in school didn't dampen my hopes of winning her in the least.

She was a beauty, Addie was; slim and graceful as prairie grass, with black hair and eyes like a summer sky. I dreamed about that girl, about her clean smell and the peek of her lashes underneath her hat brim. And I loved her for her kindness, too. Boys followed her about like pups, but she always managed to deflect their affections without wounding their pride.

For years I loved her from afar, and spent no small amount of energy convincing myself it was only a matter of time before she started loving me back. Maybe that's why what happened at the Two-Knock Inn that cool March night tore me up so bad.

I was on my third glass of Choc and feeling fine when Addie arrived. Clete was there, too, dancing with a pretty, brown-skinned girl. For when it came to the fairer sex, a sweet smile and a pair of shapely legs were all it took to turn him colorblind. Not that it mattered at the Two-Knock. Jim Crow laws may have kept Negroes and whites separated in proper Tulsa establishments, but in juke joints and speakeasies out on the edge of town, folks didn't care about your skin color near so much as they did the contents of your wallet.

The Two-Knock was a rough place, though. A place where girls like Addie didn't belong. Even so, the sight of her coming through that door took my breath away. She was a vision: crimson dress, lips painted to match, eyes all wild and bright. Clete saw her, too, and made his way to my side after the song ended and poked me in the ribs, saying, "Lookee who just walked in!"

I didn't have breath enough to respond, so Clete jabbed me again. Said, "What're you waiting for, Will? Go talk to her!"

I wanted to. Lord, how I wanted to. But Addie was too good for the Two-Knock, and I couldn't quite reconcile myself with her being there.

When I didn't move, Clete rolled his eyes and socked me on the shoulder. Said, "This is it, dummy! If you don't go over and buy her a drink, you're the biggest jackass I know."

To which I replied that Addie didn't drink. And Clete snorted, "We're in a speakeasy, knucklehead. She didn't come for tea."

I shrugged. Signaled the bartender for another glass of Choc and slugged most of it down soon as it arrived. Then I looked back at Addie and asked Clete if he really thought I should go over.

"Hell yes!" he said.

So I puffed up my chest like the big dumb pigeon I was and got to my feet. Which was when the front door opened, and everything changed.

The man who walked in was tall and handsome, muscled all over, and browner than boot leather. Something about him shone. Drew your eyes like he was the one thing in the world worth looking at. *He* only had eyes for Addie, though, and she gave him a smile like sunrise when he sat down beside her.

I dropped back onto the barstool.

"You better chase him off," Clete said. But my throat was tight, and I only just managed to mumble, "Nothin' I can do."

"You kiddin' me?" he said. "That boy's out of line!"

I stayed quiet and stared at Addie's pale hand perched atop the table. She and the man were talking. Smiling.

Laughing. With every word, his fingers moved closer to hers.

Hate balled up inside me like a brass-knuckled fist. And when he slowly, slowly ran his fingertip across her skin, every foul emotion in the world churned deep down in the depths of my belly. Glancing sideways at a white woman was near enough to get Negroes lynched in Tulsa. Shot, even, in the middle of Main Street at noon, and with no more consequence than a wink and a nudge and a slap on the back. And God help me, that's exactly what I wanted for the man touching my Addie.

I wanted him dead.

Rowan

The hole in the floor was too small to expose the entire skeleton, but a human skull and shoulders stuck out from inside a roll of stiff fabric. The body had been dumped facedown, and the skull was turned sideways enough that I could see an eye socket and most of the nose hole. A hank of matted brownish hair clung to the bone. There were crusty patches of white gunk all over the cloth and the dirt around it.

The only dead person I'd seen before was my grandfather on Mom's side. I was nine when he died, and had been allowed to decide for myself if I wanted to look in his open casket.

I did. And I remember the pretty silver and black beard hairs curling on his cheeks, each perfect and distinct, as if someone had planted them there one by one. But the hairs underneath his chin were coated with pancake makeup three shades darker than the light brown of his folded hands. That bothered me. Other than a few hurried Christmas visits and an awkward trip to Braum's for a banana split, I hadn't spent much time with my grandfather. Still, I knew he would have hated for people to see him painted up like that, lying on white satin in a fancy funeral home where the makeup person either didn't know how to match a black man's skin or didn't care enough to try.

The skeleton bothered me even more, because someone had dumped it like garbage without even bothering to turn it faceup. That felt disrespectful. Wrong. And the longer I stared into the hole, the worse I felt. I mean, the bones down there weren't props like the ones in crime shows; they'd been alive once—part of a living, breathing human being who'd loved and been loved back. I wasn't grossed out or scared, and I definitely wasn't about to pass out like some stupid girl in a Victorian novel. But I couldn't breathe right. It felt like the full weight of everything the dead person in front of me *used* to be had settled on top of my chest. It was too real, too much to handle on my own. I needed help.

I needed James.

———

Sucking in a few lungfuls of fresh air outside helped clear my head. Squirrels chittered overhead in the big sycamore tree. Mist rose off the pool. And the whistle of a train crossing the tracks north of our neighborhood made things feel more normal.

I dropped into one of the pool chairs to start calling James. I say "start" because it was James's first official day of vacation, too. He'd been busing tables after school at an Italian place on Cherry Street for the last year, and the manager had finally bumped him up to their waitstaff for the summer. Lunch only, but that meant he'd be able to sleep past nine *and* score decent tips. If I was lucky, he'd have his phone on vibrate next to the bed. Whether or not he'd actually answer it was another matter altogether.

Seven tries later, he picked up.

"Jesus, Chase," he grumbled. "Why are you *call-ing* me?"

"Come over," I said. "Please."

James snuffled like he was rubbing the flat of his hand up and down over his face. "Why? And did you just say please?"

"You'll see when you get here," I said.

A rustle came over the speaker. James must have been using his shoulder to press the phone against his ear while he sat up.

"Rowan, tell me what's going on so I know how bad to freak out," he said. James never calls me by my first name.

I glanced at the back house and over to the fence separating our yard from Mr. Metzidakis's.

"I found something. Something..."

There was no way to describe what I'd seen that wouldn't make James think I was full of shit.

"Just something, okay? Will you come?"

"Fifteen minutes," he said, and hung up. Which was fine and not fine all at once, because even though I knew he'd get there as fast as he could, and even though the sound of his voice only made me *feel* like I wasn't alone, I kind of wished he would have stayed on the phone so I could pretend.

The thing about James is, he knows stuff about me that no one else does. It's been that way since last December, when he came over to keep me company during Chase Oil's annual employee Christmas party. I'd snagged a bottle of peppermint schnapps from the bartender's supplies, and the two of us had played drunk Monopoly in the basement.

The rules were simple: Buy a railroad, take a shot. Ditto for properties. Land in jail, take two. We weren't really drinkers, so it didn't take long for both of us to get completely wasted. Neither one of us remembers who won.

What I do remember is waking up the next morning with a tidal wave headache and a fuzzy recollection of lying next to James on the floor, staring up at the ceiling while he told me how he'd gotten sent to the principal in seventh grade for kissing a girl on the playground. "I've never wanted to kiss *anyone*, girls or boys," he'd said. "I just didn't want Dad to think I was broken."

And I remembered telling him about the birthday party I'd gone to in first grade. The one at the nicest country club in Tulsa, where all the mothers drank margaritas by the pool while we swam. I told him how beautiful Mom's dark skin had looked against the pale pink of her bathing suit, and how ashamed I'd felt for wishing she looked just a little bit more like all the other grown-ups there.

We never talked about those confessions afterwards because we never needed to. James and I realized we were soul mates that night, and soul mates are okay with all the bad shit hidden in each other's dark corners.

I think that's why I called him instead of Mom or Dad that morning. To them, I was still a little girl who needed protecting. To James, I was just me.

After ten minutes, I started listening for his car. Then a siren started up in the distance and my heart jumped into my mouth. *The construction guys must have called the police,* I thought. Because that's what you're supposed to do when you find a dead body.

I considered running back to my room and pretending like I'd never gotten up. Even if the cops pulled my phone records, there was no way they could prove I hadn't called James from bed.

Which was probably an overreaction. For one thing, the skeleton looked like it had been in our back house for a long, long time. Maybe since the place was built. And even though the whole setup had a distinct crime scene vibe, there was no way I could have been involved in something that happened before I even existed.

Then again, it wasn't like there was a shortage of news stories about bad cops assuming the worst when it came to brown-skinned kids like me. So on second thought, maybe it wasn't such an overreaction after all.

Either way, the siren was moving away. My heart settled back where it belonged. My shoulder blades pressed into the seat cushion. But my hands didn't unclench until the noise faded completely, and the urge to run didn't leave until Ethel had growled her way down the street out front and gone silent in our driveway.

WILLIAM

A bead of sweat rolled down my nose and dripped onto my forearm. I watched it shine in the glow from the Two-Knock's old-fashioned gaslights as Clete eyed the Negro sitting next to my Addie.

"Will," he said in a false whisper. "If you don't do nothin', then you're a yellow coward."

I drained the last of the Choc from my glass and asked him if he had my back. "Always," he said, with something flat and mean in his eyes that I mistook for loyalty. So here's what I did: I walked over to Addie's table and I said to that full-grown man, "You best get away from her, boy."

The man pushed back his chair and stood up, and even though our eyes met on the level, I knew straightaway I'd never best him in a fight. Addie watched, her own beautiful eyes big with worry. Then a funny look crossed her face and she said, "Aren't you Will, from school?"

"William," I said, affecting a deep voice that wasn't truly mine. "William Tillman."

"Well, William Tillman," her companion said. "I'm Clarence Banks. Would you care to join Miss Dobbs and me for a drink, or have you had enough already?"

I stood there swaying, trying to figure out if he was mocking me. In hindsight, it shouldn't have taken much figuring at all.

"I told you to get away from her, boy!" I near shouted. And Addie said in her kind, sweet voice, "William, Clarence and I are old childhood acquaintances, just here to catch up with one another. If you'll go back to your friend now, you and I can have lunch together at school next week. How does that sound?"

That's when the molasses in my brain cleared enough for me to realize Addie was trying to get rid of me. And I set to blubbering like a fool, saying, "He touched you! Don't let him do that, Addie. Don't let him touch you!"

At which point Clarence moved between me and the girl I loved and said, "Now, William, I know Miss Dobbs appreciates you looking out for her, but she's fine. Everything's fine. You go on back to the bar and have another drink, my treat. Miss Dobbs and I will take our leave, and we'll all finish out our respective evenings, nice and peaceful."

I checked to make sure Clete was behind me like he'd promised, but he was way back at the bar, watching the spectacle unfold like he didn't know me from

Adam. There was disappointment in his stare. Pity, too, as if I'd failed him and every other white boy in the world. It stung so bad that something inside me broke like rotted boards under a fat man's foot. And when I swung at Clarence Banks, it was with all the broke-hearted fury inside me.

He saw it coming, of course, for I was a poor fighter sober and a downright hopeless one drunk. Clarence caught my fist and pushed me away. I stumbled backwards, landing hard on the rough pine floorboards. Pickled as my brain was, I felt no pain when my hands caught my fall. But when I lifted the left one afterwards, it flopped sideways like a dead thing.

Addie paled. Clarence looked sick, as if all his shine and confidence had snapped right along with my bones. "I...I didn't mean to...," he stammered. Then Clete was beside me, saying, "You're gonna get it now, boy! Just you wait. You're gonna get it!" He motioned towards the people around us. "You all saw it! You saw him attack my friend!"

That's when the owner came out from behind the nickel bar, saying, "Now, son, let's just settle down and sort things out."

Clete shook his head, saying *nuh-uh* and looking around for support. Only nothing came back to him but stares. That's when his face went mean and ugly, and he said he'd show us all and ran out of the Two-Knock into the night.

The bartender turned to Clarence. "That was a fool thing you did, son. Best be on your way quick before that boy comes back with the law. I'll see that missy here gets home."

He was a big man, that bartender, and could have passed for black or white. Either way, he knew Clarence Banks was in trouble.

Clarence pulled himself tall and said something I didn't hear. Addie shook her head and put her hand on his arm and told him, "Clarence, please...you have to go." Something passed between them. Something I felt more than saw. Then it was over, and Clarence Banks walked out into the night.

After that, the bartender hoisted me up by the armpits and dragged me to a stool. "Let's see what we got here," he said, straightening my wrist. That's when the first of the physical pain hit, all hot and sharp, like someone pounding a railroad spike into me. I yelped. The bartender scratched his head.

"You got folks to tend to this?"

I nodded.

"Well then," he said. "Since it ain't your leg, you can walk home just fine. And listen close: you and your friend keep clear of my establishment from now on, understand?"

I must've nodded again, for he grunted, then told me to beat it. I wobbled across the room, trying to keep my feet. And as I pushed open the door, his voice found me once more, like a kick in the pants.

"And don't you tell no one where you been!"

———

The cold, dark air hit my hot cheeks like a tonic, busting through my muddleheadedness enough so I could steer myself homeward. I cradled my hand against my chest and took a few steps.

"Will! Will, wait!" Clete hollered from somewhere behind me. I turned, trying to find him in the scant moonlight. But when I finally managed to make sense out of the shadows, there were two figures coming at me instead of one. I closed my eyes, shook my head, and looked again to make sure the Choc wasn't making me see double.

Sure enough, there were two: Clete, and a policeman who grabbed my elbow when he got to me, saying, "Hold up there, fella. Your friend here tells me you've been attacked by a Negro."

He spied my wrist and grabbed it, and the sound of my yelp tumbled down the street.

"Can't see a thing out here," he grumbled. Then we were back inside the Two-Knock. Me, Clete, and the policeman.

The place was still as a tomb. Even though Prohibition was in full swing and drinking was every bit as illegal as thieving, most coppers would turn a blind eye to it so long as speakeasy owners kept free booze and cash bribes flowing their way. Still, every man and woman in the Two-Knock that night could've been arrested on the spot.

The cop looked at my wrist, tutted, and said, "I hear a colored boy assaulted this young man. That so?"

Not a soul in the room moved save for Clete, who was practically hopping up and down, saying, "Course it's true! It's like I told you—he went after Will here just 'cause Will told him he shouldn't be pawing all over a white girl!"

The cop's lips pulled back from his teeth like the notion of such a thing made him sick. "Which white girl might that be?" he asked, looking around.

"She . . . she left," mumbled a moon-faced boy no older than myself. And the cop stared him down so hard I thought that boy would crack. Then the cop said, "Ladies and gentlemen, I'm runnin' out of patience here. Where. Did. She. Go?"

Clete cleared his throat, and for half an awful second, I thought he might just be riled enough to give Addie up. Instead, he said, "I don't know about the girl, sir, but that Negro said his name was Clarence Banks. Will, here, was just trying to get him off of her, and that boy started cursing and going after him like a mad dog. Ain't that so, Will?"

My wrist hurt so bad I couldn't think straight. My head ached. I needed to throw up. And, God forgive me, I croaked out *yes*.

The policeman looked around, asking if anybody could corroborate Clete's account. And when a few white heads bobbed in the affirmative, he said, "What about it, Ed? Was the boy called Clarence Banks?"

The bartender's eyelid twitched. The cop shook his head sadly. Said, "You're a good Negro, Ed. Never missed a payment for all the protection I give you. But now that I think about it, last week's envelope felt a little light..."

Well, that big old bartender's jaw clamped tight as a vise, and one of the veins in his neck near popped through his skin as he took the cash box from behind the bar and handed over every last cent inside. The cop stuffed bills and coins into his pocket and said to me, "Young man, I suppose we'd best take you down to the station and get a statement before we telephone your folks."

I panicked at that, stammering how I was fine and could get myself home and there was no reason to phone anyone, no reason at all. That made the cop smirk so that I felt about two inches high, which, in retrospect, was an inch more than I deserved. "In that case," he said, "I'll just head on back to my patrol."

To which I mewled *yes sirs* and *thank yous* until the cop was near out the door. Then that fool Clete yanked off his cap and slapped it against his knee, shouting, "Wait a minute! Is that all you're gonna do? You gonna let that boy get away with attacking a white man? You just gonna leave?"

The cop's eyes narrowed, and he stalked back and

grabbed Clete by the collar and yanked him onto the tips of his toes, growling: "You oughtn't question how an officer of the law goes about his business, son."

Clete shrank inside his clothes. Even still, that boy was so stubborn and cussed that he squalled like a stuck pig, saying, "I just want him to pay for touching a white gal, is all!"

The cop let go of Clete's collar and watched him work to catch his balance. "We take care of our own in this town," he said. "Understand?" And his voice was so low-down and ugly that Clete finally hushed. Then the cop took his billy club from its belt loop and aimed it around the room in a slow circle. "You all remember that," he said. "The law around these parts takes care of its own." And he smacked the club against his palm and gave me and Clete a dead-eyed stare that chilled us to our toes.

Now, soon as the door closed behind the cop, the bartender told me and Clete to clear out before we got someone killed. And Clete, knowing then that the big man was a Negro, went off half cocked, spouting nonsense about him not having any right to tell us what to do. That's when I grabbed hold of Clete's arm with my good hand and steered him out, saying to the bartender how very sorry we were, and that we'd never trouble him or his establishment again.

But he turned his back before I finished, indicating in no uncertain terms that he'd had his fill of us. Which was fine, for my thoughts were already drifting towards the selfish matter of how I'd explain my wrist to my parents. It never did cross my narrow little mind that I should worry about Clarence Banks, or be bothered by the fact that I'd just unleashed the full force and fury of Tulsa's crooked police element on a Negro.

And an innocent one, to boot.

Rowan

Ethel is James's 1969 El Camino. She's old, moody, and so ugly she's beautiful. I love the sound her engine makes—the mean, sexy rumble that turns heads on warm spring nights when we drive past the stretch of outdoor restaurant patios along Brookside. Last year, before James told his dad he was asexual and his dad stopped looking him in the eye, the two of them had rebuilt Ethel from the wheels up. They were always doing stuff like that: taking fishing trips, driving to small towns in the Panhandle to drum together at Kiowa powwows and dances. Those days were long gone, but at least James still had Ethel. The nose-in-the-air types at our private school can trash-talk him all they want for being a scholarship student, but Ethel is and always will be completely badass.

That morning, he parked Ethel behind my Acura and

sauntered toward me calmly, like I hadn't just called him in a complete panic.

"Nice look," he said.

I was still wearing the bike shorts and Tulsa Roughnecks T-shirt I'd slept in. My breath was rank, and my hair was sticking out all over the place even though I'd pressed it the day before. Not that James had a lot of room to talk; his own hair was cut into a tight fade on the sides, but it was high on top, and so flattened and messy that I knew he hadn't stopped to comb it.

Which I appreciated, because James is more than slightly obsessive about his appearance. He's this six-foot-four, part-Kiowa, part-black guy with crazy broad shoulders, a Willy-Wonka-goes-to-Wall-Street wardrobe, and more skin care products in his bathroom than Mom and I have combined. In other words, it was a big deal for him to leave the house ungroomed. I gave him shit anyway, to distract myself from the situation and make things feel more normal.

"Nice hair."

His hand went halfway to his head and stopped.

"Uh-uh," he said. "Only one of us gets to be bitchy this early in the morning and I've got dibs. Now, tell me what's going on."

So much for normal.

"Come see what I found," I said.

"You gonna tell me what it is?"

I shook my head. "You'll see."

At the door to the back house, James whistled long and low over the mess. "They tore this place up!"

"Tim and Isis Chase never do anything half-assed," I said.

We stopped at the edge of the hole and stared down together. James talked first.

"Did you call the police?"

"No. I thought maybe the construction guys would do it. But it doesn't look like they did."

"You mean they just left?"

"Yeah."

James sighed, like he had a few thoughts on the matter. But after a pause, all he said was, "Who do you think it is?"

It was such a simple question, but somehow I knew the answer was going to be anything but. I got down on my knees to look closer. With my living, breathing best friend at my side, the existential awfulness of an abandoned dead person was a lot easier to take. Bones were just bones, after all. Unless they were something more.

I reached toward the tarp. "Haven't got a clue," I said. "Let's figure it out."

James grabbed my arm. "Don't *touch* it!"

"It's been dead a long time," I said, getting braver by the second. "I think I'm safe."

James nudged my hip with the toe of his oxford. "I know. But you're the murder mystery fangirl. Aren't you supposed to leave crime scenes intact for the police?"

"It's skeletonized," I said, showing off my fangirl vocab. "And it looks like it's been here forever. My guess is, anyone who might have been looking for this guy is dead, too."

"Well, it's still nasty, and you shouldn't touch it," he said, making a face.

"Yeah. You're probably right."

I yanked up a corner of the tarp. The top layer came loose with a *thrip*. Underneath was cleaner fabric that didn't give so easy. I worked my fingers into the ground by where the hip bone should have been, found a loose-ish edge, and squatted on my toes so I could put all my weight into pulling. It gave. I fell backwards, hitting the ground hard enough to raise a cloud of dust. Once James and I recovered from our coughing fits, we looked down at the exposed body together.

"I bet that's blood," I said, pointing to a heavy spatter of brown on the yellowed shirt that must have been white once.

James nodded. "It's on the pants, too." He shifted closer to the hole. "Wait... is that a gun?"

I saw the half-buried lump of dull metal he was talking about, got on my knees, and pulled it free of the hard-packed dirt.

"What's that?" he asked.

I set the pistol down on the intact floorboards. "Like you said, it's a gun."

"No." He pointed to a rusty patch on the barrel. "That."

It looked like there was something carved into the metal. And even though I knew better than to get my own DNA and fingerprints all over the thing, I hawked a glob of spit onto the rust and rubbed. It didn't do any good; neither one of us could make out the mark.

"Maybe it's the owner's name," James said.

"Or the gun's."

"You think?"

I'd been squinting and had to blink a few times to make my eyes focus normally. "Could be. Cowboys always name their rifles in old westerns, don't they?"

James shrugged and turned the gun over. The other side was covered in white gunk.

"I think that's lime," I said. "You know—to keep the body from smelling."

He scratched at it until a big flake fell off. There was no rust underneath, and no mistaking what we saw: eight notches, carved deep.

"Somebody was keeping count," I said.

James nodded. "You think it was the skeleton, or the person who dumped it here?"

"I'm not sure," I said. "But I'm guessing whoever killed this guy wasn't interested in bragging about it. They wanted him erased, like he never even existed."

"That's dark, Chase."

"Welcome to my morning."

Then I noticed thin cracks spiderwebbing out from the hank of matted hair on the back of the skull. I curled my fingers under its edge, scraping until the whole mess came off in my hand. The bone underneath was shattered.

"That's not from a bullet," James muttered. He reached down past the edge of the hole and came out holding a brick. One of its long edges was stained dark, covered with strands of something that looked suspiciously like hair. He held that edge over the crater in the skull. It fit perfectly along the main fracture line. Warm as the air around me had gotten, I shivered.

James set the brick down and reached in again. "There's something in his back pocket..."

The gate clicked outside.

James jerked back and scrambled to his feet. I dropped onto my stomach and had just gotten hold of the thing in the skeleton's pocket when James yanked me out by the waist. He kicked the gun and the brick back into the hole. I shoved a mildewed rectangle of leather between the waistband of my bike shorts and the skin of my back.

"Keep quiet," I whispered as a shadow crossed the yard. "I'll do the talking."

WILLIAM

Not a word passed between me and Clete as we made our way west, away from Tulsa's raggedy edge and into proper neighborhoods. Years prior, when Mama and Pop purchased the house where I grew up, our street sat on the lower boundary of town. Every residence there was spit-shine new at the time, but in the years that followed, bigger and grander homes went up further and further south, casting what Pop considered to be a long shadow over our respectable foursquare bungalow.

The newest bit of town had been dubbed "Maple Ridge." It was to be a silk-stocking district where hardscrabble oilmen could build mansions befitting their brand-new fortunes and set about convincing themselves they were every bit as cultured as the steel and railroad barons back east.

My father, a shopkeep of respectable but moderate

means, took each and every one of those mansions as a taunt. He set to convincing Mama we should have a Maple Ridge estate all our own, saying she deserved it, and needed something grand to ease the grief that had consumed her since influenza took my little sister, Nell, during the epidemic three years prior.

Mama, you see, was a full-blood Osage Indian, and as such had been allotted one headright—one equal share—of all profits earned from oil pumped out of tribal land. She'd also inherited her brother's headright after he died in the Great War, and her own mother's not long after that. Mama was a woman of substantial means.

A year earlier, and just ahead of the US government declaring that every Osage without a certificate of competency would need a white guardian to manage their money, Mama gave in to Pop's wheedling and purchased a parcel of farmland from a Muscogee Creek woman at the southern edge of Maple Ridge. They commissioned a fine three-story residence soon after, all red brick and columns, and more mansion than house. Then, when that fool-headed legislation passed in March of '21, Pop was appointed Mama's guardian, and Mama lost what little voice she'd had in the project to begin with. Construction continued apace, with Pop in charge.

All that's to say that while there were plans afoot for me and Mama and Pop to move later that year, the house where Clete dumped me off after the Two-Knock was the same one where I'd been birthed.

I tried my best to sneak in quiet. I truly did. But any hope I'd had of avoiding capture died soon as I bumped the umbrella stand in the hall with my bad hand. Hearing my howl of pain, Pop called me into the parlor, where he and Mama had been sitting. And I knew soon as I crossed the threshold that there was no way to hide the reek of Choc on my breath, or the ugly spectacle of my wrist.

Nothing I said could have helped my case, so I spoke as little as I dared, gritting my teeth against the pain while Mama looked sad and Pop paced the parlor floor.

The first thing Pop asked was who I'd been with, and if all I did with my free time was drink and get into heaven-knew-what kind of trouble. When I only shrugged, he said, "You'd best speak up now or you won't leave this house on a social call until you've left it for good."

So I mumbled, "Clete," and Pop glared at me and asked why *Clete* hadn't had the decency to walk me inside. To which I replied that he'd seen me to the porch but been too afraid to go further.

Pop paced and twisted the tips of his mustache for a long while, then asked me to tell him exactly what had happened. "I fell, is all," I replied. "I wanted to see what the fuss over Choctaw beer was about, and after I'd had a glassful I got dizzy and tripped."

Then he asked was it the first time I'd drunk alcohol, and I said *yes sir* and toed the flowers on Mama's oriental carpet. Pop didn't like that response, most likely because he knew it was a lie. So he said I should look him in the eye and say it again, and I never wavered once doing it.

Mama's chair creaked. Pop gazed out the front window and told her to have the doctor come set my wrist. Mama stood up and went to the telephone stand in the hall without a word.

"I know your mother gives you money," Pop said, staring out into the dark. "And I suppose it's a woman's prerogative to coddle her son. I'll not tolerate sloth and foolishness, though. Starting tomorrow, you'll work for me every weekday from the end of school until closing. All day Saturday, too. On Sundays you'll attend church with your mother in the morning and spend the afternoon on chores of her devising."

My stomach fell to somewhere below my knees as I felt my theretofore unappreciated freedom slipping away. But I held my tongue nonetheless.

"So long as you live under my roof," Pop went on, "you'll earn your keep."

I mumbled that I understood, and tried not to look too ashamed when Mama came back and told me to go wash the stink off myself before the doctor arrived. "You reek of alcohol and sin," she said. For she was a godly woman, though of the pragmatic sort. Then Pop dismissed me with a wave of his hand, saying, "This will never happen again, William." And it wasn't a question, either; he was telling me the way things were going to be.

I was nearly out of the room when Mama's voice stopped me short. And I swear that when I spun about to face her, the corner of her mouth twitched like she was hiding a smile. But the twitch disappeared like all my pride had done, and in its place came a weary sadness that made me feel lower than pond scum.

"Chew some parsley from the pot on the kitchen sill, William," she said. "I won't have the doctor smelling that poison on your breath."

Then I slunk away, arm pressed to my belly, bearing the burden of my punishment near as hard as the sting of Addie's disdain.

Rowan

W hat are you two doing back here?"

Mom stomped across the construction mess in four-inch snakeskin pumps.

"And where the hell is that damn crew?"

Now, just so you understand the dynamic here, I'll tell you a little bit about my mother. She's the kind of woman you want to stare at but don't quite dare—striking, elegant, with a close-clipped Afro. Her makeup is always perfect, her clothes fit just so. She's a public defender with a stubborn streak, and if you ask her, she'll tell you she's nobody's girl and nobody's fool. She is a goddamned lady.

Even so, the skeleton stopped her short.

"Oh my God."

She squatted down at the edge of the hole across from us, skirt *slishing* against her thighs. One shoe slipped off her heel and knocked against the floor.

"At what point were you planning on calling me?"

The question itself wasn't unexpected, or even unreasonable. But that didn't mean I had a good answer.

"I was about to," I said lamely.

Mom wasn't convinced. "It's a good thing Judge Wilkerson has a stomach flu and canceled her morning session so we didn't have to test that, isn't it?" she said in her don't-jerk-me-around voice. "I'm guessing neither of you called the police?"

I shook my head.

"And is it also safe to assume that when *I* call them, they're going to find your fingerprints where they don't belong?"

"Mine are on the gun," I said. "I picked it up."

The look she gave me could have crushed marble.

"What about the brick? You know they can get fingerprints from bricks now?"

I shook my head.

"And you pulled off the tarp?"

I nodded. She pursed her lips and turned to James.

"What about you?"

"Just the brick," he said.

She sized both of us up like we were new clients. Which, since she mostly defends people busted on charges like drug possession and robbery and assault, wasn't pleasant. But it didn't take long before the grim line of her lips softened.

"This is a hell of a way to start your summer vacation,

isn't it?" She sighed. And before James or I could answer, she came around and turned us by the shoulders to face her.

"Are you both all right?"

James nodded. I murmured that I was and told her how the construction workers had shown up, cut the hole, and bailed.

Mom frowned. "They might have been undocumented. I can't say I blame them for leaving, but the police are going to want to talk to them."

A funny noise came out of James's throat, and I realized that must have been what he'd wanted to say earlier, when I'd told him about the workers leaving. He's into social justice and immigration reform like I'm into field hockey and volleyball and cross country. He even does ESL tutoring at the library on Saturdays. It's his thing.

Mom's eyes lingered on James's hair. "She dragged you into this, didn't she?"

"She called me, is all," he said.

"Well, then she owes you, because you're going to have to stick around and talk to the police."

James didn't seem surprised, and it wasn't until Mom said she'd have to let his dad know what was going on that he started looking a little queasy. She glanced down at the skeleton. James nudged me with his elbow, telling me that (1) even though he worshipped her, my mother scared him; (2) she was right about me dragging him into this mess; (3) I sure as hell better fix it.

He cleared his throat. "Um, Mrs. Chase, I'm supposed to be at the restaurant by ten."

Mom told him we'd make it work and sent me to get dressed while she called the police.

"Brush your teeth for everyone's sake," she yelled after me. "And, Rowan?"

I looked back. She was staring at my bike shorts, and all I could think was, *She sees it. She sees the thing you took from the skeleton's pocket.*

But then her left eyebrow arched and her lips pursed, and I knew I was safe. I also knew she was about to tell me not to come down with my ass hanging out of my shorts again.

And I was right.

———

Mom, James, and I all saw it when Mom opened the door—the slight hesitation in the policeman's hello, the split-second tightening around his mouth, the quick once-over he gave the three of us. He hadn't been expecting black people. Not in Maple Ridge. Not in one of the big houses.

To be fair, though, he recovered quickly.

"Morning, ma'am," he said. "Someone called dispatch about finding an old grave site at this address?"

Mom's voice was cool. "I did, Officer"—she glanced down at his badge—"Cooper. I'm Isis Chase. This is my daughter, Rowan, and her friend James Galvez. Please come in."

After some awkward formalities, the four of us went to the back house. One look at the skeleton and Officer Cooper was on his radio, calling for detectives. It was hard, standing there, not knowing how much trouble James and I were in. I kept my eyes on Uncle Chotch's Victrola because it was the safest place for them.

When I was little, I loved going through the fragile old records in the compartments beneath the Victrola's turntable. Its wooden cabinet was four feet tall, so I'd had to use a stool to put the records on. Then I'd wind up the stubborn crank on the side to get the turntable spinning, and dance around to the tinny, old-fashioned music it played. I'd loved that thing. Still do.

Officer Cooper let go of his radio. "Ten minutes," he said. Then the back gate clicked and the three of us stood there in this awkward silence until Dad walked in.

The shift in Officer Cooper was immediate and completely unsubtle. Clearly, having another standard-issue white guy in the room made him more comfortable.

"Glad to meet you, Mr. Chase," he said. "Now that you're here, I'd like to ask you a few questions."

Dad gave him a gee-I-wish-I-could-help-you shrug and said, "I'm really not up on the situation, Officer. You're better off talking to my wife or my daughter."

Which was exactly what he should have said, and exactly the opposite of what Officer Cooper expected. Dad's big and easygoing and almost never doubts himself. It's an old-money thing.

The policeman's Adam's apple bobbed in his throat. *Don't be an idiot*, I thought. *Talk to Mom.*

"Of course," he mumbled, flipping a page on his note-pad. "Mrs. Chase, if you'll just tell me your contractor's name..."

Wise choice, grasshopper, I thought. *You've done well.*

WILLIAM

I started working at the Victory Victrola Shop on a Saturday morning, less than twenty-four hours after the incident at the Two-Knock. And, truth to tell, the arrangement wasn't near so bad as I'd thought it would be.

I liked watching my father sweet-talk customers out of their hard-earned cash. We lured people in off the street by propping the door wide open and piping music out through it. Pop put me in charge of choosing records and making sure the demo machine stayed wound. It was a task I took to straightaway. So long as the songs kept playing, the customers kept coming.

But the best part of being at the shop was getting to watch the never-ending parade of folks strolling up and down Main Street. Tulsa had sprung up so fast and fierce during the oil boom that folks called it the Magic City. Ladies sporting fine hats and Parisian dresses walked alongside leather-skinned roughnecks in dirty overalls. Flannel-suited oilmen and jingle-spurred ranch hands bellied up to crowded lunch counters together, trading stock tips and livestock reports over plates of fried pork chops with rice and brown gravy. To the south, oil derricks pumped night and day, sucking crude from the big Midcontinent oil field. And around Greenwood Avenue, just to the north and east of where the Frisco Railroad tracks divided the city, colored Tulsans had built a boomtown of their own.

During the day you could find Negroes aplenty downtown, working as domestics in white homes, shining shoes, making deliveries. But come quitting time, the ones who didn't live in quarters behind their white employers' houses went north to sleep in homes of their own. And on Thursdays, when colored maids and cooks got the evening off, downtown Tulsa's streets turned white as fresh-bleached sheets.

Of course, Jim Crow laws kept Negroes from shopping in white stores unless they were fetching orders. But all rules have exceptions, and one of the first things I learned in Pop's employ was that his principles were far more flexible as a businessman than as a father.

"We're packing up that VE-300 for delivery," he said, half an hour before closing time on my second day. "Get its crate from the back."

I hesitated, not knowing which Victrola he meant.

"The electric one with the dome top," Pop said curtly.

"You have those model numbers memorized by the end of the week, hear?"

I mumbled, "Yes, sir," but I was confused. Just the other evening, he'd said over dinner how he regretted stocking the new electric model. Yet there we were, boxing it up for delivery.

I stood like a big lump of useless until Pop looked up from his newspaper and gave me the stink eye.

"Get the crate," he said. And I hustled off to do as I was told.

Two shoppers wandered in over the next thirty minutes, neither of them in a buying mood. At seven o'clock on the dot, we locked the front door, hung the CLOSED sign in the window, loaded the Victrola into our delivery truck, and drove north. After a few blocks, I asked where we were going. Pop said I'd see when we got there. When I asked who we were delivering to, he kept mum and left me chewing on my thumbnail as we turned east.

In the geographic sense, Greenwood was only a short walk from downtown. But for a boy like me, it may as well have been on the moon. Not that I hadn't spent my fair share of time out and about on the streets; it's just that Greenwood wasn't a place I'd ever thought to visit. Greenwood was for Negroes.

But oh, it was a sight to behold. Twilight was settling in when we got there, softening the glow against brick buildings that were every bit as impressive as the ones downtown. Smoke and barbecue smells made my stomach growl. Men, women, and children strolled the sidewalks in clothes fine as any worn by white folks on Main Street. I must have looked a fool, staring out that window with my eyes big as doughnuts and my jaw hanging slack.

In the business district, electric lights flickered on over the Dreamland Theatre's facade, and were already burning bright in the sweetshops, drugstores, diners, and hotels that lined the avenue. A few streets over, the north end of Detroit Avenue was lined with pretty, well-tended houses. Pop stopped the truck in front of a big one and told me to get out. I helped him slide the Victrola crate onto the hand truck as best I could with one arm in a plaster of Paris cast, steadying it as Pop grunted his way up the porch steps.

After he'd knocked, a little girl no taller than my belt pulled the curtain back from a side window and stared up at us. She was light brown and pigtailed, with mischief in her eyes.

Pop knocked again, and soon after that an elegant woman in a pale green dress stood in the open doorway while the little girl hid behind her skirt. "It's so nice to see you, Mr. Tillman," the woman said. "Please forgive Esther; she isn't allowed to open the door for anyone she doesn't recognize."

Pop tipped his cap in greeting and told the lady that was a wise rule indeed. She smiled, her straight white teeth standing out like pearls on jewelers' satin, and pointed us towards the parlor.

Pop pushed the cart. I followed, thinking Mama would have liked how the gold flowers on the thick rug under my feet stood out against the blue background. Pop asked if we should unpack the crate and set the Victrola up, and the woman replied no thank you, for her husband was looking forward to doing it himself when he got back from seeing patients. After which Pop cleared his throat and said then that just left the matter of payment. "Of course!" the woman murmured, and hurried off towards the back of the house, heels clicking against the polished wood floor.

I looked around, taking in the room's fancy chandelier and furniture, trying to ignore Esther's gaze. She sat in a velvet-padded chair, feet swinging back and forth a good six inches over the rug. "I got no brothers, only sisters," she said. "You got a sister?"

Pop stared overhard at a painting of fruit, pretending he hadn't heard. And a vision of my baby sister flashed through my mind, three years old, shrieking with glee as Pop tossed her into the air. "Again!" she'd cried as Mama feigned disapproval and Pop launched her higher and higher. Until he finally caught her up for good and covered her flushed cheeks with kisses.

"My sister's an angel in heaven," I told Esther in a tight-jawed voice, thinking how sometimes good memories hurt worse than bad.

Esther thought on that awhile, then looked at me square and said, "That's sad. You want one of mine?"

Little as I cared to engage in further conversation with her, I couldn't help replying, "One of your *sisters?*" And she eyed me like maybe I was slow in the head, and said, "Sure. I got two of 'em. Take your pick."

I laughed in spite of myself.

"You can't give away your sisters!" I said. "They're family." Which turned Esther's face angry and set her feet to kicking harder, right up until she heard her mother's footsteps coming back. Pop turned away from the painted bowl of fruit, smiling his best salesman's smile. And when she arrived, he counted out the bills she handed him, one by one.

There should have been three hundred and fifteen dollars in all, plus five for delivery. The VE-300 was a pricey model; not the most expensive, far from the cheapest. But when Pop was done, he handed two dollars back, saying, "It's three hundred and twenty even, Mrs. Butler."

That flustered the lady badly. "Yes," she stammered. "But I thought...for your time..."

"Delivery's five dollars," Pop said. "No tipping necessary." Then Mrs. Butler did her best to compose herself as Pop thanked her for her business and wheeled the handcart across the fancy carpet and out the front door.

He never spoke a word the whole way home. But after he'd parked the truck behind the Model T under the porte cochere, he said, "A sale's a sale, William. Things are hard now, what with crude oil prices so low. If a Negro comes to me with money in his pocket, I'll hold my nose and sell him a Victrola, Jim Crow be damned. As for tonight, we had a late customer. That's what you tell anyone who asks, your mama included. Do as I say, and I'll teach you to drive this truck once your wrist's healed."

Then he tugged down the brim of his hat and got out. And though that certainly wasn't the last delivery we ever made to Greenwood, it was the last time the matter was ever discussed.

———

I never hid from Addie. Not exactly. But Central High had enough students so that as long as you didn't share classes with a person, you could pretty well stay away from them. You couldn't avoid crossing paths completely, though, especially if they had a mind to hunt you down. And at lunchtime the day after my first trip to Green-wood, Addie did.

She found me in the cafeteria holding a cheese sand-wich in my good hand and explaining yet again how my wrist got broke. Clete sat at my side, for though things had cooled between us after the Two-Knock, habit kept us from separating completely at school. We'd even set-tled into a kind of routine where I'd tell how I'd saved an unnamed but ever-so-lovely young lady from the savage advances of a Negro cad, and Clete would nod and utter exclamations of agreement every now and again. With each retelling, Clarence Banks grew an inch, gained ten pounds, and turned two shades darker. On top of that, my pitiful punch turned into something fierce, and a baseball bat assumed responsibility for breaking my wrist rather than my own drunken stumbling. Out of all the lies I'd worked up, my favorite was the one I used to finish the story: "He tried to bash my head in, boys. My poor arm here was all that stood between me and certain death."

Addie put an end to all that.

She came at me sideways, inching up so quiet that I didn't see her until a flash of blue gingham caught the corner of my eye. Fast as lightning, she slapped me hard enough that the sound of it silenced all the lunchtime chatter around us. I can still feel the sting today, and hear her thick words in my ear: "He might die. Did you know that? They beat him so bad he might die!"

My hand went to my cheek. Addie's fury had coiled her up and washed her out, save for her red-rimmed eyes and two angry spots of color on her cheeks.

Being a dunce, I replied, "Who?"

The wrath in Addie's eyes rendered down to fat, shiny tears.

"Clarence! Clarence might die! And all because of a stupid little boy with a stupid little crush and too much Choc in his belly. You can go to hell for all I care, Will Tillman, if hell will have you."

Far as those harsh, hushed words knocked me back, they didn't prevent me from seeing our mathematics teacher, Ms. Newlin, eyeing us from across the room.

I dragged my hand from my cheek and the red mark Addie's slap surely must have left there. Ms. Newlin made her way towards us, and the next thing I knew, Addie was clearing her throat, telling her everything was fine.

The teacher surveyed us with her little piggy eyes and asked about the noise she'd just heard. I held my chin sideways, angling my struck cheek away. One of the boys beside me, a wax-skinned trumpet player named Burt, held up a library book and said, "I dropped this, ma'am. Sorry 'bout the ruckus."

Ms. Newlin looked both unconvinced and too tired to care. Word around school was that her preacher husband had run off to St. Louis with the church secretary two months prior, leaving the woman more dour than ever. Distracted, too. She glanced up at the big clock over the doorway, smoothed her skirt, and shooed us off to class. We *yes'md* her and gathered our things while she walked away. That's when Addie put herself in front of me, so close I could have kissed her.

"They whipped him yesterday," she whispered. "And beat him and left him in the street to die. Far as I'm concerned, you're as much to blame as they are. And if he does die, that's murder. Just you remember that, Will Tillman. Murder."

Rowan

Police detectives are a lot less interesting in real life than on TV. The ones who showed up at our house weren't quirky, they didn't drop smartass one-liners, and their khakis and polo shirts made them look an awful lot like accountants with guns.

After spending maybe five minutes alone in the back house, they came out and told us someone from the medical examiner's office was coming to assess the scene. Then Dad raised the umbrella on the table at the pool, and the six of us—Mom, Dad, James, the detectives, and I—sat around it. The detectives asked easy questions: What time did the construction crew show up? How long did they stay? When did I see the body for the first time? Stuff like that. They didn't even seem upset that James and I had opened the tarp and touched the gun and the brick and the actual body. I mean, I knew it was a cold case, but the way they acted, the skeleton might as well have been a forgotten ice cube at the back of the freezer.

Really, the only time things got a little tense was when the woman detective asked Mom for the contractor's contact info. Mom recited it from memory, but said that since the body looked as if it had been there a long time, and since the construction workers had taken off right after they found it, she hoped there wouldn't be any need to track them down.

The detectives traded a look. They understood perfectly well that Mom was asking them to leave the workmen alone. Then the man said they had to investigate every potential homicide thoroughly. He seemed nervous about it, though, watching Dad to see his reaction. And Dad cleared his throat and said basically the same thing Mom had, but in his I-know-a-lot-of-important-people voice. The detectives looked at each other again, only longer, and the man cleared his throat and repeated his line about being thorough, adding: "Of course, we aren't really interested in pursuing unrelated legal infractions, Mr. Chase. I can assure you of that."

Which, roughly translated, meant that since *Dad*—the guy whose family name was on a building downtown—had asked them to lay off, they would.

Funny how that worked.

The rest of their questions went quickly. Mom kept her word and made sure James left for work on time. A stubby man from the medical examiner's office showed up around eleven, smelling like Sonic onion rings and wearing what I sincerely hoped was a ketchup stain on his shirt. He snapped a few pictures, filled out some forms, and announced it was a case for the forensic anthropologist. "I'll call Genny Roop," he said. "This is right up her alley."

After the ME guy left, Dad told the detectives he'd appreciate it if they'd keep things low-key and out of the local news. They made us promise not to mess with the skeleton. We promised we wouldn't and that was pretty much the end of things.

So my very first interrogation by the police was basically a snoozefest. Or at least it would have been if James and I hadn't lied our faces off about whether or not we'd taken anything from the body.

"Oh, no, sir," I'd said when the detective asked, thinking all the while about the rectangle of leather I'd stolen from the skeleton's pocket, and how glad I was that it wouldn't end up forgotten at the bottom of a police evidence box.

"We put the gun and the brick back. Right where we found them."

———

The thing was a wallet, cracked and covered in mildew, with rotted-out stitching on one side of its change pocket. I'd figured out *that* particular little detail earlier, when

I'd run upstairs to get dressed, paused just long enough to see what my contraband actually was, and tossed it under my bed. Even before the wallet landed, loose coins clinked and rolled across the hardwood floor, giving me one of those *oh shit* moments, worrying Mom would hear the noise from the kitchen underneath me and use her powers of maternal omniscience to figure out I was up to something.

Lucky for me, either she didn't hear or she'd tapped out her powers for the day catching James and me with the skeleton. Still, I waited until after the detectives were gone and Mom and Dad had left for work to gather up the coins.

Honestly, being bad felt kind of good. James and I could be obnoxious when we wanted to, but underneath our snarky outer shells we were basically rule followers. Good kids. Nerds. Enough so that guilt kept me from looking at the wallet closely. Until I got to Utica Square, at least.

Utica's a shopping center—high-end, close to our house—where the flowerbeds are perfect and the luxury cars roam free. James made fun of me for liking it there, but he was at work, and I only had eighteen hours left before my summer of forced laboratory servitude started. I deserved a little treat.

The azaleas were in manic bloom in Woodward Park. I slowed down, watching a photographer snap pictures of a couple on the rocks above the pond. Everyone does their engagement shots at Woodward; it's practically a city ordinance. Just past that, at the emergency room entrance to St. John's, the usual cluster of worn-out hospital workers hunched over their cigarettes, sucking in tar and nicotine. I rolled up my window against the smoke, turned into Utica Square at the next light, and found a shaded parking space underneath a magnolia.

I snagged a spicy tuna roll at the grocery store where gray-haired ladies can still get their groceries carried out by bag boys, walked over to Starbucks, and sat down with an iced coffee at one of the shaded tables outside. It was a good day to watch people: tiny blond ex–sorority queens with perfect makeup, doctors in scrubs getting their afternoon caffeine, kids zoning out on iPads while their moms texted and sipped skinny iced lattes. Everyone was always so comfortable with themselves there. So confident.

Across the courtyard, two little girls chased each other around the fountain I fell into when I was three. Mom had taken me to sit on Santa's lap in the warm little cottage they set up there every year, then walked me down to the fountain to make a wish. I remember eating the cookie Mrs. Claus had given me, and Mom digging around in her purse for pennies. Then the purse was on the ground, and business cards and stray sheets of folded paper danced away like one-winged butterflies on the chilly Oklahoma wind.

"Stay put," Mom said, dashing after them. And I had,

until the wind pushed a silver tube of her lipstick toward the flat edge of the fountain.

I loved that lipstick because Mom had dotted my lips with it once as I watched her get ready to go out. "Rub them together like this," she'd said, showing me how. I'd done the exaggerated little-kid version, smearing deep red pigment all over my face. She'd told me I looked beautiful anyway, and made me feel special. There was no way I was going to let that tube roll into the fountain.

And I caught it, too—right before I tripped and went into the water headfirst. Mom caught the back of my sweatshirt, yanked me out, and rushed me to the car to get warm. My teeth chattered and my fingers went numb, but I could feel the thrum of her heartbeat and the panicked strength of her arms. That was the first time I'd ever seen my mother scared, and the memory of it has stuck with me in high-res living color ever since.

I laid two dollars and sixty-one cents in coins from the wallet out on the table. They were tarnished, and stamped with dates ranging from 1916 to 1921. Other than that, the wallet was empty. It wasn't much to go on, but at least I knew the skeleton's owner had been alive in 1921. Maybe a few years after that, too, but '21 was a good baseline.

I sipped my coffee (two pumps of sweetener, room for cream) and caught the hipster at the next table staring at me over his laptop. My phone vibrated against the metal table.

Brady tonight?

Hipster dude smiled through his beard. I smiled—just a little—and texted James back.

ok but early. work tomorrow

I swept the coins into my hand, picked up my sushi, and crossed the courtyard to my car. Hipster dude gave me a curled-finger wave as I drove past. I waved back, knowing that even though James wasn't into romance, I'd take hanging out with my best friend over flirting with a bearded lumberjack wannabe any day. And twice on Sunday.

WILLIAM

Vernon Fish had scared me from the day he parked a six-foot-tall wooden cigar store Indian outside his shop and stalked across the street to say hello. I happened to be dropping Pop's lunch off at the time, and I'll never forget the smell of hair tonic and fried onions that followed Vernon in. It had turned our familiar shop, with its scraped pine floors and fleur-de-lis-stamped tin ceiling, into someplace cold and foreign. Even the cozy glow from the Chinese lanterns Mama had hung over the ceiling bulbs couldn't warm the place up when Vernon visited. I'd feared him from the moment we met, and he knew it.

So it was a bother and a misfortune that not three hours after Addie slapped me in the lunchroom, a storm front blew dark skies and cold rain into town, and Vernon Fish into our shop. For, miserable as it was outside,

Victrolas and smokes were the last things on the minds of the few waterlogged souls sloshing their way along Main Street.

"Go stand by that window, Half-breed," Vernon said, barely glancing my way as he stalked through the door. "And tell me if I get any customers."

I came out from behind the mahogany Victrola cabinet I'd been polishing and did as I'd been told. Vernon may have been only a few years older than me, but he was not a man to be trifled with. Then Vernon went to the wooden counter that spanned nearly the whole length of the back wall and leaned his meaty forearms onto it, puffing on one of the foul Maduro Robustos he favored. Between the stink of that cigar and the way Addie's words still sawed at my gut, I was halfway to losing what little lunch I'd eaten.

"Stanley," he said in his deep Georgia drawl, "I come over to let you know I met up with some of the Ku Klux Klan's most influential leaders last night, and seeing's how you took a squaw for a wife, you ended up being the topic of some discussion."

Pop's face betrayed no emotion as he rolled an unlit Corona between his fingers. He never actually smoked them, just chewed one end and sniffed the tobacco leaves. Bad as they smelled when they burned, sometimes I wished he'd just up and light one.

Vernon tapped ash from his Maduro into the ashtray

that Pop kept for customers and drew another mouthful of smoke before he continued.

"See, the Klan may not have much of a presence here yet, but they've got big plans for Tulsa. Big enough that we decided we need upstanding business owners such as yourself too much to begrudge you your, shall we say, *exotic* choice of spouse."

Pop replied with a false smile. Though he didn't say so, he knew perfectly well that Mama's Osage roots ran deeper into the soil under our feet than his or Vernon's, either one, making her about as exotic as an Oklahoma redbud tree. Why, not thirty years prior, the land Tulsa sat on had belonged to Indians: Muscogee Creek, Cherokee, and Osage. The Perryman family alone had near single-handedly founded the place, and they were mostly Muscogee Creek. And the better part of Oklahoma itself had been called Indian Territory right up until it became a state in 1907. Far as I could tell, Indians and part-Indians like me had just as much right to be there as anyone. More, even.

"Now, Vernon," Pop said, "that willingness wouldn't have anything to do with the fact that my wife is a wealthy woman, would it?"

Vernon looked offended. "Quite the contrary," he said. "In fact, we want to *give* you money. Once you join the Klan, you'll earn a commission for every new member you recruit."

"Like the one you'll get if *I* join?" Pop asked.

Vernon shook his head and looked all sad and hang-dog, like Pop had wounded his soul. "That's not why I want you in, Stanley, and you know it," he said. "Supporting the Klan's the right thing to do. We got coloreds round these parts thinkin' they're good as white folks. Black Wall Street my foot! That strip of junk shops and cathouses up on Greenwood ain't nothin' but a blighted piece of Africa befouling our fair city."

A hint of a smile flickered across Pop's face. I'm not sure Vernon saw it, but I did. And Pop said how he'd heard tell that the Negro quarter up around Greenwood was one of the richest of its kind in the whole country. Plus they had folks like that Dr. Jackson, who'd trained at the Mayo Clinic and treated white and Negro women both. And what about John and Loula Williams, with their Dreamland Theatre and confectionery and garage that fixed as many white folks' cars as coloreds'?

Vernon turned his head sideways and spit a piece of tobacco off the tip of his tongue. Said, "Seems to me that when white men such as yourself start talking like that, Stanley, it's a sure sign folks up in Little Africa are due to be put back in their place. Besides, the Klan ain't just about keeping uppity Negroes in line, it's about making sure our town stays pure and righteous. There's white men abusing God's laws, too, and the Klan makes sure they get what they got comin'. Especially all them Catholics and Jews movin' in amongst us good Protestants, twisting the Bible round with their talk of blood and temples and such."

Pop shrugged and said people's pocketbooks interested him more than their prayers. Vernon puffed a few times, then said how Pop should be grateful the Klan was willing to forgive him his Injun wife and let him join. Pop went tight-lipped and quiet; Vernon had finally got under his skin.

"What about you, Half-breed?" Vernon said, turning to me. "How do you opine?"

I told him I didn't. And he said that was hogwash, for a boy my age ought to have the world figured out and caught up by the tail. So I looked to Pop for help, and when none was forthcoming, I turned towards the window instead, pretending to watch Vernon's shop and muttering, "I haven't got time for all that, Mr. Fish, what with school and work and all."

And Vernon pounced, saying, "Then it seems to me you oughtn't have time to be out carousing at night, getting in fights." And he weighted his words down heavy, letting me know there was more behind them than just bluster.

The shop went quiet as the rain picked up outside and the sky spit hail pebbles against the window. Vernon's lips made wet little *pwaps*, loosing smoke rings over the dark, slicked-back curls atop his head. After a while, I couldn't

help but meet his eyes. And what I saw in the milky blue-
ness of them sent a jolt through me like biting down on a
bad tooth.

He knew about the Two-Knock.

Vernon Fish knew.

Rowan

Finding a skeleton with a bashed-in skull was a bad way to start the day. Getting into a fight with my best friend was a supremely shitty way to end it.

At first, things were fine. It was one of those gorgeous Oklahoma nights in the Brady Arts District when the sun hovers low in the sky so long you wonder if it's ever going to set. Even with a Drillers game at ONEOK Field, James and I found parking spots outside the instrument repair shop that has rows of old violins hanging in the window. He wanted to catch a few innings from the five-dollar out-field lawn seats, but it gets crowded back there, and I wasn't crazy about the idea of people listening to our conversation. So we sat on one of the benches around the Guthrie Green splash pad instead, close enough to catch spray from the kids running through in their shorts and T-shirts, but far enough away from their parents to have some privacy.

James and I go to the Brady a lot. It's a few blocks north of downtown and just west of Greenwood, with art galleries and restaurants and bars and a glassblowing studio where they let you get close enough to the ovens to break a sweat. There's usually some kind of performance happening on the stage at the Green—Red Dirt bands, dancers, the symphony. That night it was actors in black leggings and white T-shirts doing scenes from *Othello*. A few families were scattered around on blankets, along with oldsters in lawn chairs and a white couple with matching dreads making out next to their bikes.

"What happened after I left?" James asked. "Anything good?"

I pretended to think hard. "Oh, definitely. Let's see ... you were there for most of our conversation with the world's least exciting police detectives, so the main thing you missed would have to be the medical examiner who spent ten minutes *not* touching the body. And—oh yeah—you didn't get to hear Dad making sure our shiny family name stays out of the news."

James's forehead wrinkled.

"I promise," I said. "It was completely undramatic. Even *this* was a letdown." I took the wallet from my purse and handed it to him, busted side up. "See for yourself."

He opened it up and felt around inside the empty bill compartment.

"Careful," I said. "One side of the change pocket is shot."

He caught two coins as they fell out. "We should have given this to the police. If they find out we took it—"

I cut him off. "Trust me, they won't. The detectives basically told Mom and Dad they're too busy with new cases to spend time on something this old. If the forensic anthropologist doesn't find anything, my guess is no one will. I'm glad we kept the wallet. At least this way the two of us can do some detective work on our own."

James jiggled the rest of the coins in his palm and turned them over one by one.

"The newest's from 1921," he said.

"Right. So unless someone snuck back to the crime scene, tore up the floor, and stuck fresh coins in the skeleton's wallet, it must have been a live human being then."

A little girl next to us gathered water in her cupped hands and threw it in a littler boy's face. The boy ran off howling. James took out his phone, punched something in, and scrolled down, muttering, "Well, that makes things interesting."

I leaned closer. "What?"

"The race riot was in 1921."

Which, I confess, was something I didn't know much about beyond what we'd covered in ninth-grade Oklahoma History. Something had happened between a black teenage boy and a white teenage girl in a department store elevator, then things melted down outside the courthouse the next night. Most of Greenwood ended up burning, and everyone pretty much tried to forget about it.

One thing I did remember was that no one knew for sure how many black people had been killed. But what stuck with me most was our teacher's description of how black survivors had been marched like prisoners of war to holding centers and forced to stay there until a white person showed up to vouch for them. Once they were released, they'd had to pin a green card onto their clothes that basically said, "I'm a good Negro." It wasn't exactly the same as the yellow stars the Nazis made Jewish people wear, but it wasn't completely different, either.

Still, I didn't see how the skeleton could have had anything to do with all that. The riot happened at the northern edge of downtown and in Greenwood—not in my neighborhood. And even more than now, Maple Ridge in the 1920s had been for rich white people.

James kept messing with his phone, twisting his mouth up on one side.

"There's a cold case database on the police department's website," he said. "But it only goes back to the 1970s." His fingers kept moving. "Jesus—did you know forty-one people were hanged in Oklahoma between 1907 and 1930? Most of them were black, and there were probably a lot more lynchings that never got recorded."

I hadn't known that, and kind of wished I still didn't.

James elbowed my ribs. "Did you hear me?"

I elbowed him back. "I did. And it's awful. I'm just glad things are better now."

A look came over James's face, like all of a sudden he couldn't recognize me. "Are they?" he said.

I swung one leg behind the bench, straddling it so we were looking at each other. "Are they what?"

"Better?"

I leaned away without meaning to. "I'm not an idiot, James. I know things aren't perfect now, but they aren't as bad as they were in the 1920s. People don't get lynched anymore. You and I can go anywhere we want. We're black, and we both go to a nicer school than most white kids."

The wrinkles on his forehead disappeared and his face went blank. "It's way more complicated than that, Chase."

I bit my tongue.

"I never told you what happened to the guy I'm tutoring at the library, did I?" he said.

"No."

"Well, his name's Eduardo, and last month he spent two weeks hanging drywall for this contractor who promised him fifteen hundred bucks cash for the work. Eduardo's got three kids. He's a good guy, and he wouldn't do things under the table if he could get a work permit. Only he can't. So he takes this job, and when he finishes and goes to the contractor to get paid, the contractor tells him sure, he'll write a check—as soon as Eduardo shows him his papers. Only he knows Eduardo doesn't *have* papers. And since Eduardo can't go to the police and report him, he also knows there's no way he'll get caught. He ripped off my friend and there's nothing Eduardo can do about it."

"That sucks," I said. "And now I get why you were worried about the workmen. But Mom and Dad wouldn't hire a contractor like that. I'm sure the one they're using pays his workers."

James was getting worked up. "That doesn't change the fact that the system's jacked against people like Eduardo and me."

He said it loud enough to make the little girl in the splash pad look over at us. I tilted my head toward her, letting James know he needed to calm down, and whispered through my teeth, "There's a big difference between a mob lynching a black man and some asshole ripping off a guy because he's undocumented, and you know it."

James shook his head slowly. "The crime's different but the problem's the same. It's about power and prejudice and shit rooted so deep that people don't see it anymore. You know we're six times as likely to go to jail as white people, right?"

"Of course I know that," I shot back. "My mother's a black public defender, for God's sake, so you can skip the lecture."

"You can't wish it away," James said softly. "Trayvon Martin, Michael Brown, Eric Harris, Laquan McDonald—they're just the ones who made the news. And I know you know that, but sometimes you disappear inside this rich-girl bubble where someone always fixes things when they go wrong, and your brown skin only counts against you until you mention your daddy's name. Most of us don't have that luxury, Chase. There's no room for us in your bubble."

Things were happening inside me. Ugly, uncomfortable things that I can't even describe. But I wasn't going to let James see me cry.

"I'm sorry I'm such a disappointment to you," I said around the tightness in my throat. James pretended to watch the actors on the stage. I got up, turned my back on my friend, and walked away. And I didn't shed a single tear. Not until I was safe inside my car, with the tinted windows rolled up and the door locked tight behind me.

WILLIAM

It was torture, staring out into the rain on Main Street while Vernon Fish savored the effect of his words. He knew about me and Clarence Banks, and clearly suspected I hadn't given Pop a full and accurate account of the circumstances behind my broken wrist. Now that he'd stuck the knife in me good, Vernon intended to enjoy twisting it.

After a while, though, the silence got to be too much even for him, and he set about unraveling the rest of his smug tale.

"See, I have this policeman friend, Carl," he said. "Works in a...well, I guess you'd call it an *unsavory* part of town. And Carl, he tells me there's establishments out there where Negroes and whites mix, drinkin' and dancin' and sinnin' together in some kind of unholy mess. Turns my stomach to think of it."

This was news to neither Pop nor me; everyone in town, even polite society ladies in their fancy hats and starched white dresses, knew about Tulsa's speakeasies and roadhouses. They also knew better than to talk about them.

But Vernon jawed on, saying, "Yep, old Carl and me met up yesterday, and he told me about a little scene he come upon in one of these places the other night. Seems a white boy tangled with a big coon, name of Clarence somethin' or other. Pissed old Clarence off so bad he broke that white boy's leg...or was it his arm?"

Vernon stopped, letting the weight of his words settle in on me and Pop. And there was nothing to fill the silence except for the sound of the rain. Not until Pop cleared his throat and said how he thought we might have a leak in the storeroom ceiling, and did Vernon have a bucket he could lend us to catch the drips?

And Vernon, he just smirked and said, "Only bucket I got's underneath a drip of my own. I ain't through with my story, neither. See, it turns out old Clarence was such a coward that when he seen what he'd done to that poor white boy, he ran away with his tail between his legs. Only, the cops found out his name, and just last night they caught him sitting down to supper with his little old mammy."

At that, my heart set to beating fast. Mostly, I'll admit, because I feared further repercussions from Pop. But I like to think that some small part of me felt a twinge of guilt over the notion that Clarence Banks had suffered a beating on my account. And Vernon kept hammering away, saying, "Cops got ways of keeping the courthouse from getting too clogged up, see, and sometimes good citizens like me help 'em. We got solutions of our own for problems like old Clarence. Ones that don't cost more'n a strop of leather and a length of sturdy rope."

Pop wiped imaginary dust from the big, gilded cash register Mama had bought for him the year prior. Vernon blew three smoke rings, *plup, plup, plup.* Said, "Remind me to show you my whipping strap sometime, Half-breed. Three foot long it is. Four inches wide. Got slits carved into the end, make it cut through skin easier'n warm butter."

I tried not to let my fear show, but Vernon saw. He saw, and from the way his close-set eyes danced about, he liked it. "You understand, don't you, Will," he said, "that righteous men take care of their own?"

I wasn't so sure that Vernon was qualified to give lectures on righteousness, but it seemed neither the time nor place to point that out.

"Yes, Mr. Fish," I said.

"And you want to overcome your own mongrel blood and be a righteous man, don't you?"

To which I whispered *yes* once more. But that wasn't good enough for Vernon, who pounded his fist against the counter, saying, "God gave you a voice, son. Use it, I tell you! Use it!"

I looked to Pop, wishing he'd say something—anything—to help me. But he just kept wiping nonexistent dust off the register.

So in the strongest voice I could muster, I looked Vernon Fish dead-on and said: "Yes, Mr. Fish. Yes, I do."

———

Whatever thoughts Pop may have had about Vernon Fish's tale, he kept them to himself. We were learning things about each other, Pop and me, and both of us had the good sense not to make a fuss over them.

As for myself, I was a seventeen-year-old boy with all the wisdom and moral rectitude of a turnip. Bad as Vernon Fish had scared me, bad as I started feeling about Clarence Banks, it didn't take long to convince myself that Clarence would recover and the whole mess would go away if only I apologized to Addie.

Two days later, I waited for her outside school after dismissal to do just that.

She must have seen me from the foyer, for she made a beeline down the front stairs and across the street, cutting westward in front of an oncoming sedan. "Addie!" I cried, thinking to stop her before she got killed. But she only sped up, forcing me into a jog.

"Addie!" I hollered. "Addie, I'm sorry! Please…just wait a minute!"

Her footsteps slowed enough for me to catch up and

fall in at her side. She wouldn't look at me, though, and I could feel her chilly disdain in spite of the warm afternoon sun. We walked side by side a good ways, me catching my breath, her refusing to acknowledge I was there.

"I truly am sorry, Addie," I said once I'd worked up the courage to speak.

She glanced at me. Barely. Said, "What exactly is it you're sorry for, Will?"

"Why, that you're upset, of course," I replied.

Addie stopped and spun towards me, and it's a testament to my ignorance that I took her doing so as encouragement.

"What about Clarence?" she asked.

And though my main concern at that moment was to set things right with the girl I loved, I piped right up: "Oh, sure. Him, too."

Addie's eyes narrowed, but I blathered on, saying it was a shame he'd touched her hand like that, and how I wished he'd known better and hoped there wouldn't be any permanent damage from the beating he took. "Everyone deserves second chances," I added magnanimously. "Even Negroes." Then I stopped, waiting for the warm flood of forgiveness I considered my due.

Only, when I looked closer to see what was holding Addie up, I finally registered the fullness of the disgust in her eyes and understood that my true love thought me no better than a pile of dog shit on the sidewalk.

Then Addie walked away.

Now, I wish I could say her reaction didn't surprise me, or that the suffering I'd caused an innocent man weighed heavier on my conscience than it did. But that would be giving myself too much credit. The truth of the matter was, I came away from the whole incident believing myself to be the injured party. For shouldn't my apology have sufficed? And shouldn't any Negro man with half a brain know that no good could come of messing with a white woman in public? What's more, I told myself that Vernon and Addie must both have been exaggerating the extent of Clarence Banks's injuries. Why, he'd probably been no closer to death after his beating than before. Vernon Fish was a braggart, after all, and Addie a hysterical girl.

With that fool line of reasoning in my head, I spent near a week feeling sorry for myself, licking my imagined wounds and scratching at the dry skin under my cast with a pencil. My path never once crossed Addie's, making it all the easier to maintain the delusion that I'd been in the right. And after those days of sulking and skulking about had passed, the delusion felt real enough that I let the matter go and moved on like the jackass I was.

It helped that working in the shop suited me. I wasn't a natural-born salesman like Pop, but I loved music. Knew all about it, too, so that when people came in able to recall a line from a song they'd heard but not the title, Pop would say, "Let's see if William here can't divine what you're looking for." And he'd ask them to hum a few bars or sing the words, and most times I'd be able to name the tune straightaway. "Swanee," "Crazy Blues," "When My Baby Smiles at Me"—I knew them all. Even when I couldn't figure out the exact song the customer wanted, I could almost always come up with something close enough to tempt them into buying a record or two.

But when it came to selling Victrolas, Pop was the man for the job. He prided himself on knowing those machines inside and out, on being able to talk a person up from only thinking about maybe buying a cheap model to knowing they couldn't live without a fancy one. If he was busy with one customer and another came in, he'd have me entertain the newcomer with records until he could talk to them himself. In terms of brass tack Victrola sales, I kept my mouth shut.

That went double when colored folks from Greenwood called up, asking if we carried such-and-such a model they'd seen in a magazine or a catalog. "Telephone sales are tough," Pop told me. "You can't tempt folks with fancy cabinets and woodwork, so convincing them to spend more than they've planned gets tricky. It's an art, describing different models for a telephone customer well enough that they end up feeling bad for wanting something simple when they could have something fine."

Occasionally, though, even Pop failed to close a deal over the telephone. When that happened, he'd have no choice but to invite Negro customers into the shop after hours to look at the different models for themselves. He never did act ashamed of what he was doing, but he sure

80

wasn't in a hurry to let nearby shop owners in on his secret. Or to stand accused of spitting in Jim Crow's eye, either.

I always liked the hushed excitement of those visits. We'd hang the CLOSED sign out front, pull the shades down over the windows, and let our customer in through the alleyway door. The first time it happened, Pop told me, "You have to pretend the back is as good as the front. We know it isn't and so do they. There's no need to belabor the point."

In general, those late-night patrons were people Pop considered to be pillars of Tulsa's Negro society: doctors, lawyers, merchants like himself. But when push came to shove, he wasn't about to lose a sale just because someone fell a rung or two short of respectable. And it was that drive in him, that will to make his business succeed, that led to my father being bested by an eighteen-year-old Negro boy armed with nothing more than a hundred dollars and a frown grave enough to shame an undertaker.

Rowan

I always train hard, but the morning after my fight with James, my run wasn't really training so much as self-punishment. I was mad at myself, mad at him, and more than a little scared that maybe he'd been right.

There's always been a love-hate thing between me and running. First off, if you don't get it over with at the ass crack of dawn, the Oklahoma summer sun will melt you into a puddle of good intentions. Plus, it hurts. I mean, have you ever seen a happy jogger? We scowl. We pant and grimace. In fact, if you ever see one of us smiling, you should assume we're a complete psychopath and run for your life.

On the other hand, running's the best way I know to clear my head and get closer to fine. Which is why I was already two miles into an eight-mile run by 6:30 AM, with the Arkansas River on my right and early Riverside Drive commuters speeding by on my left. The temperature hadn't dropped much during the night, and the humidity made me feel like I was sucking air through a wet sponge.

It was perfect.

At the start of mile three, I ditched my warm-up playlist, queued hardcore training songs, and started the fartlek run my cross country coach had posted the night before. Yes, *fartlek* is a ridiculous word, but it's basically just a fancy Swedish way of saying "play with your speed." Which I did, using landmarks along the river to separate each segment.

The first interval was a hard sprint. I switched to a jog at a downed tree limb. Went to a fast jog at a flock of Canada geese. Cranked into a sprint again at the haunted stone mansion across Riverside. Kept it going until I thought I'd die.

The sculpture of the bobcat catching a pheasant mid-flight was my turnaround point. It was also where I tried distracting myself from James by thinking about how I was about to spend the rest of my summer with safety goggles, micropipettes, and the scientists who loved them.

All things considered, working in a virology lab was better than answering phones and entering data at Chase Oil. And it beat the hell out of doing legal research for Mom while she entertained me with her all-time favorite hits, including:

Having a Trust Fund
Doesn't Make You a Success.

and

What About Your College Essay? You Know,
You Should Really Start Your College Essay.

and

Black Women Have to Work Twice as Long
and Five Times as Hard to Succeed in this
World, So Get Used to It.

All three of which were completely unnecessary, since I'd learned early on that the best way to keep her from putting too much pressure on me was to do it myself.

Then I got sick of thinking altogether and decided to fly, legs pounding, arms pumping in a dead sprint, until my muscles and lungs screamed for mercy and there was only a quarter mile between me and home. That was the best part of the whole ordeal—the part where I was too exhausted to think about anything except a cold shower, obscene amounts of orange juice, and the post-run buzz I'd have for the next hour or so. For that short, precious quarter mile, I floated along the bike path while the city woke up around me. I didn't worry about the skeleton in the back house. I didn't stress over my sucky summer internship. And I reminded myself that no matter how mad James and I got at each other, we always worked things out. Dark corners and all, we were in it for the long haul.

———

"*Which* doctor?" the receptionist at the front desk asked. Again.

I told her Dr. Kumar (again) and that my mother had arranged for me to intern with her that summer. The receptionist stared at her computer screen like it was a Magic 8 Ball. "I just started here two days ago, and I don't know any Dr. Kumar. Was it maybe Dr. Kim? We've got one of those."

By that point, I'd already pulled up my "Dr. Kumar" folder to show her the forwarded emails from Mom, the three letters of recommendation I'd gotten from teachers, and the waiver my parents had signed so I could work there. The receptionist wasn't interested.

"Hang on," she said, and disappeared into the back.

A not-unpleasant-looking man in a white lab coat came out a few minutes later and shook my hand. He seemed too young to be a doctor, but the coat made me hopeful he might actually have a clue.

"I'm Dr. Revard," he said. "And you are...?"

I told him my name and that I was there to start my summer internship with Dr. Kumar. A cute little wrinkle creased his forehead as he motioned for me to follow him to a bench near the research building's front door.

"Rowan," he said, "I'm sorry, but Dr. Kumar had to take a leave of absence a few weeks ago. Her mother's ill and…"

I stopped listening then, because no matter what words Dr. Revard used, the message was going to be *Blah, blah, blah, you're screwed.* Sure, I hadn't wanted to work there in the first place, but I wasn't exactly opposed to racking up volunteer hours and science cred for my college applications.

I was just wondering if James's restaurant was hiring when the words *opening at the Jackson Clinic* snapped my attention back to Dr. Revard's voice.

"It may not be what you'd planned," he said, "but they're pretty desperate. And I could check to see if any of the physicians up there will let you shadow them after your shift."

He jumped up, grabbed a business card from the receptionist's desk, and scribbled something on the back. "Here's the address. I can call now if you want and see if they have time to interview you this morning. Wait… scratch that. Why don't you just head up there and I'll let them know you're on your way?"

I took the card. The address was somewhere way up in North Tulsa.

Dr. Revard gave me a little grin that, under normal

circumstances, I would have considered extremely attractive. "I really think you'd learn a lot there," he said.

I smiled and thanked him and told him that sounded great, because even though working at a medical clinic in the part of town voted most likely to get you shot hadn't been on my summer bucket list, at least it was something. Maybe even something I could get a decent essay out of. Plus, I'd be helping out in exactly the kind of place James goes all gooey over, so he could pretty much suck it on that count.

Living in a bubble my ass.

———

The thing about Tulsa is, it's really three cities in one.

The newest is South Tulsa, where the houses are fresh-built and come in Tall, Grande, and Venti. People there might work downtown, but at night they escape the urban wilds and head back to comfortable developments named for the wildlife their construction displaced. *Quail Commons. Fox Meadows.* That kind of thing.

Midtown, where I live, is what you get when you squish neighborhoods from every twentieth-century decade together, starting with the 1910s. In a seven-minute drive, you can go from fancy to comfortable to small to meth-house scary.

Then there's North Tulsa.

Cross the railroad tracks and the northern curve of highways built to shunt commuter traffic away from city streets, and you're there. It's the kind of place where, if people bother talking about it at all, they either say how dangerous it is, or describe it in their it's-such-a-pity voice. Mom says North Tulsa actually has the lowest crime rate in the city, and she knows her shit. But it *is* poor, and full of people with skin a few shades darker than pale. And I can't lie—until I went up to the Jackson Clinic that day, I'd never driven there on my own.

I followed the map on my phone north past Greenwood, where businesses rebuilt after the riot but had closed one by one over the years. Beyond that, the streets were wide and quiet. There were no gang fights, no tweakers lurking in doorways or carjackers waiting on corners. It didn't feel dangerous so much as forgotten.

I passed the Dollar General store that had been on the news after a seventy-three-year-old reserve deputy shot Eric Harris in the back nearby; a used-tire lot with a hand-lettered LLANTAS BUENAS sign; a trailer surrounded by hundreds of old barbecue grills; a tiny library branch with a sign in front advertising their summer reading program. The clinic was a quarter mile beyond that.

It was new, with bright yellow siding and a freshly blacktopped parking lot. There was a fence around the perimeter, but only a short one. There were also purple and yellow pansies along the sidewalk, and a girl with a giant rainbow Afro painted on the bus stop shelter out front.

The inside was nice, with cheap but decent waiting room furniture, a stack of fresh coloring pages on a kid-sized plastic picnic table, and crayons that still had points. An old man with dirty fatigues and a nicotine-stained beard waved at me like a Walmart greeter. "Sign in, darlin'," he said. "I forgot to when I showed up last week, and they *still* haven't called my name!" His laugh was wheezy and strained, and ended in a coughing fit. I started toward him to make sure he was okay, but he waved me on. "I'm fine, young lady," he said between gasps. "You go on."

I worked my way through the crowded room toward what was apparently the reception desk. It wasn't behind glass, and there was no annoyed-looking lady waiting to check people in. There was just a man. A really tall one who looked like he'd taken a long walk through hell and survived. His skin was pocked, his nose was crooked, and a thick, jagged scar ran from his chin down into the neckline of his shirt.

Still, his eyes were calm. His face was relaxed. And the anarchy symbol tattooed on the left side of his neck was a nice counterpoint to the praying hands on the right.

"Sign in." He pointed to the clipboard on the counter.

"I'm not sick," I said. "I'm ..."

He looked up and smiled a black-toothed meth-addict

smile. "Family planning clinic runs Wednesdays and Fridays. You need an appointment?"

My face got hot. "I'm not pregnant—"

He cut me off with a raised eyebrow. "Thus the term family *planning*."

That's when I realized he wasn't serious. He was giving me shit, and I liked him for it. So I grabbed the sign-in sheet and the pen chained to the desk with a string of paperclips and wrote:

NAME	ARRIVAL TIME	APPT. TIME	CARE PROVIDER
ROWAN CHASE	NOW	DON'T HAVE ONE	HIRE ME

He took one look and burst out laughing.

A woman in pink scrubs called out, "Crystal Montoya?" and waved over the anxious-looking woman who stood up. Then the two of them disappeared behind a door.

The desk guy was still chuckling when he spoke. "Rowan Chase, I'm Truman Atwell. People usually just call me Tru. Can you type?"

"Pretty well," I said, getting the distinct impression I was being interviewed for a job I wasn't even sure I wanted.

"Can you answer phones?"

"Yes." I looked around at the waiting room full of people.

"Can you get your bright-eyed self here by seven

thirty sharp, Monday through Friday, and not complain
if I make you stay past three from time to time?"

"I guess…"

He took my right hand in both of his and shook it
solemnly. "Then, Rowan Chase, I think you and I are
going to get along just fine."

WILLIAM

In a way, everything that came next was my own doing.
After all, I was the one who watched that boy stare at
the Model 110 in our window every day for a whole week.
At first he only slowed on his delivery bike and craned his
neck towards the shop. But come Wednesday, when the
street was quiet, he got off that bike and walked right up
onto the sidewalk to look in. He was tall, with a sturdy
build, a baby face, and the look of someone who'd stop to
put fallen baby birds back in their nests.

On Thursday, I happened to be watching passersby
from a corner at the front of the store when he arrived.
He must not have noticed me there, for he leaned so close
to the shop window that I saw his eyes and recognized
the look in them straightaway.

It was want. Pure, simple want.

Come Friday, his forehead bumped the glass. He'd leaned his bicycle against his hip and was so intent on our window display that he didn't notice when I walked outside.

"How d'you do?" I inquired.

He jumped back like I'd lit a match under him. I pointed out how there was a trolley rolling towards us along the Main Street tracks and suggested he might not want to end up in front of it.

He took off his cap and gave me a lopsided grin. Said, "That wouldn't be pretty, would it?"

I laughed and replied I didn't suppose it would.

Then the two of us stood there, unsure if our conversation had come to an end, until he put his hat back on and said, "You work here, don't you?"

"Surely do," I replied.

He toed a crack in the pavement. Looked up and down Main Street, all nerves and worries. Apart from an old man hobbling along on a cane and a nursemaid pushing a fancy baby buggy, there wasn't a soul in sight.

"Well, I was...I was just..."

He couldn't get the words out. I smiled and kept quiet, which was always Pop's strategy with nervous customers. It worked, too, because pretty soon the boy said, "I'm interested in purchasing a Victrola."

I glanced inside to see what Pop was up to. Between the paper in front of him and the music from the demo machine, he didn't seem to have noticed I'd gone out. Of course, normally neither Pop nor I would have given the time of day to someone like the boy in front of me. But I was hungry to make my first sale. Maybe just a small one, but a sale nonetheless. So I said, "Well, you've come to the right place. How about you follow that alley over there around to our back door and I'll meet you?"

"Now?" he asked. To which I replied there was no time like the present, though it would probably be best if he took his bike with him to make it appear to be a delivery. He looked at his basket and shook his head, saying, "But I haven't got any packages."

I checked the street again to make sure no one was watching. Said, "You'd best hurry, then, before someone notices." And he scurried off, turning into the alley jackrabbit quick.

As for myself, I was most of the way into the shop when a clacking sound spun me about. It came from a small boy in overalls flying past on metal roller skates. He took the corner into the alley so sharp I was sure he'd lose traction and spill. When he didn't, it put me on edge bad enough that I could barely keep from running through the showroom on my way to the back. The only thing stopping me was having to pause and crank the demo machine to keep Mamie Smith singing.

> *There's a change in the ocean*
> *Change in the deep blue sea, my baby*
> *I'll tell you folks there ain't no change in me*

"Back shelves need dusting," Pop said without glancing up. I *yes sirred* him, kept moving, and closed the storeroom door tight behind me. My heart thumped so hard it near beat through my chest, but I was too flush with ambition to stop, thinking how surprised Pop would be if I sold a Victrola all on my own. This was a chance to prove myself, and though the boy waiting in our alley might have been no more able to afford a phonograph than he could a first-class ticket on the *Mauretania*, the fact that he had a delivery job made me hopeful enough that I smoothed my hair, steadied my breath, and put on my best imitation of Pop's salesman smile. It may have been just a pudgy-faced delivery boy waiting for me outside the back door, but as far as I was concerned, he was as important as the King of England himself.

———

"I'm Joseph Goodhope," he said. There was no sign of the roller skater.

I offered my hand. Said, "William Tillman. Good to know you, Joseph." Joseph hesitated only an instant before he took it. I'd never shaken a Negro's hand before. His grip felt like any other.

"Please come in," I said. "Things are pretty busy up front, but honestly, we keep all our best deals back here anyway."

I knew Joseph would peg that for a lie, but he only

said that was fine by him and came inside. Quick as a flash, the little boy was standing next to him, skates slung over his shoulder.

"Go on, now!" Joseph said. He gave the boy a shove. "I told you to get home."

The boy shook his head and skittered sideways out of Joseph's reach. Said, "I'll tell Mama where you been if you don't let me stay!" Then he stuck his tongue out and scooted further away.

Joseph gave me a look like he was asking if I minded the boy being there. I was so hell-bent on making a sale that I wouldn't have minded if Lucifer himself had been in attendance.

"I haven't got a brother of my own," I said. "Seems to me they're more trouble than they're worth."

Joseph sighed at that and said, "Sisters are worse." Which pinched at the raw corner of my heart where Nell's memory lived, and made the little boy go indignant, shaking his head back and forth so hard his cap fell off. "I ain't no boy!" he said, as two little braids wiggled over his ears.

Joseph said, "I'm *not* a boy. Talk right, Ruby."

The kid just about busted up laughing at that, saying, "I know you ain't, you big sissy!" And Joseph scowled at her so mean it scared *me*. Then the boy who was really a girl stuck her tongue out at him and hopped up to sit on a packing crate like she meant to stay.

Joseph looked all kinds of embarrassed. "I apologize,

William," he said. "Mama's tried everything, but she can't even whup the rotten out of that girl."

Ruby crossed her thin arms over her chest and stomped her foot, muttering, "Ain't never gonna, neither."

The two of them together were like a bad vaudeville act, and so loud I figured Pop would hear them and storm in any second. "It doesn't bother me if she stays," I said, which was a lie on several counts. "But we have to be quiet."

Joseph gave Ruby a nasty look that was a little bit relieved all the same, and told her to hush. Ruby smooshed her face into a mean look. She piped down, though, which I took as my cue to start.

"So," I said. "You want to bring music into your life? Well, we've got the biggest stock in town of the finest Victrolas available. Maybe you can give me an idea what you're looking to spend so I can steer you towards the model that'll best suit your needs."

It was Pop's favorite sales pitch, word for word, and it rolled off my tongue easy as you please.

"I want to know about the one in the window," Joseph said.

I launched back in, sticking to Pop's script. "You've got a good eye, Joseph. She's a grand machine. A Model 110, brand-new to the Victrola lineup this year. We've got two in stock at the moment: the mahogany beaut you mentioned and an oak version at the back of our sales floor. We can order it in walnut if you like, though to my mind, nothing beats mahogany. Of course, since the showroom's not available just now, I can't demonstrate how true her sound is or how long she'll play. But believe me, there's no surpassing the Victor Talking Machine Company when it comes to quality or reliability, either one."

The lopsided smile played across Joseph's lips again. It tripped me up. Made me forget what I was supposed to say next. Didn't matter, though, for he had something to say himself.

"I've heard it's a fine machine..."

He stopped midsentence, looking past me. Then he made himself serious again, saying, "Just as fine as the Model 14 they sold right up till this year."

"Well, I don't know...," I mumbled, trying to hide the fact that I truly didn't.

"Mmm-hmm," Joseph said. "I believe the Model 14 sold for two hundred dollars before they changed its number and raised the price to two twenty-five. Or perhaps I'm mistaken?"

That's when I felt the deal starting to slip through my fingers. Felt it so deep that I didn't even hear Pop come in. But Ruby did, and her little body jerked straight as a pole.

"What the devil's going on back here?" Pop barked.

I froze, helpless as a landed catfish sucking air. Ruby hopped off her crate and made ready to dash. Joseph stood firm. And Pop said, "William Edward Tillman, you tell me what's going on this instant or I'll tan your hide!"

Shame bubbled hot in my belly and raced up to my face. Pop hadn't threatened to whup me in years, never mind in front of strangers. I coughed to clear the embarrassment from my throat and said how Joseph was interested in the Model 110 in the front window.

Pop narrowed his eyes, first at me, then at Joseph, and asked him if that was true. Joseph said, "Yes, sir. I didn't mean to cause any trouble. It's just that William here happened to be out on the sidewalk in front of your establishment and noticed me admiring your display."

Wary as Pop was, the prospect of a sale kept him from throwing Joseph and Ruby out on their ears.

"How old are you, Joseph?" he asked.

"Eighteen, sir," Joseph replied.

"And who's that?" Pop pointed to Ruby.

"My sister, Ruby. She's ten."

Pop studied them both. Asked if they had money. Joseph said, "Yes, sir. Cash. I deliver for Rex's Drugstore after school and on weekends, and summers I help frame houses."

That piqued Pop's interest.

"Where are you a student?" he asked.

"Booker T. Washington High School," Joseph said proudly. "I graduate this year."

"Well, Victrolas are expensive, son," Pop said.

Joseph nodded, serious as all get out, and replied, "I know, sir. I've been saving a long time."

Pop pondered that, no doubt thinking of all the

colored folks he'd made money off of in the past. Finally, he said, "Well, Joseph, as you know, shops in this part of town can't sell to Negroes."

Joseph appeared neither surprised nor bothered by that. "Yes, sir," he said. "But I've heard tell you understand how difficult it can be for a person such as myself to procure a Victrola in Tulsa, there being no shop yet in the Negro quarter. They say you're the kind of man who believes every home should be filled with music."

Pop liked that, I could tell. I could also tell Joseph wasn't just some baby-faced delivery boy. Then Pop asked, "Folks say that, do they?" And Joseph replied, "Yes, sir. So I brought my money with me. And I'm prepared to spend it."

Pop took off his glasses and cleaned them with his handkerchief. "William," he said, "go up front and mind the shop. Help any customers looking for records. If they're interested in Victrolas, tell them I'll be available shortly."

It wasn't hard holding my tongue as I slunk away, weighted down as it was with humiliation. There wasn't a soul on the sales floor, either, which suited me fine. For it let me leave the storeroom door cracked open enough to hear Pop start the negotiations, saying, "Well, Joseph, what kind of budget do you have in mind?" And Joseph didn't hesitate any in telling him one hundred and thirty dollars.

Pop repeated the sum aloud. Said, "I have a nice

walnut table model that goes for an even hundred. Would that suit you?"

"No, sir," Joseph replied.

I figured Pop would lose his temper. Instead, he asked exactly what it was Joseph wanted.

"That Model 14 over there," Joseph said.

Then came silence. A long, long silence that lasted until Pop muttered something too quiet for me to make out. But I heard perfectly well when Joseph responded, "I understand, sir. Only I read how once the company brings out a new model, dealers are supposed to sell the old ones fast. I also read that if they can't get rid of those old machines, they're supposed to return them to the factory for less than they paid in the first place."

I would have given just about anything to see Pop's face at that moment, so long as he didn't know it.

"What else did you read, Joseph?" Pop asked. And Joseph replied that he knew dealers paid a hundred and fifty wholesale for the Model 14, but only got one twenty-five back when they returned them. Which meant that if Pop were to let him have the machine for one thirty, he'd cut his losses by five dollars. More, if you included the cost of freight.

Three men stopped out front to look in the shop window. I willed them to keep walking, which they did. And by the time they'd moved on, Pop had worked his way around to saying he couldn't do what Joseph was asking.

More silence.

Then, miracle though it seemed, Pop said, "I can't sell it to you for less than one forty-five, plus ten dollars delivery."

My left leg had gone numb underneath me. I didn't dare move to get blood back into it.

"You raised your delivery price?" Joseph asked.

He was patient. Clever, too. And I realized that he must have had things figured out long before he ever slowed his bike down outside the shop. I wondered how he knew about the Victor Talking Machine Company's pricing policy, how many days he'd waited to approach us. And I felt a curious mix of jealousy and admiration stir inside me for the boy who'd marched into Pop's shop and taken him on, fearless as you please.

Then Pop said, "My delivery price goes up when I'm handing out deals this good." And Joseph came right back, saying, "If you can see your way clear to charge me one forty plus the standard five-dollar delivery fee, sir, we can do business."

Now, even though I couldn't see Pop, I knew he'd have said no straight off if he wasn't thinking about agreeing. I knew he was tapping his finger against his cheek like he always did near the end of a negotiation. And I was right. For at long last he said, "You've got yourself a deal."

I drew a relieved breath. Then Joseph said, "Thank you, sir. Now, can we discuss terms?" And Pop's voice came curt, saying, "You told me you had cash in hand."

To which Joseph replied, "Yes, sir. One hundred dollars. That's a substantial down payment, I believe."

There was an uneasy stretch of silence after that, when I imagined Joseph pulling bills from his pocket and Pop eyeing them, deciding where his druthers lay. Seeing that much money in a white man's hands would have been enough to make my father accept weekly payments for the balance, no question. But Joseph was young. He was colored. And even more than that, he'd just managed to sweet-talk Stanley Tillman into selling him a brand-new Victrola for ten dollars under wholesale. The way I figured it, terms were an ask too far.

Only they weren't.

Pop agreed to take the balance in nine payments of five dollars each, plus a tenth payment of two dollars and fifty cents as a finance fee. Each payment was due by closing time on Friday. "And I won't deliver the machine until you've paid in full," Pop said. "Understand?"

Joseph said that was fine, thank you very much, and Pop told him it was to be a good-faith arrangement; he couldn't give a contract or a receipt to a Negro, for if such a thing were to fall into the wrong hands, there'd be hell to pay.

Which upset Joseph, I could tell. The words *but sir* had barely left his mouth when Pop interrupted, saying, "No *buts*. Take it or leave it. And should you miss a payment or come in late, even by a day, you'll be in default.

That means I keep every cent you've paid to that point, and the Victrola, too."

Joseph didn't protest. The terms were harsh, but just as surely as Pop had been caught flat-footed on the price, Joseph knew he was lucky to get them at all.

"That's fine," Joseph said. "Thank you, sir." And Pop replied that he'd expect the next payment in exactly one week, on the first of April.

Then Joseph told Ruby it was time to go home. I scooted fast to the front of the store and leaned against the lacquered Chinese cabinet of our most expensive model. When Pop came out, he snapped like an old alligator turtle, telling me not to scratch the finish. Then he picked up his newspaper, yanked it open, and set to reading.

I put a fresh record on the demo machine, casual as could be, and asked how things had gone. Pop would have none of it. He ignored my question and told me to go put a sheet over the Model 14 in the back. But there was no sting in his reproach. Not that time. For I knew I'd gotten the sale rolling. I knew that if it weren't for me, the Model 14 would have been going back to the factory at a twenty-five-dollar loss, plus freight. I knew Pop knew it. And those thoughts put together went a long way towards making up for the humiliation I'd suffered in the company of Joseph and Ruby Goodhope.

Rowan

The raspy singing came from the exam room next door.

I can't get no-o
Sa-tis-fak-shun

Even before it started, I'd been having trouble concentrating on the ultra-boring, never-ending tutorial about patient confidentiality, sexual harassment policy, and emergency procedures that Tru had left me to watch. There was a tax form on the desk that I didn't know how to fill out. I was hot from sitting in a tiny space with an ancient computer. And I wasn't quite sure what I'd gotten myself into.

The Rolling Stones serenade didn't help.

But then the words faded away, and deep, hard coughs

took over. It sounded like they hurt. And they went on and on and on.

I paused the tutorial and stood outside the exam room door. It was open just a crack, so my knock was careful.

"Hello?" I said. "Are you okay?"

The person inside fought to quiet himself. Even before I heard him tell me to come in, I knew who it was.

"Hey there, darlin'," said the old man from the waiting room. His shoes were off and against the wall, socks tucked inside them.

"I just heard you from the room next door," I said. "And…"

A big grin lit up his face. "And you wanted to check on me! I knew you were a sweetie soon as I saw you. I got a nose for that sort of thing, you know. It's a gift."

He looked so pleased with the whole situation that I couldn't help smiling back.

"Would you like me to get you a glass of water?" I asked. "There's a cooler in the break room."

"It's kind of you to offer, darlin', but I got my own right here." He held up an old plastic water bottle that had been reused nearly to death. "Name's Arvin. What's yours?"

I told him. Then he offered me his hand, and without stopping to think, I took two quick steps inside and shook it.

"Always a pleasure to meet a pretty young lady, 'specially when she's kindhearted to boot," he said. "I bet Doc Woods was a lot like you once. I just bet she was."

I stepped back, not quite sure if I was supposed to be there with him at all. Arvin coughed again, only that time he unscrewed the lid of his water bottle and took a long swallow.

Afterwards, he looked at me with a wicked twinkle in his eye and said, "Say, Rowan, you got a smoke I could bum?"

Before I could tell him no, the door pushed wider behind me and Arvin's face lifted into a high-eyebrowed imitation of innocence.

"Hello there, Miss Julie," he said.

The nurse behind me was not amused.

"It's a good thing I'm not Dr. Woods," she said. "You know she'll rip you a new one if she finds out you're smoking."

Arvin grinned again, and that time the innocence seemed real.

"Nah, she wouldn't. She's my angel."

"Maybe so, but I wouldn't press my luck if I were you," the nurse said, waving me out.

"Don't make my new friend go," Arvin said with real sadness in his voice. "We were just getting acquainted."

The nurse rolled her eyes. "I'm sure you'll both have plenty of time to get to know each other, Arvin."

"Prolly so," he said. "You know me—I keep turnin' up like a bad penny." Then he was laughing, and the laugh turned into a cough that even the water couldn't stop. The nurse pushed me out and closed the door, but I could hear her voice inside, asking Arvin where his inhaler was, telling him everything was going to be fine.

———

Once I'd finally finished the tutorial and faked my way through the tax form, Tru took me out to the reception desk, gave me a quick intro to the clinic's recordkeeping software, and handed me a list of questions that was supposed to help me decide which doctor or nurse practitioner to schedule patients with.

For the rest of the morning, I fumbled my way through call after call until I wasn't fumbling so badly anymore. While I handled the phone, Tru directed incoming patient traffic like some kind of tattooed, bilingual ninja-Buddha. He juggled walk-ins, bleeders, drunks, screamers, weepers, and hallucinators. Nearly every kid who came through the door ran straight to him, begging for stickers and suckers. Depending on some complex mental formula known only to him, they got one or both. The whole time, he switched back and forth between English and Spanish so fast even Señora Markowitz would have been impressed.

When things finally got a little quieter, he gave me an insurance manual and told me to read it. Ten minutes later, I set it down.

"You finished?" he asked.

"Finished? I'm not even sure it's in English."

Tru laughed and leaned close like he was about to let me in on some big secret.

"Good answer. I was just checking to make sure our evil insurance overlords didn't send you to spy on us. Any questions you can't answer about payments go straight to our billing clerk, J'Neece."

He dropped his voice. "She lives in a cave at the back of the building, and the only proof we have of her existence is the empty Diet Coke bottle she leaves in the recycling bin every night."

"Doesn't she ever come out to pee?" I whispered back.

"Never. And it's a *liter* bottle."

He stood up and stretched. I answered the phone and had just started in on the question list when Tru gave me a quick wave, saying, "Back in half an hour." My stomach barrel-rolled as I asked the woman to please hold, and pushed a button on the keypad.

"Where are you going?" I asked. Tru was already halfway to the door.

"Lunch," he said, like it was the silliest question in the world.

"But I'm..."

"You're fine. Besides, Arvin's an old hand, aren't you, Arvin?"

Arvin had been dozing in his spot by the door since his appointment ended. At the sound of his name, he bolted upright and gave Tru a salute. "You bet, boss."

Tru smiled. "See, Rowan? You've got this. And lunch is on me. You like brisket? I'll get you some brisket."

Then he was gone, and according to the dial tone coming from the phone, I'd hung up on the caller. I was also all alone except for Arvin and the little girl with Down syndrome whose grandmother had brought her in for a checkup and the roofer who'd started having seizures after he fell off a two-story house and the old woman who smelled like stale cigarettes and kept talking to the Chihuahua in her lap. Everybody there needed help. None of them had gotten a new Lexus for their birthday, or taken a spring shopping trip to Paris, or spent afternoons at the country club charging Cokes and baskets of fries to their parents' account. It was pretty much the opposite of school and everything I was used to.

The phone rang. A woman trailing four kids came through the door.

It's okay, I told myself. *You've got this.*

———

I so did not have it.

The ringing phone was the woman I'd cut off, and I got flustered enough that I disconnected her again. The lady and her four kids had no appointment, but they did have five raging cases of pinkeye between them. The Chihuahua barked at the kids. The phone kept ringing.

Then Arvin pulled a bologna sandwich out of his

backpack and fed little bits of it to the Chihuahua to shut it up. I filled the kids' hands with suckers to keep them from getting pinkeye cooties on everything in the waiting room. The nurses hustled to get people in as fast as they could. By the time Tru came back, things were basically calm again.

"What'd I miss?" he asked. And if the brisket smell coming from the container in his hands hadn't made my stomach growl so loud, I might have actually told him. Instead, I ate my lunch (which, by the way, was really good), stayed at the desk, and made it to three o'clock with no major screwups.

"Hasta mañana?" Tru asked as I dug around for my keys.

"I don't know. Is it always like this around here?"

He shook his head. "Nah. Some days it gets kind of crazy."

"Well, since you put it like that..."

He smiled.

I smiled back.

"Hasta mañana."

———

Mom and Dad were still at work when I got home, and there was an old green van parked in the driveway. Its back windows were tinted so dark I couldn't see in. The driver's seat had one of those back support wedges strapped to it, and the passenger side was full of crumpled McDonald's bags and old mix tapes. Someone had written *State of Oklahoma Medical Examiner* in purple Sharpie on an index card and stuck it between the windshield and the dashboard like a kid playing pretend. The ME guy had said he was calling in a forensic anthropologist, but the van looked more like it belonged to a serial killer.

She was on her stomach in the back house, snapping pictures of the body with an old-school camera. When I got to the doorway, she looked up. "Who are you?"

"Rowan Chase," I said. "I live here."

"Well, Rowan Chase, you can come in or you can leave, but please get out of that doorway." She started taking pictures again.

I stepped inside and stood against the wall. The woman kept working, scooting inch by inch around the hole, making tiny adjustments to the focus before each shot. She didn't seem to mind me being there, or care that her T-shirt was hiked up past the fleshy rolls around her middle.

While she ignored me, I studied her—the worn soles of her Birkenstocks, the faded list of concert dates on the back of her T-shirt, the varicose veins running like roads on a map underneath the pale skin of her calves.

I drummed my fingers against the wall.

She kept taking pictures.

I shuffled my feet and cleared my throat.

Still nothing.

Then I started wondering if maybe she was actually some delusional ex-hippie wannabe who'd overdosed on

CSI episodes and made a fake ME sign for herself. The only hitch was, unless she'd found the emergency key we kept under a flowerpot in the garden shed, Mom or Dad had to have let her in.

It was another five minutes before she spoke.

"Rowan, would you please hold my camera?"

I walked over, took it from her outstretched hand, and saw the skeleton for the first time since the day before. In the bright glare from the umbrella lights she'd brought, it was more sad than upsetting.

The woman hoisted herself up and brushed construction dust off her T-shirt, which (hello, irony) turned out to be from a Grateful Dead concert. Her arms and hands were leathery, her face pale and smooth. Best I could tell, she was somewhere between forty and seventy.

She took the camera and got so close-up in my face that I had to fight the urge to move away.

"Sorry," she said, backing off on her own. "I'm making you uncomfortable."

"No, you're not," I lied.

"Yes, I am. I'm Geneva Roop. People call me Genny but I don't like it. I consult for the medical examiner's office."

Genny. The one the ketchup-stained guy had mentioned the day before.

"You're an anthropologist?" I asked.

Geneva frowned. "I don't have a PhD and I'm not in ABFA."

"ABFA?"

"The American Board of Forensic Anthropology. You have to pass a test to join. I don't like tests."

I was about to say I hated tests, too, but Geneva didn't give me a chance.

"The police tracked down three of the workers who were here yesterday. They claimed they never touched the body, and that they left immediately after finding it because the fourth man with them was illegal. Can you verify that?"

Two seconds before, she'd been apologizing. Now she was grilling me harder than the detectives had.

"I don't know about the *undocumented* part, but they left right after they cut the hole," I said. "Probably because they didn't want to get interrogated over something they had nothing to do with."

Geneva set her camera down on top of a storage bin and picked up a stubby pencil and a Five Star spiral-bound notebook. I love those things, especially when they're new and empty and begging to be written in. There's a stack of them on the top shelf of my closet, each one filled to the first divider with stories, poems, journal entries— stupid stuff I never finished.

Geneva apparently had no such problem with persistence. Most of the pages in her notebook looked full, all the way up to the last section. She flipped there, past a sheet with our address written on it in the same purple Sharpie as the index card in her van.

"What else can you tell me?" she said.

I went over the whole story again: how the men woke me up when they arrived, how they got back in their truck two minutes after the sawing stopped. She didn't write anything down.

"Was the body in the oilcloth when you found it?"

"Yes. I'm the one who unwrapped it."

"Why?" She sounded genuinely curious.

"I'm not sure," I said, because I *felt like it* may have been true, but it would have seemed rude.

Geneva wasn't convinced.

"Why are you calling the skeleton a 'him'?" she asked.

"He's wearing men's clothes, isn't he?"

"So am I."

"Okay, but you can tell, right?" I asked. "From his pelvis?"

"Where did you learn that?"

"Netflix. Is it true?"

Her eyebrows pinched inward. "Yes. Unless it's an infant or a child, you can almost always tell from the pelvis. Women's hip bones are wider, with space inside for babies. Men's are narrower and look taller."

"So do you know if this skeleton is male?" I asked.

"Of course not. It's wearing pants."

I felt like an idiot. Geneva didn't seem to care.

"I won't know much about these remains until I get the clothes off and take a look," she said. "Oilcloth is good protection, but I'm sure that crawl space has flooded over the years. Plus, unembalmed soft tissue breaks down

115

into rot soup. Even if the anterior skeletal structures didn't percolate in that, chances are they're still degraded from ground contact alone."

The thought of spleen stew made me want to hurl, but I was, after all, a mystery junkie. Geneva had my complete attention.

"For the sake of argument," she said, "let's assume the remains *are* from a man. I'll be able to figure out a lot about what he was like when he was alive: his height, his build, which hand he used, whether he had any serious diseases or injuries before he died, and if he did much heavy labor. I'll get his age within a few years, too. And there's quite a bit of intact facial structure left on the upturned side of his skull, so I'll probably have an idea about his ancestry."

"How long will all that take?" I asked.

"Not long. But my assistant had his gallbladder out yesterday and I'm on my own."

I looked at the skeleton. The way Geneva talked, it was one big puzzle just waiting to be solved. This wasn't a show or a dusty bookshelf mystery. This was real.

"I could help if you want," I said, figuring she'd say no right away. But she only opened one of the storage bins and rummaged around.

"Would that be okay?" I asked.

"I suppose," she said. "How about you start by showing me the wallet?"

Cue my minor panic attack.

"Wallet?" I said.

"Don't be obtuse, Rowan. I can see perfectly well that the fabric of the back pants pocket is distended. Peter didn't mention finding it in his preliminary report, and there's no sign of it in his pictures. So unless you're lying to me about unwrapping the tarp yourself…"

"I'm not," I said. "Hang on."

I ran to the main house, calling myself nasty names that got even nastier when I realized our housekeeper, Gladys, had been there that day. She'd made a neat stack on my desk of everything she hadn't known what to do with, including the wallet I'd stashed back under my bed and a folded-up piece of paper I'd never seen before.

It was yellowed and brittle. I pressed it open carefully so the folded edges wouldn't crack. Inside, the blue ink was faded but readable.

Victory Victrola Shop
Payments rendered by J. Goodhope towards
one Victor Talking Machine Company
Victrola Model XIV

The columns underneath were labeled *Date, Amount,* and *Balance Forward,* and the first three entries read: *April 1, 1921; $5.00; $42.50.* Each entry after that came in once-a-week five-dollar increments, with the last on May 27. *W. T.* was penciled into the margin alongside every one, and even though there was still a $2.50 balance left at the bottom of the *Balance Forward* column, someone had written *PAID* underneath it in the same handwriting as the initials.

The best I could figure was that the paper had come out of the wallet when I threw it under the bed yesterday, and I must have been so focused on gathering up the coins that I missed it. Übermeticulous Gladys hadn't, though. Gladys never misses anything.

I folded the paper back up and grabbed the wallet. Set the paper down. Picked it up again. Set it down.

I'm still not sure why I left it there. Blame it on my detective fetish, or the fact that my day at the clinic had left me feeling salty.

The wallet and the bones were Geneva's.

The receipt was mine.

WILLIAM

A week to the day after Joseph Goodhope made his backroom deal with Pop, I was dragging my feet westward on Sixth Street, making the walk between school and work last as long as I could and thinking how I hadn't seen Addie in an age. The air was warm even for spring, and the Oklahoma wind blew stiff enough to make you hold your hat.

"April Fools'!"

Ruby popped out from behind the corner of a building, hopping up and down and giggling. I jumped myself, only out of fright.

"You should see your face, Will Tillman! Looks like you seen a ghost!" she said, cackling like a tiny madwoman.

I put my head down and tried to push past, saying, "You're no ghost, Ruby Goodhope, just a pesky little monkey."

Which made her scramble back ahead of me, scowling to beat all.

"Joseph says when white folks call black folks monkeys it shows they're ignorant."

Unaccustomed as I was to being sassed by little girls, that stopped me short. "Oh yeah?" I said.

Ruby crossed her arms over her chest and glared. "Mm-hmm."

"And how exactly does Joseph figure that?" I asked.

She glared harder.

"He says we *all* come from monkeys. Or apes, maybe. I can't remember. But people come from monkeys 'cause science says so."

To which I replied that what she'd said was blasphemy, and little girls shouldn't talk like that, and did she want to make God mad?

"I reckon it makes God madder when people don't use the brains he saw fit to give 'em," she said.

I gave her a nasty look and was about to lecture her on how she shouldn't question the Bible when a wind gust lifted the cap off my head and sent it flipping and rolling on its edge down the sidewalk. Ruby took off like a shot, zigging and zagging around parked bicycles, ducking in and out of the shade from striped store awnings, weaving through a display of shovels and rakes outside a hardware store. Each time she'd catch up, the wind would carry the cap further. I ran after her, stumbling over bootlaces I hadn't even noticed were untied. "Wait!" I hollered, kneeling quick to fix them. The cap flew into the road. Ruby followed. That's when I heard the rumble of an engine over the wind.

Everything happened so fast I can't say exactly what transpired. First there was Ruby, small and quick-winged, darting into the middle of the street with her braids flying. Then there was the big black milk truck behind her, bearing down so fast I knew it couldn't miss.

Only it did.

Or, rather, *she* missed *it*, snatching my hat midbounce and hopping away so nimbly that the driver had only just started to swerve. But swerve he did, cutting his tires hard into the curb. Glass bottles clinked and clattered. Square metal baskets tumbled out a side door, the empty milk bottles inside them shattering against the brick-paved street like icicles off a roof. And all the while, Ruby paid no mind to the chaos. She gave a deep curtsy, holding out my hat like it was grand prize at the county fair, saying, "Your chapeau, mon frère." I don't believe she even saw the white-uniformed milkman stomping towards us.

"What in hell's name do you think you're about, you little—"

I got myself between Ruby and him quick, keeping her behind me with my good arm while the fingers of my casted hand clutched my cap.

"It was my fault, sir," I blurted. Which surprised me

even as the words left my lips. "I sent her to fetch my hat without checking for vehicles first. She's a good girl, sir, doing as she was told."

The milkman's mouth clamped shut just ahead of him calling Ruby whatever ugly name had been on the tip of his tongue. His jaw hardened down like dark-stubbled granite.

"Well, she's lucky not to be dead in the street right now," he said in a way that made me think he wouldn't have minded overmuch if she were.

Ruby tried to pull free behind me. I held her arm tight and yanked her back.

"Am not!" she shouted, hopping up to try and see over my shoulder. "Ow! You let me go, Will! I wasn't nowhere close to gettin' hit!"

The milkman's skin flushed underneath the purple lines threading his drinker's nose. "I thought you said she was a good girl," he growled. "Seems to me she needs to learn her place. Her mama work for your folks?"

Ruby wriggled, and I squeezed hard enough on her thin arm that she whimpered. Our maid, Angelina, was old as the hills, and had finished raising her boy before she ever entered our employ. Still, there was no sense quibbling with the man over details, especially when they were so conveniently incorrect.

"Yes, sir," I said. "She sure does."

He mulled that over while I sent up silent prayers that

Ruby would have the good sense to keep quiet. Then he rubbed some softness back into his jaw, saying, "Somebody oughta take a strap to that girl, teach her a lesson. And you oughta know better than to send a stupid little pickaninny into the street."

An automobile honked just then, cutting off whatever invectives Ruby was about to let fly. "Get that thing out of the way!" its driver shouted. The milkman spun about sharp with murder in his eyes. But the vehicle was a beaut of a brand-new Lincoln, and its driver a goateed man wearing expensive gray summer flannels and gold-rimmed spectacles that gleamed in the sun. He looked important. Rich, at least. Enough so the milkman thought better of mouthing off and only touched his cap, saying, "Yes, sir. Just a moment."

By that point I'd made a quick mental tally of the cost of the broken bottles in the street and had dug enough money out of my wallet to cover it.

"Here, sir," I said, tossing in a few extra coins for good measure. "I hope this will cover the damage."

The milkman took the coins and jiggled them in his palm.

"Plus this, of course." I forked over my last four dollars. "For your trouble."

The creases in his forehead eased as he pocketed the coins and grunted. Then he shot me one last mean look and hustled off to move his truck. And though it would have been proper to help him clear the street, I was worried enough over what Ruby might do or say that I didn't.

"You let me be!" she howled as I dragged her off. "Or I'll tell your ma!"

I grumbled something ungentlemanly and walked faster.

"Ooh—I'm gonna tell her you said that, too. She'll blister your hide!"

And on and on she yammered, hitting at my good hand, threatening and wheedling by turns, until I finally stopped and faced her, saying, "Now, listen good, you little brat! You near got yourself run over back there, and don't think that man wouldn't have backhanded you or worse if I hadn't stepped in! You don't belong in this part of town, Ruby Goodhope. Go on back to Little Africa where you belong!"

Her big eyes fell. Her left hand rubbed at the bruised spot where I'd held her.

"He couldn'ta caught me," she said, only with none of her usual swagger and sass. And suddenly it wasn't a colored girl I saw before me, but a girl, plain and simple. And she was so small and sad and scared that my anger drained out of me like pus from a boil. I squatted down to her height. Said, "I didn't mean that, Ruby."

"Yes, you did," she whispered.

Which was partly true, but not entirely. For the man *could* have slapped or spanked her right there in full daylight. And though a few passersby might have disapproved, no one would have stopped him. To most folks, Ruby may have been a little girl, but she was a Negro first.

Still, the rest of what I'd said had gone too far. And I hadn't liked seeing Ruby cut down, never mind nearly killed. I hated it so much that I reached out and wiped away the teardrop slipping down her cheek. Counting my handshake with Joseph and grabbing her arm, it was the third time I'd touched a brown-skinned person. Fourth if you counted getting shoved by Clarence. Yet it was the first time I'd actually wanted to.

I told her I was sorry and that I shouldn't have hurt her arm or said those ugly things, God strike me dead if I was lying. And she must have sensed my sincerity, for she looked up again and said, "I ain't no crybaby. My eyes just water when I'm mad."

Two more tears slid down her cheek and darkened the fabric of her blouse where they landed.

"I came to see you 'cause I need a favor," she said. "I want you to write out a receipt for Joseph's payments on that Victrola. It ain't right, him giving money to your pa without your pa giving him any account in return. Way things stand now, he could take every dime Joseph pays, then laugh in his face when it's done. Joseph knows it's a rotten deal, but he wants our ma to have music so bad he's willing to put up with it. I ain't."

And while I wanted to answer back that Pop was an honest businessman and would never cheat a customer, the leftover shine of tears in Ruby's eyes kept me from it. Instead, I told her that the best I could do would be to write up some sort of receipt myself. It wouldn't carry any authority with Pop or anyone else, but the notion satisfied Ruby enough to win me a shaky smile.

"Joseph's bringing this week's payment to your shop just as soon as he gets a break in his deliveries," she said. "You give him that receipt when you see him, and don't say nothin' about talkin' to me. Please?"

Which took me aback, both because she'd said please and because I figured she'd want to see for herself that I'd followed through with my promise. But I told her I'd do as she asked, and she nodded and thanked me and walked away.

I watched her go, thinking how very straight her back was, how her shoulders never slumped and her head stayed high. And I wondered how it was that a girl most of the world thought so little of could carry herself so proud. Then I put on my cap, leaned into the wind, and set off for work.

———

The shop did a brisk business that afternoon. Pop sold a midpriced Victrola to a skinny roughneck trying hard to impress his girl, and four different people came in wanting a copy of Paul Whiteman and His Orchestra playing "Caresses." Two others hummed off-key versions of different songs that I recognized, and they bought the recordings, easy as you please.

But there was no sign of Joseph Goodhope; not hanging about on the front sidewalk, not zipping past on his bicycle. I was watching, too, keeping an eye on the street. For I'd made a promise to Ruby, and thickheaded as I was about some things, I was beginning to suspect that being righteous had less to do with whipping straps and beating Negroes than it did with keeping your word.

I never did see Joseph, though, and Pop neither glanced at his watch nor gave any other sign he was waiting on someone. It was as if he'd already decided the best outcome for the whole arrangement would be for Joseph to default on his hundred-dollar down payment. That way Pop would be able to return the Model 14 to the factory for $125 and still have more money in his pocket than he'd started off with. I'd told Ruby my father was honest, and to my knowledge he always had been. But I wasn't so sure he'd pass up free money, especially if it meant he wouldn't be left holding the short straw in a deal with a Negro.

Come six thirty, Pop declared it a full day's work and flipped the sign on the door to CLOSED. "Get your things," he said. "I'm ready for supper." Which didn't surprise me, since Angelina made his favorite chicken fried steak with white gravy every Friday. But food was the least of my concerns just then, what with the memory of the milk truck and Ruby's tears heavy on my mind. So, casual as could be, I said yes sir, but didn't he want to wait to make sure that Negro boy had a chance to pay his five dollars before we closed?

Pop fixed on me so hard I could near feel his eyes bore through my skull. But I'd had enough practice looking innocent and enduring skeptical glares that I didn't flinch. And that alone must have convinced Pop I wasn't up to anything too untoward, for he shrugged and put on his hat, saying, "That boy showed up ten minutes before you today, William. *He's* not a dawdler."

Then Pop went to lock up the storeroom, leaving me to gather my schoolbooks and hat and ponder why it was that I suddenly felt so much better about the world.

———

The next day found me so distracted, worrying Ruby might show up at work to read me the riot act over not giving Joseph the receipt, that by the time lunch rolled around, I'd broken one record and tripped twice over the most expensive Victrola we had in stock. It was so bad that come noontime, Pop took three dollars out of the register and laid them on the counter, saying he'd forgot his lunch, and would I please go down to Shackle's Drugstore and get him a chicken salad sandwich. Plus I should order something for myself at the counter and take my time eating it.

Normally that would have thrilled me no end. But when I got to Shackle's, my foot tapped and my eyes watched the clock as I waited for the soda jerk to work his way towards me along the crowded counter. And it wasn't until I'd near choked to death wolfing down the first half of my egg and olive that I had the sense to slow down and ponder the true and proper source of my impatience. Which, painful as it was to admit, boiled down to the fact that I wanted to see Ruby.

I made myself take smaller bites, then ordered a chocolate phosphate soda and sipped it slow. Still, I found myself reaching into my pocket every now and again to touch the receipt I'd written up for Joseph, wondering if Ruby had stopped by the shop while I was gone.

She never did show up that day, or on Monday, or the next few days after that. Yet I thought about her and Joseph more than Addie, even, which was a worry and a relief all rolled into one. So to put my mind at ease, I played hooky from my last class that Friday and made for the shop, thinking I'd beat Joseph there for sure.

Of course, it being near forty-five minutes earlier than Pop expected me, I couldn't go inside. And I couldn't pass the cigar shop's window, either, since Vernon Fish always watched the street like a hawk. So I tucked myself into a dusty alleyway, leaned against the wall, crossed my ankles, and did my best to be invisible.

It was to no avail. For not five minutes later, the stink of a Maduro Robusto crawled inside my nose and stuck there like smoke from a burnt offering. Then Vernon Fish himself walked past, stopped, switched a paper-wrapped package from his right hand to his left, and walked back.

"School let out early, Half-breed?"

The cigar smoke made my eyes water, and it took every ounce of willpower I had not to back away.

"No, sir, Mr. Fish," I said.

He pinched the cigar between his thumb and forefinger and leaned even closer. "Then what are you doing here?"

And maybe it was fear, or maybe it was all the practice I'd been getting lately, but I smiled like I was about to share the biggest secret in the world and let the lie slide off my tongue, slick as buttered glass.

"My history teacher doesn't know his ass from his armpit, and I'd had all I could stand for one day."

Vernon narrowed his eyes, wedged the cigar between his broad lips, and slugged my shoulder so hard I winced. "I like your moxie, boy," he said. "World's full of saps who think book learnin's the same as a real education. Not me. Got my degree from the school of hard knocks, I did."

I nodded, hoping the conversation would end there. But Vernon tossed me his package, scowling when I fumbled it with my bum hand. "Carry that," he said. "I'm gonna show you something."

At the door of his shop, Vernon chucked the wooden Indian on the chin for luck and said how if ever I wanted to earn a nickel an hour, I could bring my Injun headdress and stand outside in the statue's place. Then he let out a mean whoop of a laugh and flipped the BE RIGHT BACK sign on the cigar shop door to OPEN as we went inside.

I'd been in that store plenty of times, mostly to fetch Pop cigars he'd never smoke. Even so, it always surprised me how tidy the place was. On top of cigars, Vernon sold candy, cigarettes, loose tobacco, and rolling papers. The whole kit and caboodle was arranged neatly behind the counter. He kept pipes as well, from plain and cheap to fancy and not, each one polished bright and displayed alongside gleaming cigar cutters. There was never a speck of dust to be found, and Vernon worked the creaky wooden floors to a high gloss twice a week himself. Even the stink of his Maduros was more bearable inside, tempered as it was by the sweet scents of pipe tobacco and wood polish.

Which isn't to say that the state of Vernon's store made me like him more or fear him less. Truth was, the thoughtfulness behind it, the attention and care, made him all the scarier. Vernon wasn't just mean, he was meticulous.

Once he'd closed the door and hung his fedora on the hat rack beside it, Vernon told me to go to the counter. Then he settled himself onto a stool without offering me use of the spare. I stood like an albatross, awkward and itching to hand over his package just as soon as I could.

Only Vernon didn't ask for it. He said, "I'm gonna give you the honor of opening that parcel, Half-breed. I want you to see for yourself what's inside." Which made my normal fear of him bloom into full-on dread.

"Now, Mr. Fish?" I asked. Vernon stubbed out what remained of his cigar, took a fresh one from the shelf behind him, fished around in his pants pocket for his double guillotine cutter, and lined the end of the new Maduro up between its blades. "No time like the present," he said, squeezing the cutter quick so the cigar's tip dropped into the ashtray in front of him.

Well, my hands weren't all that steady to begin with, and the cast didn't help one bit. But I managed to pick the knotted string loose from the package and set it aside. I glanced up after that, unsure whether or not to keep going. Vernon lit his cigar, took a puff, and nodded that I should.

The box underneath the wrapping was plain and white. "Go on," he said. "Open it, already!"

So I did. And at first, the folded whiteness inside looked for all the world like a stack of tissue paper. But as I lifted the top piece away, a triangular outline against a bed of white fabric came clear. Then Vernon's own eagerness must have got the better of him, for he stood up, leaned over, and snatched the triangle from the box.

"Ain't that a glorious sight?" he said, all breathy like a kid on Christmas morning. The fabric in his hand fell open into the shape of a big white ice cream cone.

"You know what this is, don't you, boy?"

"No, sir," I said.

"It's a badge of honor."

Vernon set the cone down, lifted out the layers of cloth left in the box, and draped a big white choir-robe-looking thing over the counter. He smoothed the creases from it, fussing like a girl over a gown. Then he recovered a bit, straightening up and blowing smoke into my face.

"What you're looking at, boy, is the bona fide, real and true Ku Klux Klan regalia worn by God-fearing patriots across this great land of ours. And this"—he picked up the cone and laid it next to the robe—"is our crowning glory."

I looked at the getup, unsure what to say. Which proved to be a good thing, for Vernon kept right on talking about how no laundry in town knew how to starch Klan hoods proper, so until he'd found a wife and trained her to do it, he'd take care of it himself, thank you very much. Then he put the hat on, unstarched as it was, so that the tip flopped down and made him look a fool.

From the expression on his face, you'd have thought he'd just come back from war to parades and pretty girls lined up in waiting. And that's the honest truth, though it's just as true that I should have made sure my thoughts didn't show on my face. For before I knew it, Vernon was sizing me up through eyelids narrowed to slits.

"What's that sneer about, boy?" he said, all low and

quiet. Cold flushed through my insides. I lowered my gaze and said I was thinking how fine the robe was, and how proud I'd be to wear a cap like that myself. Which was a lie, but one good enough to make him take the hood from his head and cradle it close, saying: "You can forget about that, Half-breed. This cap's for white men, not mongrels. I'm just showin' it to you out of pity, on account of you not having a proper mother."

He was calm. Smug, too, watching to see how I'd react. And though the blood rushed loud in my ears, I muttered I was sorry and never meant any disrespect, hating myself a little more with every word. After which Vernon set his cigar on the lip of his ashtray and folded the robe up carefully and put it back in the box with the hood on top.

When that was done, he tucked the cigar into the corner of his mouth and propped his elbows on the counter, saying, "You shining me on, boy, or you mean it?" And I swore seven ways to Sunday that there was no living soul more sincere than I, until the side of his face without the cigar pulled up into a wicked smile.

"Good," he said. "You wait here and I'll show you what the Klan *really* means." Then Vernon disappeared behind the cloth curtain covering the doorway to the back, and I closed my eyes, thinking that when he returned, I'd say I needed to get to work. And I felt Joseph's receipt in my pocket, and hoped he hadn't already come and gone.

Only, when Vernon came back, I forgot all about

Joseph and the receipt, and about hiding my feelings, too. And he fed off the fear he'd put in my heart, letting his lopsided sneer go bigger as he aimed the pistol in his hand at my chest.

"Maybelle," he said, "this is Half-breed. Half-breed, meet Maybelle."

Rowan

I ran extra early on Wednesday so I could get to work on time, and hard enough to distract myself from the skeleton and the fact that James hadn't texted or called. Because even though I was still hurt by what he'd said, I missed him.

Since Dad's one of those annoying people who love mornings and can't understand why everyone else doesn't, he'd already left for work by the time I got back. Mom didn't even wake up until I was done showering, and when she shuffled into the kitchen as I was grabbing my keys from the hook in the laundry room, I had to decide fast whether or not to tell her about the clinic.

The night before, she and Dad had gone straight from work to a charity auction. I crashed early, they got home late. Which meant they didn't know about my internship falling through, or that I'd taken a job in the glamorous field of medical reception.

I almost told her right then and there, but the thing about Mom is, she's nonverbal until her first cup of coffee kicks in. Before that, you're pretty much taking your life into your own hands if you try to engage her in conversation. Which is why I skipped the heart-to-heart and decided to aim for an on-time arrival at work instead.

Other than a few joggers, the streets were still pretty empty at 7 AM. Instead of dodging all the fresh potholes on Peoria, I cut north through the city. Yes, there are lots of one-way streets and traffic signals downtown, but the lights are set up so that once you catch your first green you can avoid reds by keeping your speed at twenty-five. Besides, there's something about downtown that feels like home to me. The buildings there are different and beautiful and old, and they give off this Art Deco vibe that makes you wish you had a flapper dress or two in your closet.

I didn't. But I *did* have a playlist full of old jazz songs that Dad used to make me listen to on the way to school. Which (and I'll never admit this to him) I loved. So I rolled my windows down and played the music loud, all the way up to the power company's headquarters at Seventh and Detroit.

When the big brick building came into sight, I heard Dad's voice in my head: *You know, that building used to be Central High School.* It was a family joke, because he'd read some book on historic Tulsa buildings one spring break and started repeating that exact same sentence every time we passed the place. Seriously—every time. For a year.

But at five past seven that morning, there were no students gathered outside the building, only a small group of rough-around-the-edges, full-grown men. Two were drinking from foam cups. One was smoking a cigarette. And the fourth looked enough like Arvin, the guy from the clinic who couldn't get no satisfaction, that I rolled my windows up and slowed down to get a better look.

They stopped talking and watched me. Then the man, who actually *was* Arvin, got up and waved like he was trying to flag me down.

I waved back but didn't stop. And I wish I could say it was for a good reason, like I was running late, or I didn't understand that he wanted to talk to me, or I just plain spaced out. But the truth is, I didn't stop because even though Arvin seemed harmless and sweet in the clinic, he made me nervous out on the street.

Unfortunately, slowing down had thrown off my traffic signal rhythm enough so that the Sixth Street light turned red just as I got there. Arvin was coming closer to my car. The other men watched him, laughing. I glanced up and down Sixth, hoping to see another driver. A cyclist. Anybody. "Come on," I whispered to the light.

"Turn." Then Arvin was at my bumper and the light was still red.

I pretended I didn't know he was there and turned right.

The happy smile on his face faded in my rearview mirror. *It's okay*, I told myself. *You don't know him that well. You did the smart thing.*

Which was true. But that was the moment I started suspecting there might have been something to what James had said about me after all.

———

I didn't tell Tru what happened with Arvin, but I did ask about him.

"Arvin's a good guy," Tru said. "He spends most of his time downtown. Dr. Woods gives him bus tokens so he can come up here and check in with her once a week. Between his asthma and his diabetes, he's in rough shape."

"Why did he hang around so long yesterday?" I asked.

Tru shrugged. "Out on the streets, most people won't even make eye contact with guys like Arvin. We talk to him here. Plus, there's air conditioning."

Which made me feel so horrible about what I'd done that morning that it was actually a relief when Tru handed me a spiral notebook full of blank message slips and told me to go through the overnight voicemail backlog.

There were a lot of messages to take down. Enough that Tru had unlocked the front door before I got to the last one. After that, the waiting room filled up so fast I barely had time to think.

There were two full-time physicians at the clinic: Dr. Woods, and a community medicine resident named Dr. Barat. There were nurses, too, and a steady trickle of medical students. "The students are the ones in short white coats," Tru said. "A few of them are arrogant little pricks, most are great. And they're all scared to death, so be nice."

At noon I picked up lunch orders, texted NEED TO SEE YOU to James, and read a little bit about the history of my neighborhood to see if I could figure out what was going on there in 1921. And at the end of the day, Tru pulled me aside as I was checking—again—to see if James had texted back.

"Dr. Woods got a call saying you were interested in shadowing her. That true?"

Which kind of surprised me. I'd figured handsome old Dr. Revard from the virology lab had only wanted to get rid of me. But he'd done what he said, and even though there was plenty to keep me busy at the reception desk, I wasn't about to pass up the chance to learn more.

"It is," I said. And Tru walked me back to a small office filled with stacks of medical journals and told me to wait.

Two framed diplomas hung on the wall behind the desk: one from OU, one from Stanford Med. Both were summa cum laude, both belonged to Marguerite Doniece Woods. And there was music playing—a deep-voiced woman singing to a tinny guitar.

> . . . *haven't found no eggs in my basket*
> *Since my rooster been gone*

"You like Memphis Minnie?"

The tall, dark-skinned woman behind me wore a long white lab coat, jeans, and silver Doc Martens.

"I do if that's who's singing," I said.

The diamond stud in her nose flashed along with her smile. "Still, you're probably more interested in seeing patients than in getting a lesson in old music. Am I right?"

There was no handshake, no chitchat. I liked her right away.

"The music's good," I said. "But yes, I *would* like to shadow you."

"You're seventeen?"

"Yes, ma'am."

"You go to Booker T.?"

"Aberdeen."

Her forehead wrinkled a little in surprise. "And you want to go into medicine?"

I should have had an answer for that right away.

Namely, yes. Only what I said after a pause was, "I think so."

"Why?"

"I don't know. That's what I'd like to find out."

"Good answer," she said, and motioned for me to follow her up front.

At the reception desk, Dr. Woods asked Tru if he could dig up a release form for my parents since I wasn't eighteen yet. Tru made a pained face, handed me a manila folder, and said, "It hurts that you even ask, Doc."

"Get it signed and you can start tomorrow," she told me. "Say, two thirty?" She looked at Tru for approval.

He sighed. "I suppose. If she gets her work done and takes a shorter lunch break."

"You mean skip it completely?" I said.

"Yep." Tru grinned. Then he spotted a toddler bolting for the door and took off fast to snatch him up by the back of his overalls.

"That's a good man right there," Dr. Woods said.

Tru dropped the toddler into the seat next to his worn-out mother, and after he'd said something that made her nod, he picked up her wailing baby in its carrier and took it back to the reception desk. He answered the ringing phone with one hand and rocked the carrier with the other. The baby quit crying. The mother caught her wiggly toddler up and kissed the top of his head.

Dr. Woods stayed put long enough to watch the whole scene unfold. Then one of the nurses called a patient from the doorway, and Dr. Woods was on the move again. "There are some extra lab coats in the break-room closet," she said, glancing back just long enough so I knew she was talking to me. "Find one that fits. We'll start tomorrow."

———

James lives out east in a neighborhood full of flat-roofed one-story houses from the 1960s. A lot of the bigger places from back then have been remodeled with shiny wood floors and kitchens that look more like movie sets than places actual people cook. But James's house isn't one of those. His is small and cluttered and covered in old wall-to-wall shag carpet that smells like the last owner's dog no matter how many times he sprays it with Febreze.

I went over there after work even though he'd never texted me back. If I hadn't spent most of my afternoon hoping Arvin would show up at the clinic so I could apologize to him for driving away, I might not have. Only Arvin hadn't, and I was sick of feeling small and ugly. It was time to make something right.

Of course, the driveway was empty. *C'mon*, I thought, ringing the doorbell. *Please let Ethel be in the garage.* But no one came then, or after my second and third tries, either. I started getting paranoid, imagining James hiding out in his room while I stood there like an idiot. I even thought about going around to the side of the house and calling his number to see if I could hear his phone through the bedroom window.

Yes, I had completely lost it.

The only thing that saved me from utter humiliation was hearing Ethel's rumble down the street. James pulled into the driveway, cut the ignition, and stared at his hands awhile before he finally got out and stood behind the door.

"Hey," he said.

"Hey yourself. Why didn't you text me back?"

He stepped out from behind the door and closed it.

"Because apologizing by text is a dick move."

A relieved whoosh of air hiccuped past the knot in my throat. Then we were hugging, and it was like Mom pulling me out of the fountain all over again.

"I'm sorry," I said, feeling the buttons of his shirt press into my cheek.

"Don't even. I was a complete jerk."

And that was all we needed to say.

As we pulled apart, James glanced toward his neighbor's house. "We'd better go inside before Mrs. Beris gets the wrong idea. She keeps trying to set me up with her granddaughter, and I think I finally managed to convince her last week that aromantic asexuals like me really do exist—even here in Tulsa."

"Too late." I waved at the droopy woman in curlers peeking out from behind polka-dotted curtains.

"Shit," James groaned. "Now I'm gonna to have to start all over again."

"Either that, or you can just tell her you think her granddaughter's ugly," I said.

He stroked his chin. "Interesting..."

"You wouldn't."

"You're right. Now that she's seen me with you, she'd never believe I'm not into ugs."

I hit him. Hard.

"Bully."

"Asshole."

Both of us cracked up.

We were back.

———

"The skeleton must be W. T. or J. Goodhope," I said. We were on the rug in James's room—the nice one he'd bought to cover the avocado carpet—with the receipt from the skeleton's wallet pressed open in front of us.

James typed *Goodhope 1921 Tulsa* into his laptop. "It's all race riot stuff. Nothing with 'Goodhope.' But here... wait..."

He typed some more.

"Okay, so the riot started Tuesday, May thirty-first, and ended the next day, June first. That means J. Good-hope made his final payment on May twenty-seventh, four days before then. And hang on...yeah. All the payments were made on Fridays."

I searched *Victory Victrola Shop Tulsa* on my phone. Got nothing.

James retried it with the date. "Nope," he muttered. "But if there *was* a shop in town with that name, then there has to be a record of it somewhere. We're just not looking the right way."

"Nerd," I said.

He pointed to the stuff on his walls: a TARDIS poster, a wooden PLATFORM 9¾ sign, eight framed *Deadpool* covers. "*I* am a geek," he said. "*You*, Little Miss 4.0, are the nerd."

I folded the receipt back up and told him to be nice or I wouldn't tell him about the crazy anthropologist in our back house.

He pushed the laptop away, propped his elbows on his knees, and rested his chin on his hands. "You know I'm all about crazy anthropologists," he said. "Spill."

So I told him about Geneva and how she'd taken the body to her lab but managed to get the weird rust spot off the gun while she was still at our place.

"What was underneath?" he asked.

"The word *Maybelle*, etched into the metal."

He frowned. "I don't think I'd name my gun Maybelle."

"I don't think you'd own a gun in the first place."

"Good point. But listen, in related news, I read last

night how gangs of white men went through neighbor-hoods during the riot, banging on doors to make sure no one was trying to hide black people."

I sighed. "That is seriously messed up."

"Yes, it is. But what if one of those gangs found a black guy in your back house, killed him, and hid his body there?"

"Why would they bother hiding it?" I said. "It's not like anyone was going to arrest them."

James pressed the heels of his hands into his eyes and let out a long, frustrated growl from the back of his throat. "Jesus! What's wrong with people?"

I stood up and stretched. "I don't know, but I have to train really early to get to work on time. We still on for the concert Friday night?"

James took his hands away from his eyes and blinked fast against the light. "Definitely."

"Seven o'clock?"

He gave me his you-are-a-control-freak-but-I-love-you-anyway look.

"On the dot," he said. "Just like always."

WILLIAM

My knees weren't any too steady after I escaped the cigar shop. Not that it surprised me to see Vernon with a gun, mind you. *I* had one, and so did plenty of other folks. A shotgun, at least. Or a rifle. But Vernon had aimed that Colt M1911 dead at my heart and held it there, telling me what a fool the soldier he'd gotten it from had been for not marking his kills on the gun's side.

He'd set it down on the counter after a while but talked on and on, boasting how her name was Maybelle, and how he'd carved the first of her three notches the day after he got her. "I went to visit a friend at his farm," he'd said. "Caught this old nigger skulking around their pasture fence, swore he was only passing by on his way home from building pews at church. But I knew from his eyes that he was out to thieve. Weren't no eyes left in his head once Maybelle finished with him."

Which scared me good, since the weird shine in Vernon's own eyes left no doubt as to the veracity of his claim. And then he said how the second notch came after he and his Klan pals tracked down a Negro boy accused of stealing chickens from a farmer way up in Vinita, and the third after an uppity youth on the north side of town sassed him. "That boy I shot as a mercy," Vernon added with a wink. "Seeing's how mightily the poor lad was suffering after we dragged him most of a mile behind Elmer Daughtry's Tin Lizzie."

I wanted to write Vernon's claims off as him being a braggart and a liar. Wanted him to stop talking and let me leave. But I couldn't and he didn't. So I tried my best to look impressed instead of sick at my stomach, and when the chance finally came for me to excuse myself, I made such a hash of it that Vernon thought I was asking to use his john. Which worked in my favor, for, as he put it, no mongrel was going to take a piss in his establishment.

That was the point at which I stumbled out onto the street, grateful for the distracting smell of coal smoke from the brickyard ovens, and so hell-bent on getting to work that I nearly missed the person I'd played hooky to speak with in the first place.

———

Joseph was a little ways past the shop, arranging parcels in his bicycle basket for delivery.

"Wait!" I ran up to him, holding my homemade receipt. Joseph's forehead wrinkled, which I'd begun to suspect was the only display of emotion he allowed himself in front of people. Ones like me, at least.

"What's that?" he asked.

"A balance sheet," I said. "To keep track of your payments."

He asked whether Pop had written it or me. When I answered truthfully, he handed the paper back like the useless thing it was. "Thank you," he said. "I won't be needing this."

Which took me by surprise and set me to stammering how it was proof he was making his payments, and how he should take it because that was the right and proper way to do business.

"The rules aren't the same for me as they are for you," Joseph replied, shaking his head. "Don't you know that, Will?" Which put my nose out of joint so bad that I told him he was being rude, and that I was only trying to do him a favor at no small risk to myself.

Joseph's face went blank as the cloudless sky overhead. He eyed the receipt. Said, "Thank you, Mr. William. But I can't accept." And got back on his bicycle.

"That all you got to say?" I near shouted, frustrated at how easily he'd turned my good intentions into a fool's errand. And the quickest flash of hate you ever did see danced across the dark of his eyes.

I stood there, feeling awkward and a fool. Joseph put

one foot on a pedal and said, real quiet, "If you'll excuse me, I've a funeral to attend."

Only then did I notice the band of mourning black around his upper arm.

"Who died?" I asked stupidly.

Joseph's eyes were flat. "Nobody important, Mr. William. Only a Negro boy like me."

———

The Dobbs family had been rich once. Oil rich. It was a common enough thing, men born in one-room shacks coming west to dig fortunes up from underneath the hard-packed Oklahoma dirt. But just as fast as the money came in, it could all disappear in the same kind of risky business venture that earned it in the first place.

Back when things were flush, Addie's father, Richard, built a great mansion with a ballroom on the third floor where Addie and her friends would roller-skate. After he went bust, he sold the house to a banker with no children to speak of, and the Dobbs family moved into a modest bungalow a few blocks west.

That's where I found myself on Sunday afternoon, two days after my encounter with Joseph. I hadn't stopped wondering who his mourning band was for, or worrying that it might have been the boy Vernon and his pals had beat down—the same boy I knew in my heart to be Clarence Banks.

So there I stood on the Dobbses' front porch, hat in hand, knot in my throat, grateful Mama had loosed my reins for the afternoon. A black woman answered the door. She was hollow-eyed and ashen, and her black dress hung from her gaunt frame like funeral bunting.

"Yes, sir?" she said. "Can I help you?"

I told her my name was William, and that I was there to see Addie. She nodded and led me to the parlor, said I should have a seat, and asked would I like some iced tea while I waited. My throat was raw as fresh-hewn wood, but I perched on a settee and said no thank you, that I just needed to see Addie for a moment and didn't mean to be a bother. And she dropped her head and shuffled out silently.

Now, even though it was only a ten-minute walk from my house and less than five from the new place Mama and Pop were in the midst of building, I'd never been inside Addie's home. Never been alone in a room with her anywhere, in fact, which had my nerves ajangle and my temples beaded with sweat. There was plenty to look at, though, which was a distraction of the good sort.

Mansion-sized furniture filled the room to the gills. A fine rug from someplace far away covered the wood floor wall to wall. The vases on the mantel were so wide they barely fit. And instead of the tatted half-curtains that hung in the windows of most houses its size, long velvet drapes blocked out the day's heat at the Dobbses'. It was as if all those fine furnishings didn't know how out of place they were in such a modest room, or as if they didn't plan on staying for long.

The ceiling creaked overhead. Water gurgled through pipes in the wall. Then soft footsteps came down the stairs behind me, and Addie walked in wearing a yellow frock that would have shamed the sun.

"Why are you here?" she asked.

She'd painted bright circles of rouge on her cheeks; an attempt, I supposed, at hiding the pallor of her skin. But it only accented the dark crescents under her eyes and did nothing to mask the exhaustion in her voice.

"Is Clarence dead?" I asked.

"Yes," she replied.

The mantel clock measured out seconds after that, each tick louder and more awful than the one before. Birds sang outside. The smell of roasting Sunday chicken mingled with perfume from the lilac blooms in a vase on the coffee table. They were normal things, all of them, and awful for it.

"I'm sorry," I said, full expecting Addie to slap me like she'd done in the cafeteria. Or worse, to leave. Instead, she lowered herself onto the edge of a chair and said, "Good."

The clock ticked on. Addie crossed her ankles. There was a calmness to her, a tired acceptance, that I wasn't sure how to take. It might have been easier if she were angry. Easier to deal with, easier on my ragged conscience. But she just sat, watching bird shadows flit across the narrow sliver of window between the drapes. Then she did something that made no sense at all: she smiled.

"Clarence loved the color yellow," she said quietly. "Marie told me she'd wear her yellow dress if only she could bear the lightness of it. So I'm wearing mine for her."

Nervous as I was about upsetting Addie, I didn't ask who Marie was. And her eyes never left the bird shadows, not even when she spoke again, saying, "Are you glad he's dead, William?"

Which touched something curdled and tender inside me. Something I'd never known to be ashamed of before.

"No," I said, surprised at the truth of it.

Her eyes focused hard on mine. "Then you should ask for forgiveness," she said.

At that, my heart near broke along with my voice as I began pleading, "Can you ever forgive me, Addie? Please? Please, can you?" And her face pinched in frustration as she shook her head, saying, "Not from me, William. From God."

Which wounded me deeper than any slap ever could, for it hadn't occurred to me that I needed absolution from anyone other than Addie. She *saw* it, though. Saw the ugliness inside me, saw how small and stupid I was. And it shamed me to the bone.

But, kind soul that she was, Addie didn't leave me to squirm.

"He'd come down from the 101 Ranch to tell Marie

good-bye before the spring cattle drive," she said. "Even though he was only a cook, he was so happy they'd decided to let him go down to Texas with them this year. He was hoping they might teach him to cowboy…"

Her voice trailed off as the maid came in and set a tray with two glasses of iced tea in front of us. There were lace cookies, too, and a silver sugar bowl and slices of lemon.

"Thank you, Marie," Addie said gently. The maid dipped her chin and left without a word.

"He was her son," I said.

Addie nodded, picked up a glass, and stirred the ice chips round and round with a long-handled spoon.

"Marie's been our maid since before I was born. She used to live with her husband, but after he died in a mining accident, she sold their house and moved into the quarters on our property. I was two then. Clarence was four. We grew up together, playing in the yard, stealing oranges from the kitchen. Mother never seemed to mind."

Addie lifted the glass halfway to her lips, stopped, and lowered it again. Silence sucked all the oxygen out of the air between us, until it finally got so bad that I blurted out, "I never meant for him to die."

"But you never meant for him not to," Addie replied.

The gentleness in her voice was gone, and I folded in around my own shame like an accordion. She stirred her tea some more and said, "I'm sorry, William. I didn't mean to sound curt." I responded that she had every right to sound however she pleased. But she shook her head and her shoulders fell even lower.

"No, I haven't," she said.

And there was so much pain in her voice, so much sorrow, that I took her hand and squeezed it. The gesture was heartfelt, and meant to be a comfort. Addie must have sensed that, for instead of pulling away, she only sat there, chest rising and falling underneath the bodice of her dress as the clock ticked on.

An automobile puttered by outside. Addie tensed. I pulled my hand away. She looked at me, dry-eyed, and sighed and set her glass down. "I was wrong, William," she said. "Wrong to blame you, wrong to strike you in the cafeteria, and wrong not to apologize sooner."

Which left me more confused than relieved.

"The truth is, what happened was more my fault than yours," Addie went on. "I asked Clarence to take me to that awful speakeasy. He said I'd no business being there, that it wouldn't do for me to be seen with him in public. I was petulant, though, and insisted the two of us spend one last evening together before he left. My father doesn't approve of Clarence and me spending time alone, you see. And it wasn't as if we could meet somewhere private. Even *I* knew that if anyone were to spy us picnicking by the river or taking a stroll, it could very well mean a death sentence for him. But I wheedled and teased, pleading for him to take me somewhere wild, until he finally gave in."

She paused, as if she knew she should cry but had no tears left.

"That may be," I said. "But I'm the one who stirred up trouble in the first place. If it weren't for me, you and Clarence could have passed the evening together and said your good-byes in peace without anyone bothering you. I was jealous and petty. I started everything. Clarence only protected himself. It was my fault."

Addie's face darkened and her hands bunched the fabric of her skirt up tight. "Perhaps," she replied. "But you know as well as I do that if you hadn't raised a ruckus someone else would have. There was no way the other white men in that place would have tolerated a girl like me spending an evening alone with Clarence. Why, just this Friday, I heard that pinch-faced friend of yours asking boys at school to join him in a letter-writing campaign. He wants the Ku Klux Klan to start a junior branch here in Tulsa. Did you know that?"

I told her no, but that it didn't surprise me overmuch. For though Clete had a weakness for pretty girls no matter what their complexion, he harbored no love for Negro men, and had a tendency to think the world owed him more than it was willing to give.

"Well, he does," Addie said. "That's the way things are in this town, and I know it. Only I was selfish and spoiled and made Clarence give in to my whims one last time. I've always gotten exactly what I want. Even petty, silly things with prices far too dear."

She let go of her skirt and smoothed the fabric with her palms. I picked up my glass and drank deep. Not because my stomach wanted tea, but because my mouth had gone so dry I was afraid I couldn't speak otherwise.

The floor creaked behind us.

"Will your guest be staying for supper, Miss Addie?" Marie asked. Addie didn't look up, only murmured quietly that I wouldn't. Marie pressed her lips together and nodded and left the room in a rustle of black fabric.

"I should be going," I said.

"Yes," Addie replied. She rose from the chair and led me to the front door, opening it without a word. And just as silently, I walked out, knowing there would never be such a thing as a good good-bye for Addie and me. Not then. Not ever.

Rowan

When Dad asked if he could run with me the morning after James and I made nice, I knew it was time to tell him about the clinic.

He's slower than me and can't make it as far, so my mileage suffers. On the other hand, he doesn't talk a lot and lets me set the route. That morning I led us down through the southern section of our neighborhood, where the absence of sidewalks keeps the unwashed masses from strolling through. We jogged in the street.

Except for Dad breathing hard, the first two miles were quiet. It felt good going easy, especially after the pounding I'd given myself the two mornings before. Good enough that I decided to wait until we got closer to home to bring up the clinic. I'm not really sure why I worried about telling Mom and Dad my internship had fallen through. Maybe I didn't want them to think it was my fault—that I'd sabotaged things somehow, or screwed up. Not letting my parents down was a huge part of who I was. Am, really.

But then Dad started talking, and I realized I wasn't the only one who had something to say.

"You doing okay?" he huffed.

"Yeah," I said. "How about you?"

He had to work to get the words out. "Well, considering there's been a murdered body on my family's property since before I was born, I guess I'm all right."

That was his angle: Dad wanted to make sure the skeleton hadn't traumatized me.

I slowed a little so he could catch his breath.

"I know what you mean," I said. "It creeped me out at first, but I spent some time with the anthropologist the other day. She made it seem less personal and more like science."

That seemed to satisfy Dad. We ran quietly for a while, dodging kamikaze squirrels and listening to birds. As we passed a big Italian-villa-looking place, Dad pointed out a fox sitting on the walkway. It was small and sharp-eyed, resting on his haunches like a dog.

"He thinks we're beneath him," Dad said.

I laughed, because the fox really did look bored, or maybe annoyed, like who were we to be on *his* street? Which reminded me how James and I had talked about groups of men going around white neighborhoods during the riot, trying to flush out black people in hiding.

"Dad?" I said.

"Yep?"

"How long has our family owned the house?"

He side-eyed me.

"Why?"

"Well, like you said, the body's been there a long time, and I've been thinking about it a lot..."

"Since right after it was built," Dad said.

"We didn't build it ourselves?"

"Nope."

A woman pushing a stroller walked past on the other side of the street. We waved.

"Do you know who did?" I asked.

"I'm not sure. You'd have to check the title."

"How do I do that?"

"You get it from the title company."

I sped up a little, hoping he'd have to concentrate so hard on breathing that he wouldn't have the energy to be suspicious. Only it turned out I didn't need to bother.

"Ro," he said, "I don't have a problem with you playing detective. If things weren't so crazy at work right now, I'd probably do it myself. So if you want to take a look at the title, just say the word and I'll call and have them pull it from the vault."

Which earned him the kind of I-love-you-Daddy smile that still worked surprisingly well.

At 41st Street we cut over to Riverside and started north at a slow jog. Dad was nearly toast, I could tell. So

I finally nutted up and told him about the clinic, over-explaining things so there wouldn't be any questions left for him to ask. He stopped in the middle of the bike path, bending over with his hands on his thighs. "Sounds like you turned a bad situation around for yourself," he said between big, relieved gasps. "You remind me of your mother more and more every day." Then he waved for me to go ahead without him. Which I did, sprinting the rest of the way, relieved as hell and thinking how perfect it would be if Arvin showed up at the clinic that morning. He was the last person I needed to get square with.

The last thing I needed to make right.

———

Arvin never showed. Apart from that, it was a good day. Dr. Woods recognized Dad's name when I handed her the release. Not that she said anything—I could just tell from the little double take she did, looking from the signature to me and back again. "All right," she said, tossing the form into the chaos on her desk. "Let's go."

I'd chosen a long lab coat from the breakroom closet, hoping I'd look more like a really young nurse than some random high school tagalong. It was wishful thinking; with makeup, I could maybe pass for a college sophomore. But other than some mascara and ChapStick, my face was naked. I wasn't fooling anyone.

The thing was, nobody cared. Every time we walked

into an exam room, Dr. Woods would introduce me as a student and ask the patient if they minded me staying. Not a single person did. They were all so glad to see Dr. Woods, to tell her their problems and show her their rashes and bumps and where it hurt, that they barely noticed me at all.

Dr. Woods listened to every one of them. Her Spanish wasn't as good as Tru's, but she held her own. She only looked away to type quick notes into her laptop, and when she got around to the actual exam, there was something so gentle in the way she touched people—resting her fingertips lightly on a coughing man's shoulder, lifting an old woman's hand to examine her swollen knuckles—that there was no way anyone could leave feeling like they didn't matter.

It wasn't glamorous work. Mostly she did simple stuff, like adjusting prescriptions or talking with people about their diet and how much they exercised and how they should quit smoking. The only remotely exciting thing happened when we got to her very last patient of the day.

He was dressed in suit pants and a tie, and said he had chronic migraines that his old doctor in Little Rock had prescribed Vicodin for. But he'd lost his prescription during the move, so could Dr. Woods please write him a new one?

Instead of a prescription, she handed him a sheet of paper with advice for treating migraines without pills and said he should try to walk at least twenty minutes every day and eat regular meals and avoid soda and coffee and anything else with caffeine.

At first he acted sad and told her he'd tried all those things and they didn't work. I felt bad, watching him rub his temples and squint against the light from the fluorescent overhead bulbs. But when she said no, he got really insistent. Then mad. Then sad again. Dr. Woods headed him off every time, as if she knew exactly what he'd say next. She told him she'd be happy to see him again in a week if his symptoms didn't improve, and that she could get him into a guided meditation group that might really help.

He wasn't interested in any of that, and I doubt he even had migraines to begin with. He was there for pills. But Dr. Woods stayed so kind and firm that he eventually gave up, took the paper, and left.

Afterwards, Dr. Woods turned on Ella Fitzgerald in her office, leaned back in her chair, crossed her legs, and asked me to tell her what I'd seen. I knew she didn't want me to rattle off a list of diagnoses or anything as easy as that. She wanted to know what I'd *seen*. So I told her. And she listened like she'd listened to her patients—deep and thoughtful. When I was done, she said, "Not very exciting, was it?"

I thought about that awhile. Dr. Woods made me want to be . . . more. To stretch out and aim for something better than good enough.

"That depends on what you mean by 'exciting,'" I finally said.

She asked me to explain.

"Well, if 'exciting' means drama and people dying and doctors and nurses rushing around like in the movies, then no, it wasn't. But if it means doing something that seems small now but can make a big difference in the long run, then it was."

She smiled. "I'm glad you feel that way, because we're going to do the same thing tomorrow and every day after that. It's good that you're here, Rowan. You're interesting to have around."

And you know, I walked out of her office that day feeling even better than I had after my run with Dad, believing there were things I could do that were real and solid and good. It was the opposite of how I'd felt when I drove away from Arvin the other morning.

For the first time in a long time, I thought I knew where I was going. Like maybe there was something useful I could do with my life after all.

I liked it.

I wanted more.

━━━━━

Geneva was lying on her stomach in the back house when I got home, sifting dirt through a mesh screen. She lifted her head, said hi, then ignored me.

At least that time I knew she wasn't trying to be rude. Succeeding, yes, but definitely not trying. So instead of standing around feeling awkward, I poked through the odd collection of stuff she'd arranged on top of her storage bin.

Her Five Star was there, opened to a page with a sketch of the hole in the floor and an outline of where the skeleton had been. There were four numbered dots inside that, and a key to what they meant at the bottom of the page. At least I think it was a key, because Geneva wrote in some kind of shorthand I couldn't read. Not that it mattered much; the four objects on top of the bin spoke for themselves.

Two were rusty, dirt-crusted nails. Another looked like a button. And the fourth I had a sneaking suspicion about that Geneva confirmed.

"It's a tooth," she said from all fours. "A human one. Help me up?"

I gave her my free hand and pulled her to her feet. She brushed her palms off against her cutoffs and pointed at one end of the tooth with her pinky finger.

"Those are the roots," she said. "When they're intact and there aren't any signs of decay, it can indicate that the owner didn't part with the tooth voluntarily."

"You mean someone pulled it?"

"Or knocked it out."

I asked her if it could have happened when the skeleton got hit in the back of the head.

166

"Oh, no," she said. "It wasn't his. I cataloged him yesterday, and the only tooth missing was a second molar that he lost a long time before he died. He didn't have third molars, either. Those are wisdom teeth. But I don't think he had them to begin with. Some people are born like that. Would you like to know what else I found?"

I said I would. Geneva settled onto a stack of tile boxes to talk. Once she got rolling, she didn't stop.

"Well, for starters, the skeleton *did* belong to a man. I fed his long bone measurements into FORDISC—"

I interrupted to ask what that was.

"It's a forensic database that helps me calculate things like height. Your skeleton stood just under six feet when he was alive. Also, I narrowed down his age at the time of death to somewhere between eighteen and twenty-four. Usually I can get closer than that, but all the surfaces touching the ground had degraded. I had to go by how completely the growth points at the tips of certain bones had attached to the main shafts, how fully the plates in his skull had fused, and how completely his teeth had come in. But that's all part of the game. Sometimes the forensic gods smile down on you, sometimes they give you the finger."

I laughed. Geneva looked a little insulted; she hadn't been joking. "Sorry," I said. She shrugged.

"Beyond that, it doesn't look like he had any major disfiguring diseases. The size of his right humerus bone and scapula show he was right-handed. He broke his left wrist when he was young, but it healed up well. And from the marks his muscle attachments left on his bones, I'd say he had a naturally sturdy build. I don't think he did much manual labor, though. The attachments weren't robust enough for that."

"You figured all that out already?" I asked.

"Yes." She put the nails, the button, and the tooth into little plastic bags.

"It's pretty amazing that you can learn so much from a skeleton."

Geneva acted like it was no big deal. That's when I gave up trying to compliment her and asked if there was anything I could do to help.

She shook her head. "No, thank you. I have a system."

"Okay, then," I said, figuring she'd be glad if I left. "I guess I'll see you later…"

Her eyebrows went up. "Don't you want to know about the holster?"

"The holster?"

"The one that was attached to the front of his belt," she said. "I forgot you didn't see it. Anyway, I sent it off to a gun expert friend of mine along with the pistol you found. He should get his report to me soon. Oh, and I sent a tooth from the remains off to the crime lab in Oklahoma City. They're pretty backed up, so I doubt I'll get confirmation for a few weeks."

"Confirmation?" I said.

Her eyebrows went up all over again, and her head tilted sideways. "Of the skeleton's ancestry. Didn't I tell you? I'm ninety-nine percent sure the man you found was black."

WILLIAM

The Tulsa sky can turn on you quick. One minute you're rolling up your sleeves under wide-open blue, the next you're dodging raindrops and hailstones and tornadoes.

All things considered, though, that spring was gentle enough so even empty bank accounts didn't keep the Pied Piper warblings of Al Jolson and Nora Bayes from luring customers into the shop. And even though Pop couldn't keep Victrolas moving out the door as fast as he'd have liked, my own skills kept record sales brisk. Enough so that after Pop finished tallying the week's transactions in his ledger book one fine afternoon, he said, "It doesn't look as if you're harming my bottom line any, William." Which was as close to a compliment as he ever got.

But even as I was starting to earn a smidgen of respect

from Pop, there were things about the way he did business that I'd begun to question. Like his credit policy.

Never once in all the time I worked with him did I ever see Pop keep a white man or woman from taking delivery of their phonograph, even when they had a balance left to pay off on installment. "Good faith terms," Pop called the arrangement. And though more than one cheat disappeared without paying his debt, Pop considered it necessary and proper to continue extending terms to white customers.

Negroes were held to a different standard altogether. For when it came to brown-skinned customers, if they were short one single dollar at delivery, he'd load the machine back onto the truck and return it to the shop. In fact, Joseph was the only black customer I ever knew of who managed to coax a payment plan out of my father. And the fact that he'd done it ate away at Pop something fierce.

Whether it was Joseph's intelligence or his negotiation skills that bothered Pop more I couldn't say. But one thing was sure: as time passed and it became clear that Joseph was going to pay off his balance on time, Pop started taking each five-dollar installment as a thumb in the eye.

As for me, I figured those payments proved Joseph was as good as his word. Had it been my decision, we would have delivered the Goodhopes' Victrola early and been done with it. Pop had no such inclination, however, so I made sure to record each and every one of Joseph's payments on the ledger sheet I'd drawn up. Pop would have considered the exercise useless, but I most certainly did not.

And neither did Ruby, the sneak. For nearly getting hit by a milk truck wasn't enough to keep her from turning up eventually to pester me about the receipt and every other little thing under the sun. Most especially on Tuesday afternoons, when Pop had me mop the storeroom.

I resented that job, partly because the cast on my wrist made it so hard, but mostly because the ammonia I used puckered up the inside of my nose and made my eyes water. It was so bad that I had no choice but to keep the back door open, hoping to catch whatever miserly breeze might blow in from the alley.

That's how Ruby found me.

One minute I was alone, the next she was sitting on a Victrola crate with her feet swinging and a sly grin on her face. It was only a few days after the milk truck incident, and the funny thing was, it didn't surprise me to find her there. Nor did it bother me, for against my better judgment, I'd grown fond of that girl.

"Where's our receipt?" Ruby said that first day. "You promised."

I told her Joseph had refused to take it. And she grinned her silly little grin and said, "I know."

"What do you mean, you know?" I asked. And she

laughed and told me she'd been hiding nearby when I showed the paper to Joseph. "He's stubborn sometimes," she said. I grumbled under my breath how stubborn must run in Goodhope blood, which set her to giggling until I took a halfhearted swing at her with my mop. She made a face and told me not to be a bad sport, then turned serious and tried to stare me down, saying, "You should give me that receipt. I'll keep it safe."

Of course I told her no straightaway, thinking how much trouble that thing would cause if word of it got out. Mischievous as Ruby was, I figured she'd have a grand time flashing my handiwork to all her friends up in Greenwood, telling how Stanley Tillman had spit in Jim Crow's eye.

Then she hopped up from the stool and stamped her foot, saying, "You will too give it to me, Will Tillman, or I'll—"

"You'll what?" I snapped. "Get run over by a milk truck to spite me? Raise such a ruckus that Pop comes back here and tans your hide even darker than it already is?"

Which made her go quiet, searching for just the right mean thing to say in reply, until she finally gave up and blew me a raspberry.

From then on, that was how my Tuesday afternoons went. Ruby would come in the back door uninvited. The first few times she nattered on about the receipt. But before long she quit mentioning it altogether and stuck to more entertaining topics, like the neighborhood boy who'd built an airplane out of milk crates and paid his little brother a dime to climb inside before he pushed it off the roof for a test flight. Or how she let the best pitcher in class copy off her work because he was so dumb that if she didn't, their teacher would keep him in at playtime and her baseball team would lose.

And she talked about Joseph, too, so that before long I knew as much about him as I did any classmate or friend, Clete included. Like the fact that he was sweet on Eliza Clark, who'd turned him down flat for the Booker T. Washington prom. And that he'd gone door-to-door when he was eleven, taking any odd job folks would pay him a few pennies to do so he could buy Ruby the Raggedy Ann doll she wanted. Then, when he'd finally earned enough to purchase it, he'd painted its cloth skin with strong tea so that it looked more like her.

Before long, my Tuesdays with Ruby had become the best part of my week. Her stories kept my mind off the ammonia fumes, and it soothed me when she spoke of things that made her happy: how she always pinched the boys she liked up high on the inside of their arms because that was where it hurt most, and how the flowers on the blackberry bushes in her backyard were turning into little green baby berries that her ma would bake into cobblers come late June. One time she asked me did my own ma make cobblers, and I told her my pop was partial to pies, so that's what our maid mostly fixed. Ruby's eyes softened then, and she breathed the word *Peeeach?*

all quiet, like a prayer. And when I said yes, Angelina baked peach pies, she sighed, "Peach pie is my faaaaavorite. Mama bakes the best ones in the whole wide world."

And peach was my favorite, too. Only I didn't say so at the time.

What I did instead was sit on the crate beside her and take Joseph's receipt out of my wallet.

"What's that?" she asked.

I unfolded the paper. "See for yourself."

She tried to snatch it from my hand, but that time she wasn't fast enough.

"I'll hold it," I said. Which made her face start to go mad. But then she thought better of it and leaned up against my arm so she could read the entries. And the scent of her, all sweat and laundry soap and roller skate grease, was so close to Nell's that it chipped away at the frost I'd carried inside me for three long years.

"Thank you, Will," she said quietly, and stood up, leaving a cool spot on my arm. And for whatever reason, I blurted out that she should stay away from the cigar shop down the street and the man who owned it, too. *Especially* the man who owned it. Ruby squinched up her face as if she didn't know what to make of me. Then, sneaky as heat lightning, she reached up and pinched the inside of my arm so hard my eyes teared up.

"Can't boss me, Will Tillman," she said, and stuck out her tongue and darted out the back door before the sting of her pinch had passed.

Few things feel sweeter than a cast coming off, especially when you've had it on for too many weeks and the skin underneath the plaster has started itching worse than a nettle sting. After Doc Broward cut the foul thing away one warm May afternoon, Mama set me down with my arm over a washbasin and scrubbed the dead skin off with lemon juice and buttermilk. Then she rubbed warm honey all over the tender flesh, wrapped it in bandages made from a soft old bedsheet, and had me sleep that way. Which was a bother until I woke the next morning and washed the whole mess off and found pale new skin and a bone knit up good as new.

I suppose it was that fine feeling, along with the promise of a few hours' liberty in the hot spring sun, that kept me from saying no when Clete barreled out of his house before school, calling, "You been savin' up your allowance, Miss Goody Two-Shoes?"

And besides, there's only so long a boy can behave before the fires of temptation heat up all the mischief inside him so hot he's got no choice but to let off some steam. So I told Clete I did indeed have money, and when he said, "Go back inside and get it, then, 'cause you and I have mischief to be about," I did just that, hollering to Mama how I'd forgot my hat. Then Clete and me stashed our schoolbags under his back-porch steps and made for the river like the devil himself was after us.

It was a fine morning indeed, with cicadas clicking their one-note love songs and a melancholy train whistle singing low from the north. We ran across the Midland Valley Railroad tracks into the tangled thicket of green standing between us and the Arkansas River. And when we stopped in a clearing, all red-faced and out of breath, Clete punched my shoulder hard enough to push me back.

"That's for nothin'," he said. Only both of us knew it was a lie; that punch was for everything that hadn't been right between us since the Two-Knock. Far as I could tell, it was me who should have socked him, and not in the shoulder, either. And I thought about asking him if Addie had heard right, that he'd fallen in with the Klan. But I was too drunk on temporary freedom to let old grudges ruin things, and only gave him a halfhearted shove in return.

We walked south along the tracks, past the sound of hammers and workmen shouting from the unfinished rooftops of Maple Ridge's newest homes, Mama and Pop's among them. And we kept going until we reached the spot where the railroad's trestle bridge crossed the Arkansas and there were no buildings in sight. Clete dug two hooks and two lengths of fishing line out of his pocket and handed one of each to me, and we cut green switches off a bush and smoothed them with our pocketknives and tied lines at the ends to fish with bits of cheese from Clete's lunch.

The water was low and lazy, and the only things nibbling were Clete and me, finishing off what was left of the cheddar. But the lack of fish didn't bother us one bit as we sat there watching stilt-legged herons stalk across sandbars and hawks float by overhead. We didn't talk much, sensing, I suppose, that it could only lead to trouble. Though Clete did tell me how he planned to convince his father to let us drive his new Cadillac automobile out to Sand Springs Park for the Central High Junior-Senior Powwow come Memorial Day.

"Trolleys are for chumps," Clete declared, picking a length of duckweed off his hook. Then his voice went braggy and embarrassed all at once, saying, "Besides, it's what my girl wants."

"My ass, you got a girl!" I laughed, choking on my own spittle in the process so that I set to coughing near hard enough to keel over.

"Serves you right," Clete grumbled. And I could tell from the way the tops of his ears went bright red that I'd hurt his pride. So once I'd got control of my cough, I said, "All right, Romeo, what's her name, then?" And Clete got bashful again and fiddled with the duckweed and mumbled, "Eunice."

"She ugly?" I asked, mostly joshing. But Clete glowered and said, "She's the prettiest girl you ever saw. Prettier than Adeline Dobbs, and Eunice never slapped me, neither!" Which sent me to my feet, ready to fight. Clete got up near as fast, and if it hadn't been for the whistle and roar of a freight train barreling towards us, our day might have ended badly right then and there.

But that train knocked both of us back on our heels as it thundered past. Cleared our heads, too, so that after the noise let up, we dropped our fists and gave each other the evilest of eyes and let things be. Then Clete asked did I want to meet Eunice and her friend Imogene, for he'd told them just the other day that he might bring me by.

I asked how old this girl was. Clete told me nineteen and asked again did I want to go. And I said all right, since the shine had worn off of fishing altogether.

He led us north along the river, walking fast enough to let me know I'd gone soft working in the store. The sun beat down hot. The cloth of my shirt stuck to my back. And I wondered just how far north this Eunice girl lived. Clete marched on, silent, and with a set to his jaw that told me he'd more important things on his mind than chitchat.

It wasn't until we'd cut east, away from the water, that I starting thinking how little I actually had in common with my friend. We were the same age, true, and lived near each other and went to the same school and church. But past that, our similarities ran thin. Once upon a time, two mitts and a baseball had been enough to hold us together for days on end. Now even fishing hooks couldn't do the job. And it occurred to me, too, that I'd started looking forward to Ruby's Tuesday visits more than I missed the old days with Clete.

Finally, somewhere around the time I started blinking back soot from the Frisco rail yard, Clete stopped in front of a livery stable. "This is it," he said, and I near asked if his girl was a filly or a mare. But I thought better of it and followed him inside, past a greasy-headed attendant who barely nodded our way, and up a narrow flight of steps.

A woman met us at the top, saying, "I didn't expect to see you back so soon, Cletus!" And then we were in a parlor of sorts, though it was a stretch and a kindness to call it such. The stripped-down wood floor was full of splinters. Two gaudy velvet couches faced each other from opposite walls. A floor lamp threw just enough light to show that the woman had red hair and one too many buttons open on her dress. And there was a strong air of wariness about her, as if she'd seen enough of the world to know it couldn't be trusted.

Clete went bashful, asking if Eunice was in. The woman said she surely was, though she was just having her bath, and might the two of us be interested in spending time with Viola instead? Clete's face went all kinds of red, especially after a hard-looking woman in a slip and garters stepped out from one of the adjoining doorways and cocked a hip at us.

Then the red-haired woman raised her eyebrows at Clete, asking, and Clete sputtered how we'd prefer to wait for Eunice and Imogene. To which the slip-and-garters woman shrugged and disappeared back where she'd come from. And the boss lady, who I figured was the sporting sort fellas whispered and passed notes about in school, said Imogene was out for a ride on her gray. "But Eunice will see you both for three dollars apiece," she said. "One at a time, of course, this bein' a proper establishment." Then she paused a moment and added, "Unless you'd like to reconsider Viola?"

Well, Clete's ears just about started to smoke. So I jumped in quick and said how I wasn't looking for company and was only there on account of my friend. And that seemed to settle Clete enough for him to ask the madam if she minded me waiting with him. She said she didn't normally stand for dawdlers, but since Clete was such a good customer, she'd let it slide that once. "He stays out here, though," she added, aiming a look like darts at me. "Or it's a dollar fifty extra." Which even made *me* blush. Then she nodded, sealing the deal, and vanished behind a door of her own.

After that, Clete and me sat in the kind of silence that arises when two people have things to say to one another and can't figure where to start. For my part, I wanted to know if it was true he'd started running with the Klan. But when he scuffed his feet against the floor and started talking, it turned out he had something altogether more mercenary on his mind.

"Imogene was supposed to be here," he mumbled.

I replied it was fine she wasn't since I was too covered in sweat and stink to be fit for romance. Clete shrugged, not pointing out that he was in the same state himself. But he did clear his throat so long and hard that I wondered if there was something stuck in it. And he scuffed his feet again, then asked if he could borrow three dollars. That's when I understood the real reason Clete had invited me along: he was short on funds. To him, I was nothing but a piggy bank, full up and ready for the hammer.

I fished my wallet out of my pocket anyway and handed over the money. Clete was just palming the bills when a damp-haired girl with painted-on eyebrows came out the same door the madam had gone into. Even in the poor light, her eyes caught the exchange. She hid it quick, though, and smiled so bright that I understood how Clete could convince himself she loved him.

Then me and Clete stood up, and Clete introduced us. I shook Eunice's hand and said it was a pleasure to make her acquaintance. She did likewise, and Clete took her arm and dragged her away so that she barely had time to wink good-bye at me over her shoulder.

Once they were gone, I flew out of that place fast as I could, down the stairs, past the stable attendant and seedy hotels and gambling parlors and opium dens that barely bothered pretending to be anything different. I figured I'd best get off the streets before someone recognized me. So I hoofed it quick to the Royal Theatre and bought popcorn and licorice whips from a sidewalk vendor. Inside, Betty Blythe was breaking hearts on the big screen as the Queen of Sheba. I watched her, grateful for the cool dark of the place, until it was time to get to work.

I sold records that afternoon. Six of them. And after closing, Pop and me took the Model T out to an empty lot on the edge of town, and he gave me a driving lesson just like he'd promised to do once my cast was off. I made a hash of coordinating all her pedals and levers at first, but towards the end I got better. Enough so that Pop promised to let me try navigating a real road next.

Still, come bedtime, steering wheels and chassis were the last things on my mind. I lay there thinking how Clete wasn't really a friend anymore, and how close-knit and complicated the world really was, what with some folks being good and some being bad and most sitting in the middle with room to slide either way.

I thought about Clarence and what I'd done to him. About Joseph and how I'd come to know him through Ruby's stories. And I thought about Ruby, too. For I truly did care about her, pest and bother though she was. Put together, it all added up to a revelation of sorts—big enough to bust through my thick skull, sharp enough to stay there. And maybe all that pondering I did on the things that had happened since the Two-Knock would have been enough to make a righteous man out of me after all. But in the end, I never did have a chance to find out.

Rowan

The fact that Geneva thought she could tell a body had been brown-skinned from its bare skull messed with my head.

My first reaction was to assume she was full of shit. I mean, how could you possibly tell skin color from bones? Then I remembered the glob of hair I'd pulled off the skeleton, and figured maybe there had still been some skin on it. But when I asked, Geneva assured me the matted gnarl had been pure, unadulterated, flesh-free human hair.

"I know he was black from his skull," she said.

My internal you're-a-racist radar pinged like crazy, and I started hating her just a little bit. She didn't seem to notice. Then again, when it came to the living, Geneva didn't notice much.

"Skull morphology is influenced by the environment a population evolves in," she said. "I can evaluate discrete skull characteristics and match them up with typical profiles for geographically distinct human groups."

Translation: black people's skulls are different from white people's skulls.

And she didn't stop explaining there. "For example, eye orbits tend to be sloped in people with European ancestry, rounded in American Indian descendants, and rectangular in groups from sub-Saharan Africa."

Ping.

"And nasal openings evolved high and narrow in Europeans, heart-shaped at the base in Native Americans, and wider in dark-skinned Africans."

Ping ping ping.

But even though what Geneva said had rubbed me wrong in all kinds of ways, I hadn't had any trouble accepting what creaky old Mrs. Manos taught us in ninth-grade Bio—that the closer your ancestors lived to the equator, the more likely you were to have dark skin. Melanin protects you from ultraviolet radiation. More UV at the equator, more melanin. It was evolution. It made sense. So why was it hard to accept that there might be other differences? Ones that ran deeper than skin?

I've got some ideas about that now, but when I walked out of the back house that afternoon, all I knew was that I felt dirty. And since Mom keeps the thermostat pegged at sixty-seven so she can wear sweaters all summer, a long, hot shower in our house feels good even if it's a hundred degrees outside.

My shower, by the way, has four spray nozzles and an overhead rainfall faucet and is amazing. I stood underneath it a long, long time, steaming away the tension in my shoulders, washing my hair slowly. I rubbed shampoo over the bumps and ridges of my skull, wondering what it would look like after I died and all the skin and fat and muscle were gone.

I traced the bones of my face—the ridges at the tops of my eye sockets, my cheekbones, my jaw. Water cascaded over the brown of my hands, the pinks of my nails, splashing onto the white shower tiles at my feet.

If Geneva had my skeleton on a slab in front of her, what would she see? The white ancestors on Dad's side who'd left Germany and Ireland for greener American pastures? Or the black men and women from Mom's who'd been dragged across the ocean in chains and worked to death in Alabama cotton fields?

To be fair, Geneva made a point of telling me things got a lot more complicated after people from different areas started intermarrying. But anti-miscegenation laws in Oklahoma made it illegal for blacks to marry whites all the way up to 1967, which meant there were a lot fewer mixed-race kids in the 1920s than there are now. "Skull morphology is getting less and less distinct," she'd said. "But the person in your back house died around 1921. And to me, his skull features indicate that he was black."

I stayed in the shower until my fingers pruned and my skin felt raw, trying to sort out how I felt. In the end, I gave up and decided Geneva could believe whatever she wanted to. Black or white, the man buried in our back house had been smashed in the back of the head with a brick. Knowing he was black might help James and me figure out who he was, but in the end, murder was murder. No matter what his skin color, the dead man deserved to have his killer found.

He deserved justice.

———

It turned out Mom was actually kind of proud when I told her about the clinic. "I'm on Jackson's board of directors," she said. "And Marguerite Woods and I graduated from Booker T. together."

She was tearing lettuce for a salad. Dad was grilling steaks on the back porch.

"You know who it was named for?" she asked.

I didn't.

"A. C. Jackson. He was one of the best surgeons in the country, black or white. At least he was until white men shot him down in his own front yard during the riot. He came out of the house when they ordered him to, unarmed, hands in the air. And they shot him dead."

"Just because he was black, or because he was a doctor?" I asked.

She wiped her hands on the Mother's Day apron I'd finger-painted for her in first grade. "No one knows if they singled him out or if they even knew who he was. No one knows anything for sure about the riot except that Greenwood burned to ashes." She traced the outline of a thumbprint flower. "Even though your great-great-uncle on my side disappeared that night, my mother didn't hear about him or the riot until she was in her forties."

Mom never talked about her family. I wanted her to keep going, but she stopped and asked me to get carrots from the fridge. She took a sip of wine and started breaking down a yellow pepper. Her knife pattered quick and hard against the cutting board.

"Mom?"

Nothing.

"Why?"

The knife stopped. "Why don't we know more about that night, or why didn't your grandmother hear about it for so long?"

"Both."

She started chopping again. Slowly, with movements as tight and precise as her voice. "I don't know," she said.

Mom always had answers, especially to the hard questions. I didn't like how carefully she measured her words or how she kept looking at the neat pile of pepper slices instead of me. I wanted her to pull her shoulders back, lift her chin, and force everything to make sense.

"I don't need a perfect answer," I said.

She finished the pepper and leaned her hips against the sink.

"It's history, Ro. The messy kind where truth gets stretched out over thousands of unwritten stories. We don't know how many people died, or even if we should call it a race riot. *Riot* is convenient, and it's what most people use. But it isn't right."

I leaned onto my elbows. "Why?"

"Because when people hear the word *riot*—white people, I mean—they picture black people running crazy in the streets, looting stores and homes and burning things. That wasn't what happened in Greenwood. Don't get me wrong; I'm not saying black folks weren't angry or that none of them fought back. But it was white folks who rioted that night. They looted Greenwood, then burned it to the ground."

Mom's voice stayed even, but she was squeezing the knife handle so hard the tendons stood out on the backs of her hands. And the vein in her neck—the one I've always used to tell how much trouble I was in—looked ready to burst.

"What's the right word?" I asked.

Before she could answer, Dad came inside with a platter of grilled zucchini.

"Five minutes on the steaks," he said, giving Mom and me this look like he knew exactly what he'd walked in on. He squeezed my shoulder, smiled at Mom, and went back outside.

Mom started on the cucumber. "I don't know what the right word is," she said. "Some people say *massacre*, but to me that implies wholesale slaughter. It wasn't like that—plenty of folks lived and had to rebuild their lives from scratch."

She stopped cutting and stared down at the board.

"Greenwood burned because white folks—not all of them, mind you, but plenty—wanted to clear the 'bad niggers' out of Tulsa. To them, that meant any black man, woman, or child with the audacity to believe they deserved as much dignity and respect as a white person. Only, those white folks failed, because in the end, the survivors went right back and rebuilt what had been theirs from the start."

I'd never heard my mother use the n-word. It made my lungs feel too small.

She saw, and her face softened.

"Your father and I have done our best to make things easier for you," she said. "And maybe that was a mistake. But we wanted you to fill up on good things before you had to face the bad."

I tried to tell her I wasn't as naïve as she thought, that I knew what code words like *thug* and *uppity* and *urban* really meant, and that I saw the looks some people gave me when they thought I wasn't watching. Mom closed her eyes and shook her head slowly.

"I know," she said. "I do. But there is so much you haven't learned yet, Rowan. And as much as I wish I could protect you forever, I can't. So I'm glad you're working at the Jackson Clinic and asking questions. It's time."

Dad whistled outside, making as much noise as he could getting the lid on the grill and closing the grate to shut the fire down. Mom glanced toward the racket and smiled.

"There are things your father will never understand the way you and I do. Things he *can't* understand. But he tries, and I love him. I love you, too. So very much."

She smiled, and the strength I needed was there. Deeper, even, as if the roots she used to anchor our family had spread wider and sunk further as we talked.

"You're growing up fast," she said, "and that's how it should be. Just please, know this..."

I leaned closer, wishing the counter wasn't between us.

"The lives that ended that night mattered. It was a mistake for this city to try to forget, and it's an even bigger one to pretend everything's fine now. Black men and women are dying today for the same reasons they did in 1921. And we have to call that out, Rowan. Every single time."

Part II

You have to make your peace with the chaos, but you cannot lie.

Ta-Nehisi Coates

WILLIAM

I wasn't in Tulsa the day Sarah Page screamed.

It being Memorial Day Monday, Pop didn't open the shop. He was relaxed at breakfast that morning, saying how he might start teaching me to keep accounts once school let out. "I've seen worse instincts than yours when it comes to customers," he said. "We might as well let that stubborn head of yours have a go at managing sums."

Mama smiled over her biscuits and gravy, and I basked in the lukewarm glow of Pop's praise, trying not to dwell on the fact that my tenure at the shop would apparently continue through the summer.

After that, the three of us drove by the new house to check on its progress. The workers had installed windows in the main building and put red tile roofs on it and the quarters, both, and that made Mama and Pop so happy that our long drive up to Pawhuska was actually pleasant.

First thing we did when we got to town was lay flowers on the graves of Mama's mother and brother. Then we headed off to visit Mama's cousins, Margaret and Mary, who lived next door to each other on a street of grand houses built with Osage oil money. They had six children between them, and every single one made me push them about in their pedal cars. It was a good day. The kind that made you remember there's more to the world than just the town you live in.

I didn't hear about Sarah Page the next morning, either, for Pop carried his newspaper with him into the parlor while he and Mama engaged in early-morning negotiations over whether or not I could attend the Junior-Senior Powwow. Pop considered school festivals a frivolous waste of time and felt I should spend my day off of school working at the shop. Mama was of a different mind, and in the end she came out of the parlor with a shine in her eye that told me who'd won. She gave me fifteen dollars, too, which was a princely enough sum, and said I should get to work half an hour early. I promised quick, then sprinted up Boston Avenue to catch the dime trolley to Sand Springs with the rest of my classmates.

Only there was no sign of Clete. Not then, not for half an hour after we arrived at the park. That's when he pulled up in his daddy's Cadillac, Eunice at his side.

Right out of the gate, he spent a stack of dimes try-ing to win her a teddy bear at the ringtoss. I figure he just about bankrupted himself winning that thing. After-wards, she fussed and cooed and pretended to feed it boiled peanuts, looking so much like a normal girl that you'd never guess her secret.

And Clete, he made a great show of ignoring me, parading around like a cock of the walk, so that I got fed up with the spectacle of it and caught the first train back after lunch. It was better that way, seeing how sore tempted I was to tell all our classmates it wasn't just the teddy bear Clete had paid too much for.

Besides, it was Tuesday. Ruby day. And since Joseph had paid all but the two-dollar-and-fifty-cent finance fee on the Victrola and was set to receive it Friday evening, I was worried her visit that afternoon might be her last.

So it wasn't until I stepped off the train in Tulsa that I first heard a paperboy on the platform hollering, "Negro attacks white woman! Read all about it!"

Which worried me all the way to the shop. I knew, of course, that he couldn't have been talking about Clarence and Addie, for the Two-Knock incident was old news. Besides, Clarence's death hadn't warranted so much as a mention when it occurred. But the newsie's cry knotted up my mind nonetheless, distracting me so bad that I didn't notice Vernon Fish standing just inside the shop door until I'd near run him over.

He was in rare form, waving a copy of the *Tribune*

about, thundering on with fire and brimstone in his voice.

"Hanging's too good for criminals like that Rowland boy, and me and the fellas are gonna fix him good. Wanna be part of it, Half-breed?"

Then a look evil as any I'd seen came into his eyes, and his hand petted Maybelle's grip in his holster. "Gonna neuter him first. Let him dance awhile over a bonfire. Mark my words, we'll make that boy beg us for the noose."

My innards shriveled as he spoke. I thought how Ruby was likely on her way to visit. And though I'd always been irregular in my prayers, I set about asking God right then and there to keep that little girl safe.

Maybe it was the sight of me standing mute, or maybe it was just manners, but Pop got me out of Vernon's cross-hairs by saying, "Why don't you fetch Mr. Fish a stool from the back, William?"

I practically sprinted to the storeroom.

"Ruby?" I whispered once the door closed behind me. "You here?"

When no response came, I pushed open the alley door and said her name again. After that, I checked to make sure neither Pop nor Vernon had followed me back, and when I was certain they hadn't, said in the loudest whisper I dared, "Go home, Ruby. It's not safe here." Then I went inside, locked the door behind me, and made ready to face Vernon Fish.

"Everything you need to know's right here, Half-breed. Read for yourself."

Vernon jabbed his finger into the bottom right corner of the *Tribune* and smacked it down on the counter in front of me.

NAB NEGRO FOR ATTACKING GIRL IN AN ELEVATOR

A negro delivery boy who gave his name to the public as "Diamond Dick" but who has been identified as Dick Rowland, was arrested on South Greenwood avenue this morning by Officers Carmichael and Pack, charged with attempting to assault the 17-year-old white elevator girl in the Drexel building early yesterday.

He will be tried in municipal court this afternoon on a state charge.

The girl said she noticed the negro a few minutes before the attempted assault looking up and down the hallway on the third floor of the Drexel building as if to see if there was anyone in sight but thought nothing of it at the time.

A few minutes later he entered the elevator she claimed, and attacked her, scratching her hands and face and tearing her clothes. Her screams brought a clerk from Renberg's store to her assistance and the negro fled. He was captured and identified this morning both by the girl and the clerk, police say.

Tenants of the Drexel building said the girl is an orphan who works as an elevator operator to pay her way through business college.

It didn't sound good, I'll admit. But Pop surprised me, saying, "I know that boy. He doesn't seem the type."

Which set Vernon to sputtering how there was no such thing as a trustworthy Negro, and who was Pop to question the paper?

Pop said, "I'm not saying it isn't true, Vernon. It just surprises me. That boy's shined my shoes on more than one occasion and seemed the quiet type. Did a fine job, too. And I never once heard anyone call him Diamond Dick."

"Well, then you're a bigger fool than I thought," Vernon said. Flecks of spittle had gathered at the corners of his mouth. "Most of 'em know enough to hide their true nature, but all you have to do is look in their eyes to see it. They'll smile and nod, scheming all the while to take our women and everything we got. The only good nigger's a dead nigger, Stanley. And me and my boys are gonna make sure Dick Rowland's good as gold before the night's through."

Pop cleared his throat and pushed the paper back across the counter. Vernon swiped it up and stuffed it under his arm. Said, "I'm meetin' up with the boys to discuss the situation. You comin'?"

He waited, standing so still I could hear the breath coming and going from all three of us. It just about killed me, that quiet, until finally Pop smoothed his mustache with his fingertips, saying, "Not just now, Vernon. I can't leave William here alone."

Vernon's lips parted, but his teeth stayed clenched. "Close the damned shop and bring him," he said.

Pop shook his head and said he couldn't do that. Vernon's face flushed deep red. His lips went white.

"You know, Stanley," he said, getting up to leave, "the surest way to protect your business is to come with us and clear that nest of savages out of Greenwood. If you don't, they'll be comin' for everything you've got."

That notion seemed to unsettle Pop, but he held his ground all the same. Vernon stuck his smoldering cigar between his teeth and said, in a voice full of ash and gravel, "At least your son had spine enough to stand up to that boy in the speakeasy. Must be he gets it from your squaw."

Then Vernon walked out and Pop came from behind the counter, fists clenched so tight it looked as if his knucklebones might pop through the skin. And he stared out the window, looking up and down a street quiet as a cemetery at dawn.

"They won't be taking anything. Not with ten whites for every Negro in Greenwood," he said, so soft that I couldn't tell if I should respond or keep hushed. I coughed into my hand. Pop gave a start, like he'd forgotten I was there.

"Don't you have work to do?" he snapped. And I *yes sirred* him and hopped to, making for the storeroom as fast as I could, grateful for once that my mop and bucket awaited.

———

Soon as I got to the storeroom, I opened the back door wide, propped it open with a brick, and started sweeping. It was usually the part of the job I went slowest at, there being no ammonia involved. But that afternoon I felt like a mechanical toy wound too tight, pushing dust ahead of me in short, choppy thrusts. The physical movement was soothing, though. Enough that I swept the whole place twice.

And still there was no sign of Ruby.

So I sloshed out a measure of ammonia and filled the rest of the bucket with water from the spigot out back. My eyes went bleary and my lungs squeezed tight as I mopped, but that was nothing compared to the way the hate in Vernon's words chewed at my insides. I mopped the hell out of that floor, let me tell you, sweating and thinking about Clarence Banks and how even if Dick Rowland *had* done wrong by that girl in the elevator, a judge should decide his fate, not a lynch mob of Vernon Fishes.

Long after there was no dirt left to scrub, I went out back and squatted down to rinse the bucket at the spigot. Cool water spilled over my arms. I cupped my palms and splashed some over my head, closing my eyes against the drips.

"You baptizin' yourself, Will Tillman?" Ruby giggled.

It surprised me so bad that I tipped backwards onto the ground. And my heart lightened at the sight of her, then went heavy as lead when I remembered our circumstances. I put my finger to my lips to shush her and fumbled about, trying to stand. Ruby giggled harder.

"I mean it," I said. "Something bad's happening and you need to get home quick."

Her giggle quieted. "I know," she said.

Pop's voice came through the storeroom door, then Vernon's. It made me sick at my stomach knowing he'd returned. Both of them were close, like they could come through the backroom door any minute.

"Go home, Ruby," I pleaded. "There's a crazy man up front, and you don't know what he'd do if he caught you."

And she looked into me with her deep brown eyes and said, "Course I do, Will. Same thing they're gonna try and do to that man in the jailhouse."

Which made me feel sick all over again as I realized that Ruby knew better than me what was going on. She always had.

The storeroom doorknob turned. Pop and Vernon were coming.

"Get out of here!" I all but begged.

Ruby frowned, serious like her brother, then let loose the hellion's grin I'd come to love so well.

"Ain't nobody gonna catch me, Will," she whispered.

Then Pop and Vernon were in the storeroom.

And Ruby was gone.

———

We ate an early supper that night, for Pop had decided to join the crowd gathering in front of the courthouse. He ate fast, gulping down his pie and coffee before Mama and me finished our trout.

"Eat your meal," Pop said. Then he wiped his mouth off, adding, "And remember what I told you."

Mama cleared her throat. "Will's a good boy," she said. "I only wish you'd reconsider and stay home with us."

But Pop said he was obligated to go see what was what downtown. After all, the last sheriff had let a band of vigilantes walk out of the jailhouse with a murder suspect in their possession. They'd driven him out to the country and lynched him, Pop reminded us, and *he'd* been white. Besides, there were rumors aplenty that armed Negroes up in Little Africa were gathering in the streets, planning God knew what. And such a thing could not stand.

Only from what *I'd* heard, Tulsa's new sheriff was tough as nails and twice as sharp, making it unlikely he'd require the assistance of a shopkeep like my father. But Pop had made up his mind to go, and there was no persuading him otherwise.

After Pop left, Angelina cleared the table and Mama asked me to accompany her into the parlor to help wind yarn. All year long, she made caps for poor babies and orphans. Pop used to complain about the cost of it every time Mama pulled out her needles, and one evening a few months prior, he said something to the effect that it wasn't up to him to put a hat on the head of every squalling ragamuffin in Tulsa. That time Mama's eyes never lifted and her hands never slowed in their work as she responded: "I'm quite certain it's not, Stanley, which is why the yarn money comes from my own income, same as the payments we're making on that fine new house you wanted."

That ended Pop's complaints right then and there, and showed me a side of my mother I rarely saw. For though she was the quiet sort, her words had bite and heft when she wanted them to.

"Quit fidgeting," she said in the parlor. I was perched on her footstool, hands caught up in the length of soft blue yarn she was winding into a ball. I mumbled I was sorry. Mama smiled. And that was all that passed between us as she wound one skein of yarn and another. Finally, on the third, she asked would I like a cup of tea. Jittery as I was over the events of the day, I said I would. Mama called Angelina in and asked her to fetch us each a cup. And when Angelina set the china service down on the side table, Mama asked was her son's family still living up in the Negro quarter.

Now, Angelina may have been getting on in years, but there was always a hum about her. An energy. That night, though, it was quiet.

"Yes'm," she whispered.

"How many are there?" Mama asked.

"Five," Angelina replied. "Samuel, his wife, and their three boys."

Mama pondered that, then said, "I've been thinking about the violence in Chicago a few years back. How a riot broke out after those white men threw stones at that poor Negro boy in the lake until he drowned. Have you room enough in your quarters to invite your kin down for the night?"

Angelina brightened, then faded all over again. "Might be, Ms. Kathryn, but they haven't a telephone."

Mama dropped the half-wound ball of yarn into her skirt, picked up her cup and saucer, and took two ladylike sips. The china barely clinked when she set it down.

She motioned for me to give her the looped yarn, saying, "I'll take that, William. Angelina, would you be so kind as to ride along with William and show him where your family lives?"

That put the starch back in Angelina's collar, and quick. But me? Well, my jaw dropped so fast and so low I near had to scrape it off the floor. Then Mama reached into her pocket and pulled out the truck key and gave it to me, saying, "I trust your father's driving lesson was sufficient to get you safely to Greenwood and back?"

I nodded yes even though it wasn't true.

"Good," Mama said. And she took five crisp new ten-dollar bills from her knitting bag. "For emergencies," she said, handing them to me. "Be back by sundown."

The whistle from the Midland Valley Express came loud through the open parlor window. Mama set to winding the yarn herself. Angelina made for the truck.

And me?

I did exactly as Mama had bid.

Rowan

James and I started going to Cain's Ballroom together right after we met. A real estate tycoon—some founding-father-of-Tulsa type who dabbled in politics and the KKK—built it as a garage for his car collection in the twenties. After that, another someone bought the place and turned it into a dance hall. Today, it's where you go for concerts. They usually don't get anybody huge—big names go to the BOK Center downtown and charge more than mere mortals can afford. But Cain's is cheap, fun, and gets great bands on their way up.

The catch is, there's no seating. It's just this big dance floor with a few three-step bleachers against the side walls. If you want to get close to the stage, you line up a few hours before the show, rush to the front of the dance floor when they open the doors, and park yourself in the best spot you can get. And if anyone tries to push past you, it's perfectly acceptable to throw an elbow.

James and I don't bother with that. We show up just before the opening band's set and watch from the back. The view's still great, no one vapes in your face, and you can pee whenever you want without losing your spot. The barbecue place next door does decent sweet potato fries, too. And when it comes to the actual bands, James and I figured out through trial and error that the ones with the lamest-sounding names usually put on the best shows.

"They suck," James said. He'd picked me up late—just like always—and parking had been bad. So the band opening for Roy Boy and His Kentucky Kickers was maybe halfway done by the time we got our fries and squeezed in next to a be-denimed older couple on the bleachers.

I didn't think the band was that bad, but I was way more focused on all the things I wanted to tell James than I was on the music. *After* our fries, though, and after the band finished its set so I didn't have to scream over them. But James had things to tell me, too, and he didn't want to wait.

"Poke fine the rectory" and "shop" were all I could make out when he shouted in my ear.

"What?" I shouted back.

He gave me his phone. "Poke fine the rectory" was actually the "Polk-Hoffhine Directory," a printed list of businesses and people in Tulsa from 1921 that someone had scanned and put online. James reached over and scrolled down to show me an advertisement for the Victory Victrola Shop.

**Our Prices Will Be Music to Your Ears.
Victrolas and Phonograph Records.
Conveniently Located on Main Street.**

He scrolled some more and pointed to one of the actual listings.

Tillman, Stanley G. (Kathryn), prop Victory Victrola Shop, Main st r 1301 S Norfolk av

"You're a god!" I shouted. The woman next to us shot me an ugly look. James pointed to the entry beneath it.

Tillman, William E., student r 1301 S Norfolk av

At first I didn't get it. But then James pointed to the W in William and the T in Tillman.

W. T. The initials on the Victory Victrola Shop receipt. It looked like William the student was Stanley Tillman's son.

The song ended and the singer started talking about their T-shirts and CDs.

"Impressive," I told James. "What else ya got?"

"You mean I haven't given you enough already, sweetness?" James said, which I thought was weird until I noticed he was discreetly pointing at the denim couple. They were side-eyeing us, disapproval practically oozing out of their pores.

I scooted closer, put my lips to his ear, and whispered, "The anthropologist found a tooth in the dirt that wasn't from the skeleton." He giggled like I'd used my tongue for more than talking.

After the band finished their last song, James patted his lap and I climbed onto it. He winced, muttering something about his legs being sore from working out that morning, and the denim couple started quietly shitting kittens. Then the roadies came out to set up Roy Boy and His Kentucky Kickers' gear, and I told James everything Geneva had said about the skeleton.

"Uh, racist much?" he grumbled when I got to the part about her using the skull to decide the skeleton's race. Denim man cleared his throat and said something to his wife. All we heard was "trashy" and "typical."

I wrapped my arms around James's neck, saying, "Maybe. But Geneva kept saying how even though race might be an artificially created construct, patterns of evolutionary differences in skeletal morphologies from isolated geographic areas are measurable and real."

James's eyebrow went up. "What?"

"I think she was trying to say it's complicated. And that she's not a racist."

He brushed my hair away from my ear and whispered, "Speaking of racists, shall we?"

I pointed to the OVER 21 wristband he'd gotten with his lousy fake ID at the door. "Only if you buy me a beer."

James smiled, stood up, took my hand, and planted a big, wet kiss on it. Then he turned to the denims, flashed them my most favorite of his wicked grins, and said, "Don't worry, folks. It's not serious. I'm just her baby daddy."

And then we walked away, leaving them to sputter and grumble over the sorry state of Negro youth in America today.

———

I didn't get home from the concert until after one, so I skipped my run the next morning and slept late. There was a sticky note on the fridge when I got up saying Dad was at the office and Mom had gone to the gym. I showered, threw on a T-shirt and basketball shorts, and pulled up directions to the title company. Dad had kept his word and called them, and since I hadn't been able to get there during the week, Saturday before noon was my big chance.

It was a nice morning. Not too hot, not too sunny. I stopped for a chai at the coffee shop James thought was pretentious—the one next to the barbecue place where people line up for ribs an hour before it opens. Gray clouds hung low around the Art Deco spire of Boston Avenue Methodist. Semis on the Broken Arrow Expressway made the overpass vibrate under my tires.

Half a block past that, I clipped the edge of a pothole hard enough to send hot chai splattering down the inside of my thigh. I cursed and set the cup down quick. Then I saw the cat—frozen in the middle of the road, staring at my car with its tail tucked and its hind legs sunk low.

I hit the brakes.

Slammed forward and back as the seat belt locked.

There was no thump, no yowl. Out the corner of my eye, I saw it bolt, unhurt, toward the sidewalk. Relief and adrenaline jacked through me all at once. Then I was rocketing forward again, so hard that white-hot pain sang through my ribs as they hit the seat belt again. My chin jammed down into my chest before the back of my head whipped, slingshot fast, into the headrest behind me.

The world went black. And when the light came back, everything was slow. Blurry. Quiet. Then a man's voice was trampling my ears. It was muffled, but loud and angry enough to make my eyelids flutter open against light that seemed too bright to be real.

"...the hell are you doing, stopping in the middle of the street?"

I rolled my head toward my window. The man was waving his arms, cell phone in one hand, running his words together so fast I couldn't make sense of them. A knob of pain pulsed at the bottom of my skull. The man opened the door and snapped his fingers in front of my face, his cheeks pale with anger.

"Hey! Don't pretend you can't hear me. I'm sick of you people acting like..."

Wisps of pain wrapped around each syllable in my head. He kept shouting, on and on and on. The chrome grill of his massive pickup was in my rearview mirror. So was a second figure coming toward us—grizzled, black, and dressed in a dirty shirt and fatigues three sizes too big.

I knew him.

Arvin.

"Hey, you're my girlie friend from Jackson!" he said, peeking around the truck's driver. The black and gray stubble on his chin reminded me of my grandfather's funeral, of the smell of candles and gardenias.

"Back off, buddy," the driver barked. "Go back to the gutter you crawled out of!" Arvin ignored him and tried to get closer to me. "Gotta get you to Dr. Woods, young lady," he mumbled in his raspy voice. "She'll make you all better."

"Arvin..." My voice floated in the air like a ghost.

"I said back off!" the driver shouted. And when Arvin didn't, the man put both hands against his chest and shoved.

"Goddamned nigger."

That time his words were calm. Deliberate. Cruel.

Arvin's arms flew up. He pedaled backwards, tripping and stumbling into the second traffic lane behind him on

214

the one-way street. Then there was a horrible crunching thud, and Arvin's body flew up and over the hood of an old gray Suburban. The back of his head hit the street. The Suburban lurched to a stop. The woman inside was screaming.

Arvin didn't move. Sirens wailed louder and louder, ping-ponging around in my thousand-pound head as flashing red and blue lights filled my mirrors. The siren stopped. The wisps turned into angry fingers of pain squeezing the sides of my head. Then a policeman was coming toward us. The truck's driver watched Arvin's body like he expected it to stand up and come at him.

He didn't need to worry.

Arvin wasn't ever going to stand up again.

WILLIAM

Our trip to Greenwood was touch and go at first. It took me three tries to back the truck out of the driveway. Two to start forward. And every time I managed to gather a little steam, a stop sign would show up and throw a wrench into the works. Angelina sat behind me in the truck's cargo space, out of sight and holding on for dear life as we jerked along. It was for her sake as much as my own that I started ignoring the stop signs altogether.

The sun was only just starting to drop at that point, meaning sunset was still a ways away. But there was a quietness to the streets I didn't like. People were about, to be sure; men, mostly, headed in the direction of the courthouse. A few children played in yards, too, and every now and again we'd pass a woman sitting out on her front porch, snapping beans or darning socks. Even so, the air had a hushed feel to it, like the city was holding its breath.

It was a different story altogether in Greenwood. As soon as I headed north off of Archer, the tension in the air got thick enough to chew. Shopkeepers and clerks stood in doorways. Men huddled in groups of threes and fours, talking. Until they caught sight of me, that is. Then everything stilled as their wary gazes followed our progress up the street. After Angelina realized where we were and came up to sit beside me, those gazes turned curious.

More than anything else, I wanted to find Angelina's family quick so we could turn around and go home. For though the truck was unmarked, the white of my skin made us stand out bright as a signal fire. As soon as the Dreamland Theatre marquee came into sight, though, I knew things wouldn't go easy. There were cars on the street in front of it, and more black men than I'd ever seen assembled in one place. Enough so I hadn't room enough in the street to pass.

It felt like a thousand faces were staring at me as the truck lurched to a stop. Looking back, I reckon there were fewer than a hundred, but fear makes everything bigger and worse. It didn't help that some of those men held rifles and shotguns. Pistols, too, though many appeared unarmed. And I'm not ashamed to say that the sight set my hands to shaking, especially when a man tall as a chimney and dark as soot came to my window.

"You oughtn't be here," he said. Then Angelina spoke up with an authority I'd never heard in her voice before, saying, "You let us through, now. We come to fetch my boy and his family, and you got no business stopping us."

The man didn't back off one bit, only asked who her boy was. "Samuel Brightwater," she replied, after which the man turned and pointed, saying, "You mean that Samuel Brightwater over there?" Then Angelina was out of the truck and marching into the crowd, parting it like Moses did the Red Sea.

I wish I knew what words passed between her and her son, and that I could say he joined us in the truck. Only I don't, and I can't. For after a conversation that seemed to go on forever, Angelina returned alone and got in without looking back.

"You'll want to take your next left, Mr. William," she said.

I asked was he coming. Angelina motioned with her chin towards the opening in the crowd in front of us and said, "He's got plans of his own. Best be on our way."

And you know, that was the first time I ever managed all the levers and pedals just right, so that we started up Greenwood without so much as a sputter.

———

Other than offering a word here and there to guide our progress, Angelina kept quiet until we stopped at the curb in front of her son's house. It was small, with an outhouse in the back and a yard full of dirt and bull nettles. The porch was swept clean, though, and the little boy who ran out onto the front stoop to greet us had creases ironed into the sleeves of his shirt. "I'll just be a minute," Angelina said. Then she left me alone in the truck, pretending there weren't eyes watching me from behind every curtained window on the block.

True to her word, Angelina came back out quick with the boy from the porch plus two more. All three wore caps and faded overalls, and each carried a sack over his shoulder. The older two looked worried and angry all at once. The littlest one was bawling.

"Get in," Angelina told them when they got to the truck. They did as she said, sitting on the floorboards. The youngest sniffled and hiccupped, and Angelina said, "Hush now, Freddy," and shut the back door. I asked what was wrong. "Doesn't want to leave his dog," she replied through the passenger side, pointing to a scruffy brown mutt straining against its chain to peek around the back corner of the unpainted shack. The little boy snuffled. "That's enough!" Angelina snapped. The boy did his best to be still. And though Pop had never let me have a dog of my own, I was about to say how Freddy should fetch the thing and bring it with him. Only before I could, Angelina marched back, unlatched the chain, patted the dog's head, and left it standing there with its ears perked high.

"Dog can take care of herself," she muttered when she

got back. Then she motioned for Freddy to come closer. She wiped his cheeks and nose with her apron, kissed his forehead, and told him that was the end of the matter.

Only it wasn't. For as soon as Angelina returned to the house, the boy started crying all over again. "Shush," the oldest said. "Lulu'll be fine." And Freddy came back at him angry, saying, "You don't know that, Sam. You don't know nothin'!"

I turned around just in time to see the littlest boy's heel come down hard on the top of Sam's foot. It must have hurt, too, for Sam winced. But he held his tongue and didn't kick back.

"I'm Will," I said, hoping the interruption would settle things down.

"Samuel Jr.," the eldest replied. "This is Marcus and that's Freddy. Where you takin' us?"

"To my house," I replied.

Which made him knit his brow and ask, "Why?"

I had no good answer for that. I knew bad things were brewing. I knew there was a Negro man at the courthouse who some white folks wanted dead. I knew there were Negroes gathering outside the Dreamland, too. And, more than anything, I knew I was half out of my mind with worry over Ruby. But that's not what I told Sam. To him I said, "In case something bad happens, I suppose." Which made his forehead pinch even tighter. "That's not what I mean," he said. "I mean why are *you* taking us to *your* house?"

"Because my mama told me to," I replied, for that was the honest-to-God truth of the matter. And it must have made sense enough to Sam, for he leaned his back against the side of the truck and kept quiet. Then it occurred to me that maybe I should ask *him* if he knew what was going on in front of the Dreamland.

Sam nodded when I did.

"Well then, what?" I asked.

And he told me how folks were worried that white men were going to lynch Dick Rowland before he was tried in court, and that the people gathered at the Dreamland—his pa included—were trying to decide what to do about it. "Some of 'em believe it'd be best to send an important man like Mr. Gurley down to talk to the sheriff," he said. "If it weren't for Mr. Gurley, there'd be no such place as Greenwood at all. But there's others who think things have gone too far for talk."

I asked him which side of that debate his father was on. Sam shrugged and said his pa didn't figure any man deserved to die until God, or at least a judge, had decided he should, no matter what the color of his skin.

Then the Brightwaters' front door slammed shut, and a short, slight woman locked it up. She and Angelina came to the truck together, carrying a heavy-looking sack between them.

"Mr. William, this is my daughter-in-law, Grace," Angelina said. I tipped my cap to her and hopped out to hoist the sack into the truck. Grace looked surprised.

Then her lips trembled and she thanked me, which made my cheeks turn hot.

After that, Angelina climbed in and told me to drive due west, as that was the quickest way out of Greenwood. And it seemed such a fine idea that I was clear to Cincinnati Avenue before I recognized the opportunity I was wasting, stopped the truck, put it in idle, and faced my passengers.

"Any of you folks know Joseph or Ruby Goodhope?" I asked.

Five worried sets of eyes peered back at me. Three heads shook no. But the middle boy, Marcus, grimaced and reached up to the inside of his arm like it pained him. "Do you know them?" I asked him direct. And he squinched his lips up tight and nodded a little and said, "Don't know Joseph, but I know *her.*"

"You know where she lives?" I asked. Marcus shook his head. But Freddy sniffled and wiped his nose on the back of his sleeve, saying, "He's lyin'." Marcus scowled, and Grace looked at him stern and told him he'd best tell me the truth. Marcus hung his head and hunkered down further. "Yeah. I know where she lives," he said. "Only I don't wanna go there."

Then Grace turned stony like only a mother can, and Marcus shrank even smaller.

"I'll show you," he said. So I turned the truck around, stalling once, and steered back towards the heart of Greenwood. And over the engine's putter, I heard Marcus grumble to anyone who cared to listen, "I can't stand that Ruby Goodhope. She pinches."

———

In the end, Marcus never did get pinched. Leastways, not that night. For the only person we found at Ruby and Joseph's house was their mother, distraught over her two missing children and scared near to death by the sight of a six-foot white boy standing on her front porch.

Angelina smoothed things over. She introduced herself and asked the woman's name, which was Della. Then she told Della how I knew Joseph from him making deliveries to my father's store, and Ruby because she tagged along. She didn't know to say anything about the Victrola, for that was a surprise I wasn't about to ruin. Then Angelina said my mama was a kind soul willing to open her home to Negro women and children until the trouble down at the courthouse blew over.

Looking at Ruby and Joseph's mother, so scared and worn in her faded blue dress, I knew I had to invite her along. But after I'd done it, she looked as if the idea made her sick at her stomach. "Thank you kindly," she said. "But I'll just wait here till my babies come home." Then she forced a smile for my sake and cast a worried look up and down the street. And Angelina patted her arm and told her we'd be praying her children got home soon. "Best be going now, Mr. Will," she said after that, nudging me towards the street. "Sun's almost down and your own mama will be worrying."

I didn't want to leave until I'd found Ruby, but I drove straight home anyway. And Mama *had* been worrying; I could tell by the nervous chirp in her voice when she met us in the driveway. "Back the truck up to Angelina's door, William," she said, loud enough for every wag-tongued busybody in the neighborhood to hear. "I don't want you dropping that mattress in the dirt."

Which I understood straight off was her way of telling me we couldn't let anyone catch sight of Angelina's family, so we should pretend we were unloading a mattress into her quarters. And though I made a hash of the job, stopping and starting and stalling and cursing under my breath, I eventually got the truck's back end close enough for Grace and her family to scoot inside without being seen.

After that, Mama had me park the truck where it belonged. Then the two of us went into the main house, and Mama wrapped a plate of sandwiches inside clean bed linens and told me to carry them out to Grace and Sam and Marcus and Freddy, who I found cramped and sweating but grateful nonetheless. While they ate, Angelina came back into the big house with me and fetched a glass of lemonade with mint in it for Mama. And Mama said it was dark enough then for Angelina to take a whole pitcher of the stuff back to her guests.

As for me, I was too full of nerves and worry to stay

inside. So I took my ragged school copy of *Macbeth* out onto the front porch and set about trying to make myself read. Only the bulb was flickering and there were so many mosquitos that I felt more like a snack than a scholar. I kept at it, though, swatting and muttering and watching a steady trickle of automobiles roll by.

Some stayed closed up and quiet as they passed, others were so full there were passengers standing on the running boards. Those were the rowdy ones, with men whooping and carrying on loud enough so I could make out each and every word they said.

"Gonna put 'em in their place tonight!" one man hollered. And a few minutes later: "Sheriff better turn that boy over if he knows what's good for him!"

Even without the mosquitos, those voices would have been enough to make reading old Mr. Shakespeare near impossible. Yet I sat there pretending to try, wondering what was afoot at the courthouse, until maybe half an hour had passed and one of those sets of headlamps coming down the street turned into our driveway so fast the tires squealed.

It was Pop in the Model T. Him and the iron in his eyes. He wasted no time on greetings as he strode past, saying I should follow him inside. And when he led me to the parlor where Mama was waiting, her gaze fell on me first, calmer than it had any right to be.

Pop asked straight off if Angelina was in her quarters. Mama replied yes. Then Pop said I should go out and tell her to lock her door and stay put for the night. I looked to Mama, who nodded and said she'd have no further need of Angelina anyway. So I hustled back, and Angelina cracked open the door before I'd even knocked, just wide enough for me to hear sniffling behind her. It was Freddy, I supposed, still worrying over his dog. Then I delivered Pop's message to Angelina, adding, "He doesn't know your kin are here." And the whites of Angelina's eyes shone scared against the dark as she whispered, "I can hear them, Mr. Will. Even through the window glass, I can hear those men driving by, calling for that poor boy's blood."

There was nothing I could say; leastways, nothing that would make her feel better. But it didn't matter, for Pop's voice boomed across the yard, telling me to come back inside. And Angelina shut the door so quick I near lost a finger.

I crossed the lawn at a jog, shaking my hand and gritting my teeth from the pain. But I forgot all about it as soon as the porch light came on and Pop stepped outside with the long barrel of his Remington resting against his shoulder.

"Fetch your Springfield," he barked. "Now!"

Which loosed the invisible strings holding me back and sent me hustling inside to get my hunting shotgun from Pop's gun rack. Back in the parlor, Mama sat, white-lipped, watching Pop slide a round into the Remington's chamber.

"Load it," he told me, pointing to a box of shells. Mama's expression went faraway distant, and the color drained from her cheeks altogether. When I hesitated, feeling suffocated by all the things I didn't know about or understand, Pop picked up the box of shells and rattled it in front of my nose. "You deaf?" he snapped.

I said I wasn't and cracked open the Springfield's barrel, thankful Pop was too busy filling his ammunition belt to notice the shake in my hands.

"Hurry up," he said. "We've got work to do."

And I did as I was told because he was my father. And because it hadn't yet occurred to me that I had any other choice.

Rowan

The rest of the day that Arvin died was a blur of uniforms, ambulances, and sirens.

I spent a long time at the hospital—five hours, maybe six. One CT scan, lots of different people asking me to rate things on a scale from one to seven, seven being the worst.

How much did my head hurt? Seven.

How nauseated was I? Three.

How hard was it to concentrate? Eight.

Nobody asked how it had felt seeing the Suburban hit Arvin, or hearing his bones shatter. I guess there wasn't any scale for that.

I cried a lot, too. "Post-concussion symptom," the neurologist said.

Bullshit.

After the hospital, Mom gave me enough painkillers

to muffle the bad thoughts and set them adrift. She curled up next to me in her pajamas, and when I woke in the middle of the night, sobbing, she gave me two more pills, kissed my forehead, and feathered her fingertips against my back until the drugs kicked in and I fell back to sleep.

The next day, the police came.

Detective Bennet was a youngish black woman dressed in a pantsuit that pulled tight across her hips. Her partner, Detective Bland, looked like a mall Santa shaved clean for the off-season. I was propped up on the leather sofa in Dad's darkened study with an ice pack on my neck and a blanket pulled up to my chest. Mom had pushed the coffee table back and moved two armchairs close to me. She stayed at the foot of the couch, resting her hand on my ankle. Dad leaned against the bookshelves by the door.

Detective Bennet had me describe the accident. After that, she asked what the other driver had done when he got out of his truck. I didn't want to talk about it. Didn't know if I could. Dad asked the detectives if he could speak with them in the other room.

When they came back, Detective Bennet apologized for having to interview me when I wasn't feeling well, and said she just needed me to tell her what I remembered after Mr. Brightwater showed up.

I had no clue who she meant.

"The indigent," she said. "Arvin Brightwater."

I wanted to scream at her that he wasn't Arvin the indigent, he was Arvin the person.

Mom squeezed my ankle gently. Instead of screaming, I kept my voice calm and told them Arvin had come over to the car to try and help. "He wanted to take me to see Dr. Woods," I said. "She's a doctor at the clinic where I work…"

I lost it a little then. Mom handed me a Kleenex, and everyone waited until I could start again.

"That's where I met Arvin," I said. "Dr. Woods takes care of him."

Detective Bennet nodded and asked if Arvin had said anything to Mr. Randall.

"Mr. Randall?" I said.

"The other driver."

I started to shake my head. Bright ribbons of pain reminded me to stay still.

"No. Arvin was only paying attention to me. But the man—Mr. Randall—he was so angry. He told Arvin to get away, and when Arvin wouldn't, he pushed him and…"

I swiped at my tears. Detective Bennet glanced at her partner. Mom caught the look and said, "We need to wrap this up, Detectives."

Detective Bennet started to argue, but her partner stopped her, saying, "That's fine, Mrs. Chase. We'll come back when Rowan's feeling better. For now, I'd just like to know if there's anything else she can tell us about Mr. Brightwater's death. Anything at all."

I kept my eyes on Dad as I spoke.

"When he—Mr. Randall—pushed Arvin, he called him a goddamned ni…" The word stuck in my throat like the last thing you feel before you throw up. "He called him the n-word."

Dad didn't look away. But something shifted in his eyes, and Mom's grip tightened on my ankle.

Detective Bland's lips pinched into a tight frown. He didn't believe me.

Mom stood up. "I'm going to have to insist that you let my daughter rest now, Detectives." Her voice was smooth and cold—a frozen plane of ice with a river of anger flowing beneath it.

Detective Bland looked like he wanted to say something. Whatever it was, he kept it to himself and stood up.

"Thank you, Rowan. We appreciate your help," he said. Detective Bennet looked unhappy, but she didn't argue. Dad led them to the study door. Once they were gone, Mom sat back down.

"You did good," she said.

"It doesn't feel that way," I whispered.

"You told the truth." She handed me another tissue. "Will you drink some orange juice if I get it for you?"

"I don't think I can."

"You'll try."

I needed to blow my nose but knew it would hurt too much.

"This is what you meant about things being complicated, isn't it?" I said.

Mom nodded.

I closed my eyes. The pain quieted, and I felt the air shift as she moved away.

"I'll be okay," I said.

Mom came back and knelt beside me. "I know you will, sweetheart," she whispered, and kissed my temple so softly it didn't even hurt.

———

James brought me balloons and a stuffed elephant on Monday morning. At first he sat far away, like I'd break if he breathed on me too hard. I pointed at the chair closest to me and told him not to be an asshole.

"Your mom wouldn't let me in yesterday, and she threatened bodily harm if I stay too long or upset you today," he said, switching seats.

"She's just worried. I spent most of yesterday crying," I said.

"I'm not surprised. How are you?"

"Today? Mad. Really mad. A man I should have treated better is dead, and I'm not sure whether it's because he was black or because he was poor or because some people are just plain evil. And you know what? I'm starting to think no one's going to do anything about it. Arvin's probably going to end up just another murdered black man whose killer gets to walk. They may as well dump his body at a construction site and forget about it."

James seemed surprised at first. Then he leaned closer with this really intense look on his face.

"So what are you going to do about it?"

"About Arvin?" I said. "There's nothing I *can* do except hope the DA will press charges. But that still leaves another dead black man who deserves better than he got. I want to figure out who the skeleton was. For real, James. And I want to know who killed him."

"I'm in," James said. "Where do we start?"

"With minor fraud."

"Um..." He was appropriately concerned.

"Relax. All I need you to do is go to the title company, pretend to be me, and pick up the title to our house. It's what I was on my way to do Saturday morning."

"That seems a tiny bit illegal," he said.

"It probably is, but no one there knows I'm not a guy. Rowan goes both ways."

James gave me his wickedest smile. "Quit talking dirty, Chase. You know I'm not interested."

It was the first time anyone had treated me normally since Saturday, and I had to roll my eyes to keep from bawling. It hurt so bad I nearly cried anyway.

"I need you to do this for me," I said. "Even if I could drive myself, that asshat nearly totaled my car."

James was quiet. I think he was only pretending to think it over, but my skin was too thin to deal with teasing just then.

"Please," I said. "If I hadn't been on my way to get the

title, there never would have been an accident in the first place."

James tried to say something. I cut him off.

"The police buried the skeleton's file at the bottom of their cold case stack, and the only real investigator trying to figure out who he was can barely carry on a conversation with the living. If we leave this thing unsolved, Arvin will have died for nothing."

James was quiet. I could hear Dad and Mom talking in the kitchen. Not actual words, just their voices rising and falling.

"If I get arrested for impersonating you, your mom had better go all pro bono on my ass," James said.

"Don't be stupid. If you get arrested, Dad will make a phone call and fix it."

James stood up. "Okay. I'll give it a try. But if they ask me for ID or act suspicious, I'm out of there."

"Deal."

"You know you're the only person in the world I'd do this for," he said.

"Because you love me, right?"

He tilted his head, serious and soft all at once.

"Yes, Chase. Because I love you."

———

At first, I thought Mom was just checking on me when she peeked in later that morning. But when she saw I was awake, she told me I had a visitor and opened the door wide for Tru.

"It was a pleasure meeting you, Truman," Mom said.

Tru gave her his full-on smile. "Yes, ma'am. And don't worry—I won't stay long. My nephew's a wide receiver at Booker T. and took a late hit last season that knocked him out cold. I know all about concussion protocols."

Mom tilted her head and gave him her you-interest-me look before she left. People don't surprise her very often. Not in a good way, at least. I think she kind of likes it when they do. Then she ducked out, and Tru put a clean mayonnaise jar full of black-eyed Susans on the table next to me and said the best thing he could have: "Rowan, I am so, so sorry."

I burst into tears. He sat down and waited quietly until I was done. At the exact right moment, he started talking again.

"Mama Ray sent the flowers. And I came to tell you in person that you shouldn't come back to work until you're ready. But if you're up to it, Arvin's funeral is Thursday at six, and all of us from the clinic are going."

He offered me a tissue and took one for himself.

"If you can make it," he said, "it'll be your big chance to see J'Neece from billing. We're having a reception at my house afterwards. She's bringing the Diet Coke."

I laughed, ignoring the pain it sent shooting through my head.

"I'll be there," I said. "And, Tru?"

"Hmm?"

"I'm sorry I didn't call in sick."

He looked at me like I was nuts. "Are you kidding me? Besides, your mom called Dr. Woods to tell her what happened. Did you know they went to high school together?"

"Only since Friday."

"Well," he said, "even as we speak, a completely overwhelmed lady from the temp agency is at the reception desk trying to deal with Mrs. Penfield. That woman shows up like clockwork every Monday with some fatal disease she read about online. Someone really does need to cut off her internet."

I laughed again. It still hurt, and it still felt good.

"Thank your mother for me, please," I said. "For the flowers, I mean."

Tru winked and grinned. "Mama Ray's gonna like you," he said. And suddenly I understood why he never kept his meth-wrecked smile hidden. It showed where he'd been, what he'd gone through.

It was proof he'd chosen to survive.

I ditched the prescription painkillers Tuesday morning and switched to ibuprofen so the sharp edges of my grief could come into focus.

It was awful.

So was the headache that started up as soon as I

opened my laptop. But I was sick of lying still, trying not to feel things all the way. If the neurologist could have seen what I was doing, he would not have been pleased.

I started with the Victory Victrola Shop listing in the 1921 Polk Directory, then backtracked—1920, 1919, etc.—until the listing disappeared in 1916. That meant the shop had opened in either late 1916 or early 1917. After that, I worked forward. In 1929, there was a Victory *Radio* Shop listed instead of the Victory *Victrola* Shop. The address was the same, though, and the proprietor was still Stanley Tillman. His home address never changed in all those years, and he stayed married to Kathryn. But there was no William E. Tillman, student, listed under Stanley's entry past 1921, or anywhere else in the directory for that matter. And in 1937, Stanley Tillman and the Victory Radio Shop disappeared from it altogether.

After I'd poked around for an hour, it felt like a roller derby was going on inside my head. I set my phone alarm for thirty minutes, closed my eyes to rest, and made it a full fifteen before I got impatient and turned the alarm off.

That's when I started digging around the Tillman family tree, found a historical newspaper database, forked over $19.95, and read the obituary.

> **Mr. Stanley George Tillman** of Tulsa suf-
> fered a fatal heart attack the morn-
> ing of Friday, September 3, 1937,
> in the Victory Radio Shop on Main

Street that he had run successfully for twenty years. Mr. Tillman moved to Indian Territory from Cuyahoga County, Ohio, in 1899 and married Kathryn Elizabeth Yellowhorse in 1902. He is survived by his widow, who resides in Pawhuska. The whereabouts and disposition of his son, William Edward Tillman, are unknown.

That made for an awful lot of question marks around William Tillman, including why his initials were all over the Victrola receipt from the dead man's pocket.

Payments rendered by J. Goodhope towards one Victor Talking Machine Company Victrola Model XIV

J. Goodhope.

I pulled up the 1921 directory, scrolled to the *G*s, and found one entry.

Goodhope, Della (wid Theodore), cook
Nut-n-Honey Café, Greenwood av, r 114 Jasper st

It was close, but that was D. Goodhope, not J. I tried to find 114 Jasper anyway, just to see where Della had lived, only there was no such address in Tulsa anymore. I did find a historian's map outlining the boundaries of the area affected by the race riot, though, and there, inside the shaded zone where everything had burned, was a little stretch of Jasper Street.

Which meant Della Goodhope's house had probably been destroyed in the riot. But since her husband's name had been Theodore, and since there was no other Goodhope listed, I let that particular thread drop. Besides, any woman living and working in Greenwood had to have been black. And I remembered enough from Oklahoma History to know that Jim Crow laws would have kept black people out of a Main Street Victrola shop anyway, so J. Goodhope must have been white.

Still, I liked the name Nut-n-Honey Café, and that got me wondering about what Greenwood must have been like before the riot. I found pages with stories from survivors. Descriptions of what happened. Photos of smoke pouring out of the Mount Zion Baptist Church roof and of black men walking down Greenwood as white men held guns to their backs. I also found statements from white Tulsans denying there had been anything more than a few scuffles that night. But when I stumbled onto digital copies of a black-owned newspaper called the *Tulsa Star*, I felt like I was really getting a glimpse of what life in Greenwood had been like before the riot.

There were stories about how bad race relations were, not just in Tulsa, but all around the country. I found an editorial that argued toy companies should make brown-skinned dolls, and a bunch of others calling on black people to stop settling for second best. The writers questioned the way things were and talked about how much better they could be.

And there were advertisements that painted a picture of life in Greenwood: luxury rooms at the Red Wing Hotel, top-notch service at the Alexander Laundry, laughter and tears on-screen at the Dreamland Theatre. There was even an ad for radium water treatments at the Washington Bath House, which couldn't have ended well for anyone. And then, on the last page of a December edition from 1921, I found an ad for the Nut-n-Honey.

When You Ask What's For Dinner
And She Says, "Nothin', Honey,"
Take Her To The Nut-n-Honey Café.

FINEST IN HOMESTYLE COOKING
YOU MUST TRY OUR PIES

And that was all my bruised brain could take. So I closed my laptop, shut my eyes, and dreamed of pie.

WILLIAM

You can think yourself into all kinds of trouble when you're alone in the dark, especially when there are mice in the walls, and creaky wood floors, and a gun on your shoulder, plus your own heart thumping so loud in your ears that it near drowns out the rest.

The Springfield was loaded and I had two full boxes of extra shells thanks to Pop. Any other day, I'd have been tickled pink if both he and Mama had sent me off driving on the very same night. But sitting there in the shop under Pop's strict orders to shoot anyone who tried to come through the door, I was anything but. Still, push come to shove, I'd have done as he said. For if there was one thing I knew, it was that you didn't carry a firearm unless you were prepared to use it.

Back at the dining room table, Pop had told Mama

and me how the crowd of white men around the court-house was growing by the minute. How carloads of armed Negroes had come and gone, offering to help Sheriff McCullough keep Dick Rowland safe. And how three white men had gone inside the courthouse to try and drag Rowland out, only to be ejected posthaste by the sheriff's men.

"This whole city's a tinderbox waiting on a match, and I'll be damned if I let a bunch of hooligans ruin everything I've worked for!" Pop said. "It doesn't help that there's a group of white rowdies heading across Sixth Street, aiming to snatch weapons from the National Guard Armory. If they manage it, every fool and scoun-drel east of the Arkansas'll be armed and up to no good. We have to protect what's ours, William. If anyone tries to come in the shop, you shoot first and ask questions later. Understand?"

I'd nodded that I did. Mama bit down on her lip and fought back tears. And Pop glared hard at us both.

Then he stood up and said for me to follow him, and told me I was to drive straight to the shop, park in the alleyway, and take up a post in front of the counter. Mama stood with us, asking why Pop didn't guard the shop him-self. Pop replied that he needed to keep an eye on the situation at the courthouse. "I'm a tolerant man," he said. "And good to Negroes. But I'll not stand for armed gangs of them coming into proper Tulsa."

After that, Mama kissed me and held me so long that

Pop grumbled it was time to go. We drove north, him in the Model T, me in the truck behind, until Pop turned left onto Seventh and I continued on. And though a few empty cars were parked along Main Street by the shop, that part of Tulsa was quiet as a ghost town.

I parked in the side alley like Pop had said and used the moonlight to find my way inside. Then I stood guard for near an hour before calling Mama, just to hear her voice and tell her I was fine. She said she was glad, and that she loved me and I should be careful.

After we hung up, I was alone in the quiet and the dark again, wishing I knew if Ruby was safe.

Until the shot sounded.

Just one, far off.

Then another.

Two after that.

Then so many that I couldn't count. And I stood there with my gun in my hands, frozen with fear and numbed by a sudden, overwhelming awareness of just how fragile the life I knew really was.

———

Eleven minutes ticked by on the old pocket watch Pop kept near the register. I tightened my grip on the shotgun as a pair of headlamps moved north along Main Street. More gunshots sounded, then three northbound vehicles passed by. After that, the street stayed empty, though shots pecked and popped at the air like Fourth of July fireworks. I ground my teeth so hard my jaw ached. Only, so far as I could make out, the sound was moving away. And by the time twenty-three minutes had passed, my breathing eased and my muscles unclenched.

At minute twenty-four, the telephone rang and near scared me to death. It was Mama, checking to see how I was. I could hear the relief in her voice when I told her the gunfire was too far north to be a worry. Then she said it was good I hadn't let word slip to Pop about his surprise, and could I keep it secret just a little while longer. Which made no sense at first, though I did have my wits about me enough to eventually figure out that Mama was speaking in code. She did that sometimes, knowing any one of the other four households sharing our telephone's party line could listen in on our conversations whenever they pleased. And whether or not we heard a click or a cough to let us know they'd picked up their receivers to spy, we always assumed they had.

Mama waited patiently until I caught on that she was talking about Angelina's family. I said of course I could keep the surprise a secret, feeling guilty over how completely Grace Brightwater and her children had slipped my mind. But they were safe as any Negroes in Tulsa could be, tucked away in a white neighborhood full of lawyers and bankers and merchants. It was Ruby I was scared for, knowing she might be out on the streets in the middle of a gunfight.

And perhaps Mama heard something in my tone, or perhaps she understood me better than I knew, for she asked was I all right. Then a dark shape sped by outside, and when I gave her a hesitant *yes*, Mama asked was I sure.

I eyed the Springfield on the counter. Said, "I'm sure, Mama. Don't you worry." Then I hung the earpiece up, set the telephone down, and grabbed my gun. Whatever was outside had been moving too fast to be a person and too slow to be an automobile. I crouched down and waited until a soft rapping came from the storeroom. Shotgun at my shoulder, I made sure the front door was locked.

The rapping came louder.

My feet moved against their better judgment. My throat seized up. My palms went clammy. But I kept walking until I got to the storeroom door, where I stopped and put my ear to the wood and heard it again.

Knock, knock, knock.

KNOCK, KNOCK, KNOCK.

The storeroom was pitch-black save for a patch of moonlight shining through the high-set ventilation window on the back wall. Thankfully, all my afternoons mopping had taught me where every last crate and stool in the place was. Enough so I could get to the back door without so much as stubbing my toe. I leaned towards it, waiting for another knock. A kick. *Something.* Only what I heard was a grunt, then metal scraping overhead. Warm air blew across my cheek, and a deep voice came, hushed and desperate, but a relief to me nonetheless, calling out for the girl I hadn't been able to get off my mind all night.

"Ruby? Ruby, are you there?"

———

I found Joseph in the alley, standing atop a wobbly stack of crates from the stationer's next door. He'd got himself just high enough to catch hold of the back window's sill, but not high enough to see in. It was a precarious arrangement even without the surprise of me opening the door. The crates underneath him swayed and swung, then the stack toppled like so many jackstraws.

Joseph didn't fall. He hung there, fingertips hooked over the sill, whispering a blue streak of curses that surprised me more than seeing him there had done in the first place.

"That you, Will?" he asked when his curses had run their course. I replied it was, and that he'd better come inside quick before someone heard the ruckus he was making and decided to investigate.

He let go of the sill, landing heavy on his feet.

"Ouch!" he grunted, shaking out his ankles and rubbing his knee.

"I bet," I said.

Then we stood there, Joseph casting a wary eye towards my Springfield, neither one of us knowing quite what to do.

He spoke first.

"You gonna call the police?"

"Why?" I replied. "You gonna rob us?"

He sighed. Said, "You know full well I'm not."

Which I did. Far as I was concerned, Joseph had paid off all but the finance fee on the Model 14 and would have been perfectly within his rights to carry it home. But both of us knew he hadn't come about the Victrola. And both of us knew he couldn't go home.

"You seen Ruby?" he asked.

I told him I had, only much earlier that day. Then I said again how he'd best come inside.

"Word of honor you won't call the police?" he said.

I swore it. Even so, Joseph deliberated long enough that I got tired of waiting and told him he could stay or go as he pleased, but I wasn't saying another word about Ruby until we were safe inside with the door locked behind us. He sighed and followed me into the shop. And I bolted the door and told him to stay put while I went to fetch the old oil lamp and matches Pop kept on a shelf next to the cleaning supplies. Then I carried the lamp back to where he was and lit it and turned the wick low, praying no one would notice its glow from the alley behind.

After that, Joseph and I sat down on the floor. By the look of him, he was even more scared than me. Yet he started right in talking, saying how Ruby had been miss-ing since noon. As a rule, she never played hooky until the last hour of the school day; noon was early enough that her teacher had telephoned their mother at the café to let her know.

"Peach pies," I murmured.

"What's that?" Joseph asked.

So I told him how Ruby had been visiting me for the last two months, and how she'd said their mother was a baker who made wonderful peach pies. Joseph let out a sob disguised as a cough, and my own throat swelled up tight. But it didn't stop me from saying I was worried about Ruby, too, and that I wanted to help him find her.

"You mean it?" he asked.

I replied that I did, then pointed to the Springfield and said I knew how to use it.

"Maybe so," he replied. "But would you do it on her behalf?"

I thought about Ruby, and the carloads of armed men who'd driven past our house, and the marks on Maybelle for the Negroes Vernon Fish had shot. And there was no hesitation in my voice when I replied *yes*. Yes, I would.

———

That was the moment things began to change between me and Joseph. Not in any way I could define, more in a way I could feel. He told me what he'd seen that night; how he'd been too far away from the courthouse steps to hear everything that transpired, but that he knew enough men had come down from Greenwood to make the white folks assembled there nervous.

"I didn't see who fired the first shot," he said. "But it turned everyone still as statues. Second one got them moving, and by the third, they were screaming how they'd chase all us Negroes out of Tulsa for good."

He went quiet, then cleared his throat and began again.

"They started moving up Boulder. I ran east along a side street. Plenty of those men from Greenwood are soldiers come back from the war. They know how to fight, but they weren't at the courthouse for that; not most of them, leastways. They just wanted to make sure Dick Rowland lived long enough to stand trial. But now… well, if a white man shoots at them first, they'll shoot back. Only do you know how many white men there are for every one of us, Will?"

"Near ten," I replied.

Joseph nodded. I asked him did he know any other places where Ruby might hide. He shook his head, saying, "I've checked all her usual haunts twice already, including here."

Then it occurred to me that Joseph must have been worried about his mother on top of everything else. So I told him I'd seen her earlier that night. "She was afraid for you both," I said. "But she was safe."

"How'd you know where I live?" he asked. I replied I'd been helping our housekeeper's family and one of her grandsons had told me the address. He frowned like he didn't quite believe me, but the space between us softened even more.

Then I asked did his family have a telephone. Joseph said no, but their neighbors Mr. and Mrs. Tyler did. Only, when I took him up to the store's counter to call, the Tylers didn't answer. Neither did anyone at the Nut-n-Honey Café, which Joseph said normally didn't close till midnight.

"I'm sure your ma's fine," I said, aiming to make him feel better.

"How do you figure that?" Joseph replied.

And the God's honest truth was that I had no idea if Mrs. Goodhope was fine or not, nor any reasonable basis for making assumptions either way. So I changed the subject, suggesting that if the crowd at the courthouse was moving north towards Greenwood from downtown, maybe we could take the truck out wide to the east, turn north, and come down into the area from above. "You ride in the back of the truck so no one sees you," I said. "With any luck, we'll get to your house and find out Ruby got home long ago."

Joseph looked at me, his face more open and true than ever I'd seen it. "Why would you do that?" he asked.

Which was a question I couldn't answer. Nor, as it turned out, did I have to. For just as I was about to mumble how I only wanted to help, headlamps lit up the shop window, passed by slow, and stopped.

Joseph went still as a possum. "Get down!" I whispered, blowing out the lamp. "Stay low, crawl back to the storeroom, and wait for me there."

When he didn't move, I said it again, loud enough to shock him into dropping to the floor. Then he made for the back, leaving me there with the Springfield clutched tight.

Please go, I thought to myself, praying the automobile would move on. Seconds ticked by. Minutes. Enough of them so that I switched to whispering for Joseph to stay put in the back. For if he tried to sneak out through the alley, whoever had parked across the street was bound to see him.

I patted my pocket and felt the fob ring holding the truck's keys. Then I slipped out from behind the counter and pressed my back against the north wall. Fast as I dared, I slid forward, keeping to the shadows all the way up to the front corner of the shop until a rap came at the glass so sharp my belly dropped clear to my boots.

I looked down the length of the front windows and saw Clete's profile. And past him, someone taller with his cap pulled low.

"Will?" Clete hollered, cupping his hands around his eyes to peer inside. "I know you're in there, Will!"

I stepped away from the wall. Then Clete saw me, and I noticed the rifle at his chest. He smiled and motioned with one arm, shouting: "C'mon out, Will. We got some huntin' to do!"

I resisted the urge to look back towards the storeroom,

and hollered through the glass how Pop had told me to stay put and guard the shop.

"We come to grant you a reprieve," Clete bellowed. "Besides, ain't nobody gonna mess with white men's property tonight!"

"I can't leave," I replied. Then Clete elbowed the figure next to him and the two of them laughed. "You let me in right now, Will Tillman," Clete hollered. "Or I'll tell your pa you were too lily-livered to come out!"

"I told you," I hollered back. "Pop said to guard the shop." And Clete looked straight at me with a predator cast to his eyes, saying, "Who do you think sent me here in the first place?"

Then the man beside him moved out of the shadows and tipped back his cap. He held up a wicker fishing creel stuffed full to overflowing with bullets, shaking it so I could hear the clink of them through the glass. And he smiled around the cigar between his lips and pressed his horrible face close to the glass, saying, "Open the door, Half-breed. Or I'll smash it in myself."

Rowan

J ames showed up Tuesday night with gelato and a grin.

"Petty crime's my calling," he said, handing me a dish of half-melted coconut and chocolate. "And by the way, that's très chic." He meant the hideous neck brace I'd finally given in and put on.

Smartass banter didn't feel natural yet but I played along anyway, hoping it would help get things back to normal.

"Good. That's what I was going for. Do you have the title?"

James lifted the strap of his messenger bag over his head. "Of course. Because yours truly possesses one of the great criminal minds of the century."

"They just gave it to you, didn't they?"

He took a thick sheaf of papers out of the bag. "Didn't even ask for ID."

Now, it turned out that reading our house's title was only slightly easier than reading the clinic's insurance manual. But it was definitely more interesting. The first few documents were typed on paper as thin as an onion skin. They showed that the land our house was built on had been signed over to the Muscogee Creek Nation by President Millard Fillmore in 1852. There hadn't even been an Oklahoma then, only Indian Territory.

After that, we read from the yellowed pages how the tribe had given my family's lot to a seventeen-year-old girl named America Manuel, who was listed as a freedman—a black slave who'd belonged to the Muscogee Creek Nation but had been freed after the Civil War. Which meant that the first person to own our property was a teenage girl with brown skin.

I set the empty gelato cup aside and took the title from James's hands so I could see her name up close. "That. Is. So. Cool!"

He reached across me and flipped the page. "No doubt. I don't think she ever lived here, though. She leased the land to a farmer first, then to the Anchor Oil Company. After she sold it in 1904, it changed hands"—he took the title back and flipped pages quickly, counting under his breath—"eight times. But there's nothing about a house until"—more flipping—"ha!"

"What?" I peeked over his shoulder. He pointed out two names at the top right corner of the page.

Stanley G. Tillman and Kathryn E. Tillman

"No shit!" I whispered.

"Yup. Stanley and Kathryn bought the lot in 1920. And here's a construction mortgage in their names for twenty-five thousand dollars, so apparently they built the house, too. Only…"

"What?"

James kept reading. "I'm not sure, but I think…wait. Yeah. Here. Stanley and Kathryn owned the land and built the house, but if they lived here, it wasn't for very long. See?"

He pointed to a tiny line of type. In November of 1922, my great-great-grandfather and great-great-grandmother, Flowers and Ora Chase, paid twenty-nine thousand dollars cash for the house James and I were sitting in and the land underneath it. Which meant that since the Victrola receipt and the newest coin in the skeleton's pocket were from 1921, there was a good chance the body was in the back house before my great-greats ever moved in.

"Maybe there isn't a murderer in your family tree after all," James said. "You relieved?"

I flipped the title closed and rolled my eyes, saying, "Oh, so very."

And you know? I actually kind of was.

———

William Tillman's parents built this house. He left home sometime before the Polk-Hoffhine Directory came out in 1922. No one could find him when his father died. And he almost definitely would have had access to the back house while it was under construction. Bottom line: there was a good chance he was either the skeleton or the guy who'd put it there.

Only the more James and I talked things through, the less likely it seemed that the body could be William's. For one thing, we didn't see how he could have been black (yes, uncomfortable as it made me, I was willing to give Geneva's race theory the benefit of the doubt). His father, Stanley, must have been white, otherwise Tulsa's Jim Crow laws would have made it impossible for him to own any business on Main Street other than a shoeshine box. And when we tracked down the Tillman family tree on Ancestry, William's mother turned out to have been one of the original 2,228 Osage Indian tribe members given a headright allotment and 160 homestead acres in 1906. That meant she'd had money, because the Osage had made sure the mineral rights for tribal land—translation: the oil rights—stayed communal. And *that* meant all the profits from oil pumped out of Osage land went into one big account, and four times a year, everyone with a head-right got a check for an equal percentage share.

"Now I get how they could have afforded this house," James said. "I thought it was pretty fancy for a guy who sold record players."

I took my computer from him and ignored how the glow from the screen made my eyes ache. "It could explain more than just the money," I said. "Those headrights were valuable. Maybe William tried to claim his mother's after she died. If he did, we might be able to track him down through tribal records."

James spotted something on the page I was looking at. "Can I see that for a sec?" he asked. I handed him the laptop.

"Okay, I thought I remembered this," he said. "A bunch of Osage, especially Osage women, were murdered in the 1920s after the government decided that anyone who was half Indian or more needed a white guardian to manage their money."

"Lovely," I said.

James sighed. "I know, right? So, anyway, a lot of white men married Osage women just to get control of their fortunes. Then a bunch of those women started dying in weird ways—drowning in shallow creeks, falling out of third-story windows, turning up with bullet holes in their skulls. No one really looked into the deaths until the FBI finally stepped in. *After* the white guardians had inherited the women's money and headrights, that is."

"Figures," I said. "But what does it have to do with the skeleton?"

"Well, I know your anthropologist friend said it's from a black man, but what if she's wrong? The DNA tests haven't come back yet, have they? Maybe she isn't as great as she thinks at telling Native American skulls apart from African American ones. Or it could be that she's just completely full of crap about being able to judge someone's skin color by their skulls in the first place."

I shrugged. "That doesn't change my question: what does any of that have to do with our skeleton?"

"Well, I was thinking that maybe, just maybe, Stanley Tillman was a cold-blooded bastard and killed his own son to keep him from inheriting Kathryn's money and headright."

"That doesn't make sense," I said. "We know Kathryn didn't die until 1976—way after Stanley. If he was willing to kill his own son to get her money, wouldn't he have killed her, too?"

James clicked back to the family tree. "This says that Kathryn Yellowhorse Tillman died in 1976 in *Pawhuska*—not Tulsa. And she was there when Stanley died in 1937. That's more than an hour north of here. What's to say old Stanley didn't knock off William, let his wife go out of her mind worrying about her missing son, then ship her off to relatives up north while he stayed here in town? He was in charge of her money anyway. Maybe once the son was out of the way, it didn't matter to him if Kathryn was alive or dead."

I closed the computer. "Don't you think your theory might be just a tiny bit influenced by the messed-up father-son dynamic in your house?"

"Maybe," he said. "But maybe Stanley was a racist prick and didn't want a half-Indian son to begin with."

I shoved the computer to the foot of the bed with my toes. "I guess it's possible, James. But I'm too tired to deal with thinking about that right now."

He gave me a guilty look. "You're supposed to be resting."

"I know. But you could be onto something with the Osage connection."

"Yeah?"

"Yeah. Kathryn didn't die until 1976, so there's a good chance *somebody* in Pawhuska remembers her."

"You're right!" James said. "In fact..." He opened my laptop back up and typed something into the search bar, clicked a few times, and scrolled. "Look."

He spun the screen toward me. And there, on the Osage Tribal Museum website, was Kathryn Yellowhorse Tillman, staring out from 1898—where she'd been waiting for us all along.

———

I dreamed of Kathryn Yellowhorse that night. That's how I thought of her, because *Tillman* didn't fit the girl in the picture—not the black shine of her hair, or the open kindness of her face, or the way her smile played out in her eyes more than her lips. And even though she may never have lived in our house, it's where I pictured her, gliding through the halls in a white flapper dress and pearls.

When my phone went off just after eight the next morning, I was in the dream myself, doing the Charleston at a party in the Philcade Building downtown that would have made Jay Gatsby jealous.

I squinted at the unfamiliar number on the screen. "Hello?"

"Ms. Chase?"

I sat up. My neck was still stiff, but it was better. "Yes?"

"Ms. Chase, this is Michael Mercury from News-Hacker Media. I was wondering if you could share your insights into Arvin Brightwater's death. And maybe you'd like to let our readers know how you're doing, too?"

"What?"

"You're Rowan Chase, right?"

"Yes, but..." I swung my legs over the edge of the bed.

"The seventeen-year-old driver involved in the car accident that occurred prior to Arvin Brightwater's death?"

I stood up, wide awake. "How did you get my number?"

"I can't tell you my source," he said. "But if you'll just..."

"No. I won't *just*."

I hung up and sank onto the window seat. With the morning sun glinting off the back house windows, the only thing I saw in them was the reflection of a redbud tree.

I blocked the number that had just called, then searched *Arvin Brightwater*. The first hit, a CNN story about candlelight prayer vigils scheduled across the country for that night, was a surprise; I didn't know anyone outside Tulsa had even heard about Arvin's death. At the same time, it was good. I liked the idea of people holding flames up against the dark in Arvin's honor. And if that had been all I'd found, maybe I could have let things go.

But it wasn't. And I couldn't.

Pages and pages of hits came back.

Jerry Randall was a racist and pushing Arvin in front of the car was a hate crime. Jerry Randall was the victim and had been defending himself against a crazy homeless man. The mental health system had let Arvin fall through the cracks. It was the teenage driver's fault for causing the accident that led to the confrontation. If the police didn't go after Randall, Tulsa would be Ferguson all over again.

And on. And on. And on.

Nearly every single person who wrote about Arvin in articles, tweets, and comment sections acted like they knew what had happened. *They* got it. *They* were appropriately sad or angry or confused or forgiving or whatever. *They* understood. Which was funny, because I'd been there, and I was mixed-up as hell. Angry, too, that no one had told me Arvin's story was blowing up. Mom and Dad, Tru, James—they'd all kept it secret, as if I was too fragile to handle reality.

The more I thought about it, the more I realized that reality was exactly what I'd needed all along. It would have helped to know that people were talking about Arvin, remembering him. It mattered. It made his death matter. And it was exactly the kind of thing I had to know if I was going to make sense of what had happened.

I took Geneva's business card down from the bulletin board over my window seat and ran my finger over the lettering next to the five-pointed Oklahoma star.

It wasn't even in purple Sharpie like the medical examiner sign in her van.

Geneva was odd, but she'd been straight with me from the start and had never treated me like a child. Maybe she'd learned more about the skeleton or had ideas of her own about who he'd been. Maybe she didn't.

Either way, it couldn't hurt to find out.

WILLIAM

Vernon turned on the overhead lights and lit up a Robusto as soon as I let him inside the shop. He handed one to Clete, too, and Clete near burst from pride as Vernon lit it for him. Then Clete sucked in a big lungful of smoke that turned him green as springtime in the light from Mama's Chinese lanterns. Vernon cackled and smacked his back, saying, "Ain't s'posed to inhale, son!" Then he offered one to me. I declined, and Vernon shrugged. Said, "Here's the story: me and my friends've been deputized special to help shut down this Negro uprising we got goin' on. And as a duly sworn officer of the law, I'm enlisting your help."

I must have looked as dubious as I felt, for Clete said, "It's true, Will. Some old coon down at the courthouse wouldn't hand over his pistol when a white deputy told him to. Next thing you know, there's guns firing and seven kinds of hell breaking loose, and all because those Greenwood boys don't know their place."

Vernon grunted, then started in like General Pershing himself, talking about skirmish lines and battle plans and how the Negroes had made their stand just south of Third Street. "Turns out some of 'em fought in the war and picked up a thing or two about combat," he said. "We aim to show 'em they'd have been better off learning to duck."

At that, he took Maybelle out of the holster on his belt and carved two more notches into her with his pocket knife. Clete grinned and looked back and forth between me and Vernon, asking did I know what the notches meant.

"He knows," Vernon said, squinting against the wavering column of smoke from his cigar. Then he blew the filings off of Maybelle. Said, "Now that we got the ammo we came for, the three of us best get moving. We got a long night ahead of us."

Only I didn't want to go anywhere with Vernon and Clete and their guns. So I said again how Pop had told me to guard the store, and Clete insisted Pop had sent them to get me.

"He truly said that?" I asked Clete direct. "He said for you to fetch me?"

Clete's eyebrows furrowed. "Well, he didn't get a

chance to come right out and say for us to *fetch* you," he said, "but that's only because we got separated once the fighting heated up."

Which told me straight off that Pop hadn't said any such thing, and that I'd been suckered into opening the shop door in the first place. Though, of course, there would have been hell to pay if I hadn't.

After that, Clete yammered on about war and duty and white men needing to stand up for what was theirs. Vernon's dead eyes stayed on me until Clete finally shut up. Then Vernon said, "Listen to me and listen close, Half-breed: there's good niggers and bad ones. Good ones know their place. Bad ones don't. What's happening here tonight is an old-fashioned purge. We're gonna flush the bad ones out of Tulsa once and for all."

I gave no response, for there was nothing I could think to say. Then Vernon pushed his face so close to mine that I felt the heat from the tip of his cigar against my cheek. "I'll brook no cowardice, boy," he said. "Now you quit pissin' and moanin' like a damned woman and come fight!"

I thought of Joseph and Ruby then, and Angelina and her grandbabies, and knew in my heart what I believed.

"No, sir, Mr. Fish," I said softly. "I can't do that."

Clete was silent beside me. Vernon's face went white with fury. He walked to the demo machine Pop and I used to play music for customers and, casual as could be, pushed it over. Wood splintered. Metal twisted.

"Let's try that again," Vernon said. "You're going to come with us right now or so help me God I'll destroy every last thing in this place and tell your pa you weren't man enough to protect it from rioters. Clete here will back me up, won't you?"

Clete focused on his boots but mumbled *yes* quick enough. And though the thought of Vernon ruining the shop was none too pleasant, it was my fear of what he'd do if he found Joseph in the back room that tipped the scales on my decision once and for all.

"All right, Mr. Fish," I said. "I'll come."

"Good," Vernon muttered. Then he spun me about by the shoulders and shoved me out the door. I stopped on the sidewalk, saying I had to lock up. And I went slow as I could, leaning my Springfield against the door, dropping the keys, pretending the bolt was stubborn. So that by the time I looked up and across the street, Clete had got behind the wheel of his daddy's Cadillac and Vernon was climbing into the seat beside him. Their cigars glowed red in the hot night air. And though darkness cloaked Vernon's features, I could still picture the smile on his face. The one saying he'd won, and I was nothing but a stupid boy.

Shots sounded to the north. So many I lost count. Then silence, until Vernon Fish broke it.

"Let's go, Half-breed," he cried. "The night's young, and we've got killin' to do."

The Cadillac's engine growled to life. My pulse quickened. And without letting myself overthink the matter, I loosed a curse loud and vivid enough to make Vernon and Clete spin around, mouths open in surprise.

"Forgot my shotgun shells," I hollered. And before either one of them could say a word to stop me, I was through the door I hadn't locked in the first place.

"Joseph!" I yelled, running to the storeroom. But there was no sign of him there, and my heart sank, worrying he'd gone out through the back. I called his name again as I swapped the door keys in my hand for the truck key in my pocket. And just as I was about to go look for Joseph in the alley, I heard my name from the darkest corner of the room.

There being no time to chat, I shouted for him to follow me to the truck. Then the two of us were outside in the warm night air, running on the balls of our feet to keep our heels from clipping the concrete. I got in my side and jammed the key into the ignition, praying the engine would catch easy. And for once the heavens listened, so that as soon as Joseph had got beside me with the passenger door shut, I hit the reverse pedal and dropped the throttle level hard. The truck bucked and squealed onto Main Street like an unbroke horse. I swung its nose north. Went to neutral. Stomped the clutch. And promptly felt the engine go dead.

There we were, ass backwards to Vernon and Clete, motor stalled, Clete shouting, Vernon sputtering, the Cadillac's engine revving. I stepped on the starter. The truck's motor churned and refused to catch. The Cadillac backed towards us. I saw Vernon Fish in my rearview mirror, looking angry and exhilarated all at once. Then he caught sight of Joseph next to me, and the look turned into something else altogether.

At that moment, everything felt far away and quiet. I had no heartbeat. No breath. There was only the heavy night air against my damp skin and the stubborn whine of the truck's engine. I hovered in that nothingness, suspended somewhere between where I needed to be and where I was, until a bullet stripped the haze from around me.

It passed by so close that the percussion of it hurt my ears. I turned and saw Vernon's hand raised, aiming Maybelle's muzzle at the truck.

Joseph shook my arm and screamed for me to go. I pressed the starter one more time. The engine rolled and caught and roared. I pushed the clutch in. First gear took. And finally, finally, we were moving north.

"Faster," Joseph said, quiet at first, but louder once Clete got the Cadillac moving behind us. Headlamps shone in the windscreen glass. I revved the engine high and shifted into second. Then Joseph was pointing left and saying to turn so we didn't drive straight into the battle line of white men fighting black. I did as he said at the next street, cutting hard enough that the whole truck tilted into the turn. Our tires held the road, though, carrying us west with the twin orbs of the Cadillac's headlamps close behind.

Joseph leaned forward with his hands on the dashboard and said something I couldn't hear. "What?" I shouted. "Rain," he replied, which made no sense at all. Only it did make me think on water and how we were heading towards the Arkansas River and the long, flat stretch of road running alongside it out to Sand Springs. On a straightaway like that, the Cadillac would catch us in no time. So I banked hard right at the next street and accelerated, near bouncing out of my seat as we crossed the Frisco tracks.

The Cadillac stuck tight.

Then a whistle sounded loud in my ears and Joseph said "rain" again, only that time I heard the *t* in front of it and understood he'd been saying "train" all along. For there was a train just ahead of us on the Katy tracks, coming fast.

I knew I couldn't turn right because of the gun battle, or left because the Cadillac would catch us. And backwards? Well, that was no option at all.

The Cadillac was gaining. The train whistle shrieked louder. Joseph's hand was in front of my face, pointing to the freight engine barreling towards us on our left. "STOP!" he screamed. "STOP!"

Only I didn't. I mashed the throttle lever down,

and gasoline flowed wide open into the truck's gullet as we barreled towards that oncoming train. And its light shone blinding white into my window, and the roar of its whistle rattled my heart in its cage. Our front wheels hit the tracks, and we were in the air.

Then we were plunging forward, crashing nose-first into the ground. The rear tires hit after, hard enough so the truck bounced up and down as train cars thundered behind us in a fury of screaming metal and brakes. I eased the throttle back. Joseph slumped on the bench beside me.

"You're crazy, Will," he whispered. There was fear in his voice, but admiration, too.

I clenched my right hand into a fist and opened it wide, freeing up the muscles that had locked down on the steering wheel. Did the same with my left. And there was no denying the truth in what Joseph had said.

"Nice evening for a drive," I said, two blocks later.

Joseph smiled, which made me smile, too. And it was good that we didn't have a clue what lay ahead of us. Elsewise we might well have stayed a northward course, driving until our gas was gone and the Oklahoma state line was nothing but a ghost in the dust behind us.

———

The first family we saw fleeing Greenwood was on foot: two children, a man, a woman with a babe clutched tight to her chest. The man hunched forward, struggling under the weight of a lumpy, flower-embroidered sack. It was a tablecloth, loaded up, I supposed, with the family's silverware. China. Pictures. Things they'd worked hard for. Things meant to be handed down.

More came after them.

"Where are they all going?" I asked Joseph.

"Into the hills," he replied.

Some drove. Most walked. A few pedaled bicycles. There were children, too—so many children. And old women and old men and everything in between, struggling under the weight of their belongings and their situation. I thought about the Brightwaters, huddled together in the dark of Angelina's quarters, and wondered if Freddy had stopped crying over his dog.

Then Joseph was pointing to a figure ahead of us, telling me to stop. "I know him," he said. "Please."

The young man had an ancient musket slung over his shoulder, so rusty I doubted it had been fired since the battle at Gettysburg. Even so, he shrugged it off into his hands as we drew near.

"Gideon?" Joseph called out. "Gideon Wright, it's me, Joseph Goodhope." The musket's muzzle dropped, and Gideon squinted against the headlamps as he walked to the passenger side. Then he must have seen my pale skin in the moonlight, for he backed up a step and raised the musket high.

"It's all right," Joseph said. "Will's helping me."

Gideon took a step closer, face dark with suspicion, saying, "Why?"

"I don't rightly know," Joseph said.

"Why are you helping him?" Gideon asked me direct. And though I wasn't exactly sure, his rusty musket inspired me to come up with an answer quick.

"Because of Ruby," I said.

At that, the musket dropped and Gideon scowled even better than Joseph could, saying, "That girl's like a skeeter bite on the ass!" He stared at me hard, and I looked from him to Joseph and back again until suddenly the three of us were laughing. Nervous and quiet, but laughing nonetheless. Then Gideon slung the musket over his shoulder and leaned against Joseph's door, tapping a finger on the metal. He told us there was a line of armed colored men at the southern edge of the Negro quarter, fighting to keep bands of renegade whites out of colored neighborhoods. "There was some fighting down at the Frisco tracks earlier," he said. "But it's been pretty quiet for a while now."

"Then why're you leaving?" Joseph asked. Gideon said how his ma had gone up to stay with her sister in Claremore earlier that day, and it didn't seem worth risking a belly full of lead just to stick around and see what would happen. "Plenty of folks took off already," he said. "But there's others staying, thinking what happened at the courthouse was just a misunderstanding. They're locked in their houses now, praying for sunrise to put things right."

I could tell by the way he said it that Gideon considered those people fools. Far as I was concerned, he was right; I'd seen the hate in Vernon's eyes and heard the evil in his voice at the shop. For men like him, the old normal wasn't an option anymore.

Then Joseph asked had Gideon seen Ruby or his ma, and Gideon's face pinched up.

"I thought you knew," he said.

Joseph stiffened. Said, "Knew what?"

"Well... that they took her," Gideon replied.

Then Joseph opened the door of the truck so hard it pushed Gideon back. And he grabbed Gideon's collar and yanked him up and shook him, shouting, "What do you mean, they *took* her?"

Gideon kept calm. "Three white men. They found your ma looking for Ruby down along Archer and they took her. Leastways, that's what I heard."

Joseph let go. Whispered, "Where?"

Gideon said he wasn't sure, but word had got round they were holding Negro prisoners in Convention Hall. Then Joseph turned even quieter, asking had they hurt her. Gideon looked at the ground.

"Well, did they?" Joseph demanded.

And Gideon looked sorry as could be, saying, "She was alive. That's all I know."

I leaned over towards the passenger side, saying Joseph's name loud enough for him to hear. He looked at me, all dull and numb. Then Gideon put his hand on Joseph's shoulder and said he was sorry.

"We have to find Ruby now," I said, strong as I dared. Joseph nodded and got in the truck, and Gideon turned north and started walking.

"Eliza Clark turned me down for prom so she could go with Gideon," Joseph said as we pulled away. "It's tomorrow, you know. She was supposed to be with the decorating committee at the Stradford Hotel ballroom tonight, getting things ready. She was so excited."

I tried saying I was sorry, and not just for the Booker T. Washington prom that seemed unlikely to occur. But I had to stop and clear my throat and try again. The second time it came out right.

"Do you think they got Ruby, too?" Joseph said by way of a response.

I had no answer for that. Joseph looked out the window and didn't seem to notice.

"Won't be any colored folk dancing in Tulsa tomorrow night," he said. Then he swiped at his eyes with the back of his sleeve and let me drive on.

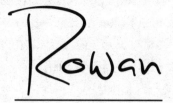

Rowan

H ello?"

Geneva's voice was wary when she answered the phone.

"It's Rowan Chase," I said.

Insert awkward silence.

I tried again. "The one with the remains in her back house?"

"I know who you are," she said. "It's just that people don't usually call me."

Which was sad and honest and perfectly Geneva.

"I don't have the genetic results yet, if that's what you're after," she said. "I won't have them for at least another week."

"It's not," I said.

"Then what do you want?"

She didn't mention the accident or seem to have any idea I'd been there when Arvin died.

"I was just wondering if you had any new information," I said. "About the skeleton."

Nothing.

"Hello?"

"Sorry," she said. "There's a big hawk overhead. I'm on a dig in Tahlequah."

Again, perfectly Geneva.

"So is there anything new?" I asked.

She was quiet. Maybe she was thinking about how to respond. Maybe she was still looking at the hawk.

Eventually, she cleared her throat and started talking in the calm, clinical voice she used when the subject was her work. "As a matter of fact, my friend Bob—the one I sent the pistol and holster to—finished his report yesterday."

"Can you tell me what it said?" I asked.

"I don't see why not. He used the original manufacturer's marks and serial number to trace the gun. It's a Colt M1911, purchased by the US Army and stamped by someone named…"

I could hear her notebook rustling.

"A. L. Hallstrom. He inspected military M1911s from 1916 to 1917. Bob says the gun parts were all original, and the gun itself was produced in 1917. The holster was standard issue. It was stamped with initials, too…"

No rustling that time, just a pause.

"Here it is. The initials were *V. F.*, but Bob said the first letter was modified at some point after the gun was distributed. He isn't positive, but he thinks it was originally an *R*. He searched World War One draft registration cards, and the best match he could come up with was a Raymond Fisher from Decatur, Georgia."

I scribbled down what she said on an empty page at the back of my Calc notebook and asked if Bob happened to mention anything about Raymond Fisher coming to Tulsa.

"No," she said. "But it's possible. He went AWOL while he was on leave for his mother's funeral in 1919 and was never found."

"Did she live in Tulsa?"

"Decatur."

"Still, he could have been the killer," I said, more to myself than to her. My hand had cramped from writing so fast, and all kinds of scenarios were playing out in my head.

"Or the killed," Geneva said. "According to his draft card, Raymond Fisher was black."

———

I didn't go to Arvin's candlelight vigil in Reconciliation Park that night. Part of me wanted to be around other people who cared that he'd died, but another part knew the funeral the next day would be hard enough. So while people gathered in Greenwood to remember him, I sat on one of the chaise lounges by our pool, listening to peepers and staring west at the glow of the refinery lights along the Arkansas.

Their flare stacks were dark. Some nights, flames shot out, burning off waste overflow. I used to pretend those stacks were dragons breathing fire into the night when I was little. I knew better; my father was an oilman, after all. But even as a kid, I'd liked the idea of dragons better than the thought of burning petrochemical waste.

Dad came out after a while and lay down on the chaise beside me.

"How you doing, kiddo?"

"Okay," I said.

"Cloudy tonight."

It was a nothing comment. Dad isn't usually big on chitchat unless he's working his way up to something bigger. I knew the best thing to do was ignore his small talk and let him get to the big reveal on his own. That night, it didn't take long.

"Your mother just got a call from her friend in the district attorney's office," he said. "They haven't announced it yet, but they're not charging Jerry Randall. They're calling it self-defense."

I looked at the clouds and blinked back the stupid tears in my eyes.

"What are you thinking?" Dad asked.

"Rowan?"

"Yeah?"

"Do you think they made the right call?"

"They didn't believe me, did they?"

He sighed. "I don't know. But even if they did, I'm not sure your statement would be enough to prove the case. Then again, your mom's the lawyer, not me."

"What does she think?"

"You'd have to ask her. But one thing I *do* know is that she believes you, and so do I."

A train whistle sounded up where the tracks crossed Peoria.

"Are you okay, kiddo?"

"As okay as I can be," I said.

We sat there for a while, looking west, until a column of flames flared up into the western sky.

"One of your dragons is awake," Dad said.

"There's no such thing as dragons, Dad."

"Don't be so sure," he said softly. Then he left me alone to stare at the sky, imagining the flames were for Arvin, wishing dragons were real after all.

━━━━

There hadn't been any public announcement about Arvin's funeral, so the size of the crowd at the cemetery surprised me.

"Let's stay in the car," Mom said. "You can watch from here."

Some of the people were from the clinic. A few more looked like they might have known Arvin from the street. Other than that, everyone was a stranger. They were black, mostly, and went from a toddler in a miniature three-piece suit all the way up to an ancient jelly bean of a woman pushing a walker in front of her.

"Who are they?" I asked.

Mom looked out the window. "Family. Folks he grew up with."

I watched people get out of their cars and walk slowly to the fresh grave. It was my fault I was surprised. I'd never stopped to think that just because Arvin lived on the street, it didn't mean there weren't people who loved him.

There were no reporters in the crowd, though, or anyone else who looked obviously out of place.

"I want to be with them," I said.

Mom and Dad traded a quick look of parental concern. Then Mom dug out her lipstick for a fresh coat, and Dad got out to open my door. Tru waved when he saw me. Mom excused herself to go say hello to Dr. Woods.

Once the service started, Mom and Dad stayed at my side—through the pastor's homily, the kind words and memories from childhood friends. The last person to speak was a short woman in a dark blue suit and a peacock-feathered hat who turned out to be Arvin's aunt Tilda. Her eyes stayed dry, but by the time she was done, the rest of us were a mess.

Afterwards, Tru came over to say hello and offered to drive me to the reception in his boat-sized Cadillac. "I can bring her home, too," he told Mom and Dad. "It's really no problem." They gave each other the look again, but I could tell they were relieved not to have to go.

"I'm good with that," I said.

Mom asked if I had my phone, which was like asking if I'd remembered to bring both kidneys. Then she and Dad took off and Tru drove me to his house. And even though we barely said a word to each other, there was nothing uncomfortable about it.

We ended up in Brady Heights, an old neighborhood that had been just white enough and just far enough away from Greenwood to escape burning in the riot.

"Home sweet home," he said, swinging the Caddy into the driveway of a yellow bungalow with a magazine-worthy garden. "Welcome to Mama Ray's."

For the record, my knowledge of gardening begins and ends with the name of the guy who does ours. But even I could tell that Tru's front yard was something special. There were flowers everywhere, and bushes, plumed prairie grasses, and trees with blooms cascading from their tops like Fourth of July fireworks.

Inside, the house was like one of those reconstructed historical rooms at the Smithsonian. The purple velvet sofa and chairs were old and formal. The floor and tables were made of dark, heavy wood. The lamps looked like they'd been around since electricity was invented. And there was an abundance of doilies. Seriously—they were everywhere.

"Mama Ray?" Tru hollered.

"Be right there!" came a voice from the kitchen. Based on the garden and the furniture, I was expecting a rosy-cheeked, unscarred, grandmotherly version of Tru.

I was way, way wrong.

For one thing, Mama Ray was black, and as far as I knew, Tru wasn't. Plus, she wasn't even that old. Forty, maybe forty-five, with a short-sleeved gray silk shirt that showed off seriously ripped arms. Her hair was in a medium-length Afro pushed back off her forehead with a silver headband.

The surprise must have shown on my face.

"You did it again, didn't you?" she said.

Tru grinned like he'd just pulled off the best prank in the world.

"Shame on you, Truman!" Mama Ray smacked his shoulder, then shook my hand with both of hers. "He does that sometimes—lets people think I'm his mother just to see their reactions. But he ought to know better after everything you've been through."

"Aw, she likes it when I tease her," Tru said. Then he got all fake serious. "For the record, Rowan, Mama Ray didn't give me my life, but she did save it."

"That's not true," Mama Ray told me. "Truman saved himself."

Tru got serious for real then. "Mama Ray's the youth pastor at Grace Emmanuel," he said. "I used to go to their Tuesday soup kitchen. It took three months of sitting next to me while I ate grilled cheese sandwiches and tomato soup, but she finally talked me into rehab. Gave me her spare bedroom when I got out, too. If it weren't for Ray, I'd have been back out on the streets and using again inside of a week."

Mama Ray smiled. "We all make choices. I just gave you a few options that hadn't been available before."

A car door slammed outside. Voices carried in from the driveway.

"Truman, sit this poor girl down before everyone arrives," Mama Ray said. "She looks wrung out."

Tru led me to a loveseat. Mama Ray opened the front door and let in Dr. Woods and a stiff-looking black woman in a black suit. Both of them hugged Mama Ray like they'd known her forever and started toward me. Tru kept behind them, mouthing something I couldn't make sense of. Then I noticed the bottle of Diet Coke in the unfamiliar woman's hand and smiled. I'd finally spotted the mythical J'Neece.

Who, as it turned out, was very sweet and apologized for not introducing herself at the clinic. "I meant to," she said. "There's just always so much to do."

Dr. Woods put an arm around her shoulders and squeezed. "J'Neece is a miracle worker. We couldn't survive without her." Then she asked about my symptoms, how I was doing, and said I should call her if I needed anything.

More people came after that. Lots more. The ones who knew me said hello, the ones who didn't I watched. At one point, there were so many bodies streaming in, arms full of hams and casseroles and desserts, that Mama Ray just threw open the door and got out of their way. And it hit me then that, for the first time in a long time, I was in a room full of people whose skin looked like mine. School, the country club, Utica Square, the Brady—in most of the places I went, I stood out. Yes, Dad was white, but Mom wasn't. Which meant that to the rest of the world I was black. At Mama Ray's, I wasn't the awkward line in a poem. I fit the meter. I rhymed.

And suddenly, I was breathing deeper than I had since Saturday. Mourners sniffled and hugged and talked quietly. I liked that some of them wore bright colors. One woman had on a green pantsuit and a scarlet hat. Another had chosen a flowered dress and support stockings that stopped at her knees.

Arvin's aunt Tilda was one of the last people to arrive. She zeroed in on Tru straightaway and pushed through the crowd, using the pie carrier in her hands to nudge people out of her way. Once she got there she hugged him, holding on so she could speak straight into his ear. Tru pointed to me, and Aunt Tilda raised a you-stay-right-there-young-lady index finger before she disappeared into the dining room with the pie.

What? I mouthed at Tru. He gave me an eyebrow wiggle and went to greet people with Mama Ray. Next thing I knew, Aunt Tilda was on the loveseat beside me.

"Hello, Rowan," she said. "I'm Tilda. It's good to know you."

Guilt, frustration, and helplessness started up a nasty free-for-all in my chest, and the headache I'd been fighting all day thumped with my pulse. This woman had loved Arvin. By failing him, I'd failed her, too.

"I'm so sorry for what happened," I choked out.

She patted my hand and studied my face calmly, saying nothing about the tears in my eyes or the way I was pressing my lips together and blinking fast to keep them from falling.

"The newspaper didn't give a lot of details," she said. "But I know you're the one who was there. You gonna let it keep you down?"

It wasn't what I'd expected at all; her nephew was dead, and there she was, asking about me.

She leaned sideways, pressing her shoulder into the velvet of the loveseat. "What I mean to say is, are you the sort that stays down or the sort that gets back up?"

It wasn't something I'd ever considered, but my answer came out before I knew it was there: "I get back up."

The skin around her eyes crinkled as she smiled. "Good. Too many young folks these days think life owes them. I was hoping you knew better."

She looked around the room. "Arvin was such a

gentle soul," she said. "Loved making people happy. I remember once when he was just a little thing, he walked the two miles between his mama's place and mine to bring me birthday flowers. Prettiest bouquet of dandelions and poison ivy you ever did see. But he was so pleased with himself, standing there on my front porch, itching, that I didn't have the heart to disappoint him. So I put on my dishwashing gloves and dumped that poison ivy into an old coffee can with some water and set it out back. Washed the poison off his hands and arms as best I could, too, but by the next morning, he was covered in blisters up to his armpits."

It was easy picturing Arvin as a little boy. And I should have laughed at Tilda's story for her sake, but a tear ran down my cheek instead.

She handed me a tissue from her big patent leather purse. "Never knew anyone so good at making you laugh and cry all at once as my nephew. He was something special."

"I didn't know him very well," I said. "But I'm going to miss him."

She patted my arm. "We all will, honey. Now, there's something I need to know, and you're the only one who can tell me."

"Yes, ma'am?"

"Did he suffer?"

She sounded strong, but her lips trembled.

"No," I said. And I sounded strong, too, and my lips did not tremble. I owed her that much.

Tilda closed her eyes and whispered a thank-you prayer, and when she was done, said quietly, "Thank the Lord. That boy shouldered more than his share of hurt as it was."

Then the softness in her disappeared, and she put her purse strap in the crook of her elbow and stood up.

"You're a skinny thing," she declared. "I'm getting you a slice of my pie before it's all gone."

I thanked her and said I wasn't very hungry.

"Oh, you don't want to miss out on my pie. Took me forty years to pry that recipe out of my friend Opal's hands. It was her gramma's."

She winked at me.

"Best peach pie you ever had."

WILLIAM

I knew from my earlier visit to the Goodhopes' house that it was small but tidy, with tended grass and a dish of pansies on the porch steps.

When Joseph and I arrived together, clouds blotted out the moon and the street was dark as pitch. It was quiet, too. So much that if it weren't for the sound of gunshots in the distance, you could have convinced me easy that Joseph and I were the only two people left in the world.

"Ruby?" Joseph called once we'd got inside.

No reply came.

"Stay here," he said. "I'll look around."

It didn't take him long, but in those few lightless minutes, I felt the walls of the tiny house press so close around me that I understood why Joseph wanted a Victrola for his mama. Music opened up space where there wasn't any, and lit up skies inside you that ceilings couldn't hold in. Suddenly, I wanted there to be music in that house, too. And not just for Mrs. Goodhope, but for Joseph and Ruby, as well.

The floorboards creaked, and Joseph was back at my side saying Ruby wasn't there. I asked where we should look next, and he'd just managed to say "The Dreamland Theatre, maybe," when lantern light peeked through a side window.

"Don't seem worth the trouble, Eugene," came a loud voice. "These are just shanties." A second chimed in, "Aw, horsefeathers. Your family's place ain't no bigger, Jack. Besides, maybe we'll find keys to that truck inside one of 'em. I could sure use a new truck."

Joseph and I pressed against the wall, standing so close our shoulders touched. Fists knocked against wood next door. The voice that went with Jack hollered, "Kick it in!" Then the lantern light bounced like crazy, and there were thuds and a *crack* and both those boys set to whooping and hollering, "We got you now! Ain't no use tryin' to hide!"

"Mr. and Mrs. Tyler," Joseph whispered. I saw anger in the set of his shoulders, heard it in his quick, shallow breathing.

"Your shotgun loaded?" he asked.

I said it was, but that I'd left my shells at the shop and only had the one round. "It'll have to do," he replied, and told me his plan, asking if I thought I could pull it off.

I didn't. But I said yes anyway.

Then Joseph opened the door and stepped onto the porch. I got behind him. Squeezed my eyes shut. Pressed the Springfield's muzzle to his spine. And shouted: "Make one wrong move and I'll shoot you dead!"

———

Next thing I knew, a big punkin-headed boy not much older than myself was in the Goodhopes' yard, double-barreled shotgun in one hand, lantern in the other. He had a thick look about him, like maybe his mama had dropped him on his head a time too many. But he was big as a bull, and muscled like a sideshow strongman.

"That boy giving you trouble?" he asked.

"Nothin' I can't handle," I replied. "I'm just lettin' him know what's what."

A jack-o'-lantern grin spread across his face. "'Bout time *someone* did," he said. "My name's Eugene. Wait here."

He turned and lumbered back inside the Tylers' house.

"We're fools if we don't make a break for it," I whispered. "Couldn't agree more," Joseph whispered back. But neither one of us took so much as a step towards the truck. And when the gray-haired couple stumbled out onto the porch, lantern light silhouetting their thin, bowed legs through the cloth of their nightshirts, I knew we'd been right to stay.

A lean, hollow-cheeked white boy came out of the

house behind them. After he and Eugene had forced them to march over to us, Eugene set the lantern down and said his friend's name was Jack. Jack had a rifle. And even though Eugene was big enough to give anyone pause, Jack scared me more. For his eyes were hooded and blank, and his expression never changed as he pushed the old man hard enough to send him sprawling down the stairs onto all fours.

"Evening," Jack said.

I told him hello, and we all watched Mr. Tyler pull himself onto his knees. Eugene slapped the back of his head when he got there.

"Lookee what Methuselah here tried to hide," he said, dangling a gold pocket watch from one hand. "We found it wrapped up in oilcloth and hidden in the flour bin. Thought you were bein' clever, dincha, boy?"

He slapped Mr. Tyler again.

"Answer him!" Jack barked. And Mr. Tyler's mouth opened to speak, but Jack smashed the butt of his rifle into the man's temple before he could. His frail body crumpled sideways onto the dirt. Mrs. Tyler cried out and fell to her knees. Eugene planted the thick sole of his boot in the curve of her back and kicked, sending her forehead into the ground.

Still, Joseph didn't move.

Mrs. Tyler whimpered.

"Shut up," Jack barked.

I cleared my throat loud and nudged Joseph's shoulder with the Springfield, saying, "At least you got somethin' for your trouble. Ain't nothin' in this one's house. He's poor as dirt!"

Eugene laughed a dullard's laugh. Jack's lips pulled back from his crooked teeth. "Best take what you can out of his hide, then," he said. By which I figured he meant I should beat Joseph, or shoot him, or both.

"Nah," I said, lies flowing off my tongue like God himself put them there. "I know a fella over to Convention Hall, gives me five dollars for every live Negro I deliver."

Which piqued Eugene's interest enough to make him look at the Tylers like maybe he'd let them live after all. Jack appeared dubious. And though his rifle stayed pointed at the ground, I knew he'd have it at his shoulder quick as could be if he felt the need.

"Why would anyone do that?" he asked. To which I replied I didn't know, but I wasn't one to look a gift horse in the mouth. Then a shot rang out nearby, and every one of us in that yard tensed. And there was nothing but threat in Jack's voice when he spoke into the quiet that followed, saying, "Come to think of it, neither am I. So I'm wondering if maybe Eugene and I oughtn't just take your truck and deliver these three to Convention Hall ourselves."

And I never will forget that moment so long as I live, for it was the first time I ever contemplated taking another man's life. But there was the small matter of Eugene's shotgun and Jack's rifle, and the fact that neither boy seemed opposed to using them. So instead of shooting him from over Joseph's shoulder, I said I'd advise him against it.

"Oh you would, would you?" he replied.

"Yes," I said, and asked did he remember how a gang of men had dragged that white car thief, Roy Belton, out of jail last year and lynched him while the police kept a lookout.

Jack nodded. Eugene's eyes got big in the lamplight.

Then I said how the man paying me for live Negroes had been the leader of that gang, and that he knew me and my truck since we'd delivered ten to him already. "And he don't take any more kindly to car thieves now than he did back then," I added. After which I pulled all five of Mama's ten-dollar bills from my pocket and fanned them out for Jack to see.

The money shifted something in Jack.

"Here's the fifty he gave me already," I told him. "Cash. And since I'd hate to see the two of you get your necks stretched for stealing my pop's truck, what say I just give you the fifteen dollars I'll get for these three Negroes, right here and now, with five more thrown in for good measure?"

Eugene glanced at Jack. I shifted the Springfield's muzzle higher on Joseph's back. Jack saw, and tilted the barrel of his rifle with his left hand, making ready to shoulder it.

"What say we make it fifty?" he asked. Only he wasn't really asking at all.

Joseph's hand twitched. Jack lifted the rifle higher.

I nodded big. "Fifty, then. Fifty sounds fair to me."

At which point Jack shouldered his rifle all the way and dropped his cheek down and squinted at me through the sight.

"Get it from him," he told Eugene. "And don't block my shot."

Eugene came around Joseph and swiped the bills from my outstretched hand. "Got it," he said.

Jack told him to get back. I poked Joseph with the Springfield, saying, "Help 'em up, boy."

Joseph hesitated. I prodded him again. "Help 'em up, I said!"

Which changed the feel of the air between me and Jack and Eugene enough so all three of us could feel it. Joseph must have, too, for he helped Mrs. Tyler to her feet, then gathered Mr. Tyler into his arms. And he lifted the old man's body out of the dirt as if it were a child's, and carried him to the truck with Mrs. Tyler limping alongside.

I followed, gun to their backs. And I never did look behind me. Not as I walked. Not as I waited for Mrs. Tyler to pull herself into the truck. Not even as I made a show of binding Joseph's wrists together in front of him with a length of the twine Pop kept in back. For by the second-hand glow of the lantern on the porch, I'd seen Mr. Tyler's eyes open and blink against the blood from his temple and stare up at the inky sky.

He was alive.

We were all alive.

And for that one brief moment, alive was enough.

———

Ghosts walked the streets of Tulsa that night. Banshees, too. Back when she'd been alive, Granny Tillman loved telling me how her family's banshee in the old country would keen warnings two days prior to a death. The ones haunting Tulsa weren't so generous, for not a block after an ice water wail had pierced the warm air around me, I found a dead man on the street.

Judging from the swatch of uncharred skin between his shirtsleeve and the burned stump of his right hand, he'd been a Negro once. A length of rope looped around his neck and snaked along the street behind him. His body was broken, his suit in tatters. Someone had dragged him behind an automobile, though whether or not he'd been alive when it happened was a detail I chose not to ponder overmuch.

His killers had left him splayed across the middle of the street so that there was no way to pass without hitting him. And though my main worry was getting the Tylers to a doctor, driving over a dead man was something I could not do. So I stopped the truck and got out, and not thirty seconds later, Joseph was kneeling at my side, praying aloud as he shucked off the loose-bound length of twine I'd wrapped around his wrists. I bowed my head and listened.

"We have to move him," Joseph said when his prayer was done.

"Where?" I asked, and we searched each other's faces in the glow of the headlamps for answers neither one of us had. Then I climbed into the back of the truck to fetch one of the oilcloth tarps Pop kept there. Dark as it was, I couldn't see the Tylers. But I could hear the missus gently shushing her husband's groans.

"Won't be long now," I whispered. "We'll get you somewhere safe."

"Ain't no place safe for us," she whispered back. "But I heard tell there's a white church on Boston Avenue giving sanctuary."

I told her I'd do my best to get us there. Then I carried the tarp back to the burned man, and me and Joseph rolled him onto it and wrapped the fabric around him twice. After we'd lifted him into the truck, Joseph handed me the twine and said I should bind his wrists again just in case. "Makes me a more credible prisoner," he added, ignoring the way both our hands shook.

"You think Ruby might be at the Dreamland?" I asked, mostly as a means of distraction.

"Might be," he replied. "But if she is, there's men better than us looking out for her. Trained gunmen and soldiers, I mean to say. For now, I suppose we'd best get the Tylers somewhere a doctor can tend to them."

I asked was he sure. He said yes, so I told him I knew a place. Then Joseph climbed between the Tylers and the burned man, and without so much as asking me where, said, "I trust you, Will. Let's go."

———

We traveled east, far enough that the buildings got sparse, the streets turned dusty, and soft smells of hay and manure replaced the sharp edge of city air. I figured then that it was safe to turn south.

I was wrong.

For where the Frisco tracks crossed Kenosha, a line of cars and white men with rifles and flashlights and bike lanterns blocked the road completely.

They were rough and refined by turns; nine in number, alike only in the whiteness of their skin. Two wore old US Army uniforms. Several had written *DEPUTY* on scraps of cloth and pinned them to their shirts. And while none wore Klan hoods, a thick whipping strap hung from the belt of the best-dressed man among them.

"We got trouble, Joseph," I said, doing my best not to move my lips.

One of the men flagged me down.

"Evening," I said as he ambled towards me. The hand-rolled cigarette between his lips waggled as he responded in kind, then asked why a young man such as myself might be out and about in that part of town.

"I'm hunting Negroes. And yourselves?" I said, with nary a blink nor a stutter.

He laughed at that, and took off his hat and wiped the sweat from his forehead with the inside of his sleeve. "Hear that, fellas?" he hollered over his shoulder. "Boy says he's hunting *Negroes!*"

Then the men behind him were laughing, too, all except the fancy one in the pressed white shirt and fresh-shined Florsheim shoes. I knew that's what they were because Pop had purchased a pair just like them not two weeks prior, saying no one wanted to buy high-end items like Victrolas from a man in cut-rate shoes.

I touched the brim of my cap, first to the laughing man nearest me, then to the Florsheim man direct.

"Just stating my business," I said.

The laughter died quick.

"Any particular reason you're alone?" the man beside me asked. I replied that I preferred it that way.

"You find any?" the Florsheim man said, his words clipped.

"Any what?" I replied, feigning stupid.

Then he was striding to the back of the truck so fast that by the time I'd scrambled out and caught up with him, he was already shining his light inside.

Joseph and the Tylers were pressed up against the rolled tarp, which Joseph must have pushed behind them. Mr. Tyler's eyes were closed. Joseph and Mrs. Tyler shielded theirs from the lantern's glare.

"Where'd you find 'em?" the Florsheim man asked. I replied they'd been in the root cellar of the old folks' shack. He narrowed his eyes and peered back so that I was sure he'd see the tarp and want to know what was inside. Only it turned out he was looking at the gash in Mr. Tyler's temple. "You responsible for that?" he asked. And I replied that I was, adding, "He tried to run."

The Florsheim man clapped me on the shoulder. Said, "Well done." But then something new caught his eye, sending him straight into the truck to snatch Joseph up by the collar.

Joseph didn't resist being dragged. His body fell like deadweight from the back of the truck onto the hard-packed dirt street.

"Didn't anybody ever teach you how to tie a proper knot, boy?" the Florsheim man growled. Then he kicked dirt into Joseph's face so that Joseph couldn't help but bring his hands to his eyes, and he pointed at the loose strands of twine around Joseph's wrists, saying I was lucky I'd caught a stupid one, elsewise he would have escaped. The Florsheim man knelt down and yanked the twine tight, handed the loose end of it to the nearest of his friends, and stuffed his handkerchief into Joseph's mouth.

Then the Florsheim man nodded at one of the make-shift deputies, who took out his pocketknife, slit Joseph's shirt clear up the back, and jerked the fabric wide onto his shoulders. The Florsheim man pulled the strap from his belt, slow enough for me to make out the three Ks burned into its handle. And he ran the side of that handle down Joseph's cheek, saying, "String him up, boys."

As they dragged Joseph off towards the nearest telephone pole, the Florsheim man put his hand on my shoulder. My skin prickled. The hairs on my neck stood up as the heat of his whiskey-tinted breath touched my ear.

"Watch close, young fella," he whispered. "Watch and learn."

Rowan

There were seven messages on my phone the next morning from numbers I didn't recognize, all saying they were so-and-so from such-and-such website or newspaper, all wanting to know if I'd be willing to talk to them about Arvin. I deleted every one, turned off my phone, and went downstairs. Mom was dressed for work, reading the newspaper at the dining room table.

"It's official," she said, handing me the front page.

I skimmed the story just enough to see it wasn't going to tell me anything I didn't already know. The DA's office hadn't found sufficient evidence to prosecute Jerry Randall. People were angry. I was still a "female teenage driver whose identity is being withheld." Arvin was still dead.

"How are you feeling about everything?" Mom asked.

"Lousy." I headed to the kitchen for my juice. Mom followed, pressing me to say something more.

"I liked being around people who knew Arvin yesterday," I said. "But in some ways it made everything harder. His aunt Tilda told me what he was like when he was a little boy, and there were people who went to high school with him, and his friends from the Day Center for the Homeless…"

Mom looked out the window, giving me time to finish. When I didn't, she turned back and said, "Your father and I have been talking. We're not sure the DA made the right call on this one."

I drank some juice to clear the lump out of my throat.

"Was it self-defense?" she asked.

"No."

"Do you think he would have done it if Arvin had been white?"

"I don't know. But he definitely wouldn't have called him a—"

Mom put her hand up. "Okay," she said. "That's all I needed to know. Got plans for today?"

"Just laying around, following doctor's orders."

She gave me a dubious look.

"Call if you need anything," she said, giving me a quick kiss on the cheek. "And no digital screens until Monday."

I smiled, poured another glass of juice while she gathered up her stuff, waited until her Mercedes backed out, and got my computer.

I had work to do.

Thanks to Geneva, I knew Raymond Fisher was from Decatur, Georgia, and that he and his gun, Maybelle, had gone AWOL from the army while he was on leave for his mother's funeral. So I started my digging with the 1910 census, which was the last one taken before 1919.

Sure enough, Raymond Fisher was there, in the same household as his mother, Ava. Both of them were listed as being Negro, but other than that, the census didn't have a lot to say. There was a link to Ava's death certificate, though, which told me she'd been a seamstress who died of pneumonia in January of 1919. There was also a little window on that page with the names of her children. Raymond was there, born 1902, and so was Virgil, born 1900. There wasn't anything more about Virgil, who I assumed must have died young.

Raymond's 1917 World War I draft card was even more helpful. According to that, he'd been single, childless, had dislocated his shoulder when he was sixteen, was tall, stout, and had blue eyes. The top right corner of the page was torn off, and even though there was no specific line for it, the person filling in the card had written *Light-skinned* and marked it with a star.

There was no death certificate for Raymond, but that wasn't a big surprise. He'd probably changed his name after he went AWOL, trying to stay out of the army's way. From 1919 on, Raymond Fisher was literally a dead end.

After that, I searched Arvin's name and got sucked into reading the online craziness that followed.

There was good stuff, yes. But it didn't take long to wander into comment threads and forums full of crap so hopelessly messed up that I couldn't stop reading. Neo-Nazis, white nationalists, racist skinheads, neo-Confederates, the KKK—up until that morning, I'd had no idea those were all different things, or that there were so many different ways to hate black people. Racists, it turned out, were into diversity after all.

Fortunately, the doorbell rang just before ten. Otherwise, I might have spent all day getting sucked into the world's most depressing wormhole.

It was James, dressed in a pink plaid shirt, Bermuda shorts, and Top-Siders with no socks.

"Road trip," he said.

I asked if the yacht club knew he'd escaped. He ignored me and came inside, grabbing my hand on his way past.

"C'mon. I was a busy boy yesterday, and it's my second day in a row calling in sick. We've got a lot to talk about on our way to Pawhuska."

I let him pull me toward the staircase. Other than moving out of Gladys's way when she came to clean that afternoon, I didn't exactly have plans.

"Why would I want to go to Pawhuska?" I asked.

He started up the stairs, pulling me behind him. "Get dressed. I'll tell you in the car." At the top, he pushed me into my room—gently—and closed the door. "Hurry, Chase. It's a long drive, and he's expecting us."

"Who is?" I hollered, digging through my closet for something clean.

"William Tillman's son."

Sixty seconds later, I was fully clothed, yanking the door open so fast that James stumbled inside. My sandals were in my hand. The Victrola receipt was tucked into an envelope inside my purse.

"What are we waiting for?" I said. "Let's go."

———

There's not a lot to look at between Tulsa and Pawhuska other than fields, hawks, and sky. We roared up Highway 99 north of Cleveland with the windows down and wind whipping our hair. 1969 El Caminos didn't come with AC, and even though the backs of my knees were damp and a fine layer of Oklahoma dirt had settled on my skin, I felt free.

I kept James's phone in my hand as we crossed into the Osage Reservation. If I'd turned it on, the screen would have filled with William Tillman's picture. But I didn't need to do that—I had every curve and line of his face memorized already.

While I was at Mama Ray's, James had been faking sick so he could talk to a historian at the Osage Tribal Museum and dig through the high school yearbook collection at the main library branch downtown. He'd found William Tillman inside the pages of the 1921 Tulsa Central High School *Tom Tom*, looking out from underneath black hair that was slicked back and parted down the middle.

If Geneva was right about the skeleton belonging to an African American, it wasn't William's. His features in the picture were round, with broad cheekbones and a softness that somehow came across as strength. He definitely wasn't black, though. Brownish, maybe, with skin that would darken quickly in the sun. But not black like Mom, or even me.

All that aside, his eyes were what held my attention for so many miles. They were deep set and calm, laughing all on their own as if the photographer had just cracked a good joke and told him not to smile. They were kind, too. Like Kathryn Yellowhorse's.

James slowed down when we hit the outskirts of Pawhuska. We passed through downtown, with its low-slung brick buildings set against the sky's wide-open blue. A few storefront windows had displays. Plenty were empty, others had been boarded over. I pulled up directions to Parkside Manor, and we followed them to a depressing one-story building overlooking City Cemetery.

"Shouldn't they have built their nursing home someplace with a nicer view?" I said.

James jangled the keys in his cupped hand. "I bet they put toe tags on people as soon as they check in."

Neither one of us unbuckled.

"We should take him something," I said.

"What?"

"I don't know. Just…something. What do you think?"

James shifted into reverse. "I think we should see what we can find."

———

"Mr. Tillman?"

The sign next to the door said JOSEPH TILLMAN & HERBERT EBERSOL. I knocked quietly in case either one was asleep.

"Hello?" I peeked inside and saw the ends of two beds. The one next to the window had feet underneath its blankets.

"Mr. Tillman?" I bumped the door with the box of grocery store cookies in my hand. Behind me, James had a potted fern.

The feet moved. A soft voice told us to come in.

"You must be James and Rowan," the man said. "Please, sit down."

His shaky hand pointed to a blue plastic recliner and a folding chair. I went to the recliner, trying to ignore the nursing home smell of warehoused human beings. James shook the man's hand, saying, "Thank you so much for seeing us, Mr. Tillman."

"I'll take any visitors I can get," Mr. Tillman said. "Especially ones who bring me presents." He eyed the cookie box and patted the top of the hospital tray table next to him. "What have you got there, young lady?"

"Cookies." I opened the lid and held them out. "Would you like one?"

"I would indeed," Mr. Tillman said. "There are paper towels in the bathroom. Do you mind?"

By the time I got back, James had set the fern on the windowsill and was sitting in the folding chair. Mr. Tillman tilted the top half of his bed to sit upright. I moved the tray table across his lap and set a cookie on a paper towel.

"I can't eat all of these myself," he said. "Won't you have some, too?"

I took out one apiece for James and me.

"That's better," Mr. Tillman said. Then he stopped, drawing a deep breath in through his nose and closing his eyes. As his wrinkled face tightened in pain, I noticed how long his body was underneath the covers, and how broad the gaunt shoulders underneath his hospital gown were. He felt for a cord looped over the bed railing without opening his eyes and pushed the button at the end of it. A few seconds later, his face relaxed and his eyes opened.

"Sorry about that," he said. "I've got a touch of cancer, and sometimes the pain gets to be a bit much." He pointed at the IV bag hanging from a hook above his bed. Morphine, I figured. The heavy-duty stuff.

308

"But enough about that," Mr. Tillman said. "I believe you mentioned you have some questions about my family, James?"

James came forward onto the edge of his chair. "Yes, sir, Mr. Tillman," he said. "Rowan and I—"

The old man interrupted him. "Joe. Call me Joe."

James smiled. "You got it, Joe. So, Rowan and I are researching the history of her house, and I think your grandparents might have been the ones who built it."

"Stanley and Kathryn," Joe said. The smile on his face was so sad and sweet that I could see a young man underneath the wrinkles. Once upon a time, he must have looked a lot like the picture of his father on James's phone. And even through the morphine glaze, I could see he had his father's eyes.

"That's quite a house you live in, young lady," he said.

I smiled. "It's been in my family a long time. My great-great-grandparents bought it from Stanley and Kathryn."

"Imagine that," Joe said. "Granny Kathryn wouldn't set foot in that place, you know. Though I suspect the two of you might not be surprised to hear that."

He looked back and forth between James and me, and I swear he was trying to get information from us as much as we were from him.

I asked him what he meant. He closed his eyes again, only that time he didn't jack into the morphine. I got the feeling he was doing some kind of complex mental cal-culation instead, deciding what to say. And when they opened, his eyes weren't just clear, they were alive.

"I mean you've found it, haven't you?" he said. "After all these years, someone's finally found the body."

WILLIAM

The Florsheim man's gang was so fired up and rowdy that not one of them heard me the first time I shouted for them to stop. Second time, either. Third one did the trick; they all looked to me, then to their leader, who eyed me like I'd sprouted horns. "What did you say?" he asked in a growl that made the hackles on my neck stand up.

I swallowed hard. Said it a fourth time: "Stop." And his growl dropped even lower as he asked me, "Why?"

"Because I promised him to Vernon Fish," I replied. And the whole lot of them stared with their jaws aflap. All except the Florsheim man, that is.

"You know Vernon?" he said, coming so close that the bootleg whiskey on his breath set my eyes to watering.

I stammered that I did. Then my voice steadied, and I

spun a yarn about how Mr. Fish was a friend of my father's and liked to tease me about not knowing how to handle Negroes properly. I said how I'd argued back earlier that day that yes I did, and that I'd go out and hunt one down myself to prove it. I even told him Mr. Fish had promised to let me use his whipping strap if I succeeded, adding, "I reckon he'd be pretty sore if I showed up with this boy already whupped."

The Florsheim man ran the leather of his own strap across his palm, caught the end of it, and snapped it tight.

I swallowed hard. Said, "I sure do want to join the Junior Klan once they start up here in Tulsa."

And he snapped the strap again, saying, "So you've never schooled a nigger?"

A shudder passed through Joseph's body.

"No, sir," I said. "But Mr. Fish told me all about how he handled that chicken thief up Vinita way, and how Maybelle shot an old man's eyes out."

I stopped then, for something had eased in the Florsheim man's countenance. He even chuckled, saying, "I doubt Vernon Fish ever will love a girl so true as he does that Colt of his." Which set a few of the men around Joseph to tittering. Then he yanked Joseph's head up by the chin and said, "What do you think, boy? Should I leave your hide to Vernon?"

Joseph said nothing.

"You answer him, boy!" one of the uniformed men shouted. Another hauled back and kicked Joseph in the stomach so hard the air rushed out his mouth. But Joseph kept his eyes down and did not move.

"I sure would appreciate it if you'd let me handle this boy myself," I said, stepping closer to the Florsheim man. "I've been struggling lately, bucking rules and acting all kinds of awful. If you were to let me deliver him like I promised, it might prove to my pop and Mr. Fish that I'm on track for real. And, well...I'd just be awful grateful, sir."

The Florsheim man looked from Joseph to me. Said, "Who's your pop?"

"Stanley Tillman," I replied.

And he tipped his head sideways and looked surprised, saying, "The same Stanley Tillman who sold me my Victrola last year?"

"That's him," I replied.

"The one Vernon's been trying to bring into the Klan for months even though he's married to an Osage squaw?"

I told him yes. Then I felt the thin ice under my feet starting to crack as the Florsheim man came at me. And just when our chests were near close enough to touch, he laughed and slugged my arm so hard my teeth clattered.

"Why didn't you say so, Half-breed?" he boomed. "Your pop saw the light and joined up tonight. He's one of us now!"

———

Pop had filled out his application, paid his fee, and joined the Klan right there on the courthouse steps, in front of God and Vernon Fish and the Florsheim man. Whose real name, I learned, was Reggie Gould.

Reggie told me the whole tale with relish, saying how Pop's view on Negroes being harmless had changed soon as he saw the first armed carload of them drive up to the courthouse, and how Pop said that if they were willing to confront the sheriff with guns, they surely wouldn't hesitate in doing the same to him at his shop. Which sounded close enough to Pop's sort of reasoning for me to believe it was true.

But bad as it hurt to hear them tell about Pop's change of heart, some good came of the exchange. For Reggie and his boys let me drive off without harming the Tylers or Joseph, believing as they did that I was about to deliver all three to Vernon Fish. That's how I ended up driving down the outer edges of the city like a madman, desperate to get Joseph and the Tylers safe.

———

Turned out I'd no choice but to stop again, when a second body turned up in the street with a fist-sized hole blown out of its chest. For even after all the trouble we'd run into so far, my instinct was to pick it up and see that it was buried proper. But Joseph peeked up as the truck slowed, and when I pointed to the corpse, he said, "It isn't safe, Will. Keep driving...please?" His voice bobbled about, which was understandable given what had nearly been done to him not five minutes prior. And there was no question it would be risky to stop.

So I drove on near a half mile until the next obstacle presented itself. Only that time it wasn't a corpse, but a living man.

A living man who I hit with the truck.

It happened at the intersection of Fifth and Detroit. He'd only intended to step out into the street long enough to flag me down, that much was clear. But he misjudged my speed and distance by a good ten feet, so there was no way I could avoid him. Fortunately, I only clipped his hip. The man and the shotgun he'd been holding spun through the air separately and landed hard on the ground. Then came an awful silence, followed by the sound of Mrs. Tyler's sobs and a moaning from the street. I told Joseph to stay put and got out.

Judging by his grease-stained overalls and the black under his fingernails, the struck man was a roughneck. That didn't account for the red spot blooming on the leg of his pants, though, for even in Tulsa, there was no mistaking blood for oil.

"Help me," he wheezed. "Please!"

Then his gaze jerked to something past my shoulder. It was Joseph, standing behind us with his legs set wide and the roughneck's shotgun aimed at its owner's head.

"Give me my gun and get away from me, you goddamned nigger," the roughneck hissed.

Joseph pressed the muzzle to the man's cheek, whispering, "How many goddamned niggers have you killed with this gun tonight, *sir?*"

I leaned away out of sheer instinct and contemplated telling Joseph not to shoot. But given all we'd seen that night, it didn't seem right, me trying to influence his decision one way or the other. So I rose, silent, and stood at his side.

The man's dry throat clicked. Joseph's finger came out of the trigger guard, flexed, and went back in.

"Might be this is my chance to even up the score a little," Joseph muttered, though whether to me or the roughneck I couldn't say. And his hand trembled so bad I feared he might fire whether he meant to or not.

He squeezed his eyes tight, opened them, resighted down the barrel, and spoke so there was no doubt he was talking to me: "I've spent my whole life forgiving white folks, Will," he said. "And I am so very tired of it."

Then he lifted his head from the sight, lowered the shotgun, and carried it back to the truck without another word.

"Who shot you?" I asked the roughneck once Joseph had got safely in the back.

He was silent.

I poked my toe into the flesh of his leg near the bullet hole. He gritted his teeth. Said, "I ain't tellin' you nothin', boy."

It was a poor choice.

I pressed the sole of my shoe down square over the bullet hole. He roared in pain and set about expanding my repertoire of curse words until I lifted my foot to stomp him again. At that, he quieted and held up his hand, breathing ragged. And he feigned contriteness, saying how he was bleeding bad and couldn't move because the truck had broke his other leg, and wouldn't I please help him.

"Only if you tell me the truth," I replied. "I bet it was white men who shot you, wasn't it?"

He spit on my shoes and told me to go to hell. Only I went to the truck instead, to fetch twine and the handkerchief Reggie had stuffed in Joseph's mouth. And I caught that roughneck as he cursed and howled and tried to drag himself away, and I tied his hands tight behind his back and stuffed the handkerchief in his gob. For it was at that moment that I realized how very much I wanted to be a righteous man, just like I'd told Vernon Fish lo those many weeks ago. And a righteous man would never leave another human being to bleed to death in the street.

Of course, a truly righteous man *would* take pains to keep the roughneck's ruined legs from knocking against the truck bumper as he loaded him in, so I can't say I was quite there yet. But I kept that miserable so-and-so alive and did him no permanent harm. Which, in my book, was at least a step in the right direction.

———

The church was dark and locked up tight when we arrived, and the clouds overhead had cleared enough for the moon to shine on the empty roadway. Still, there were dark shadows and corners aplenty.

No one came when I knocked. So I knocked again, and the lock turned and hinges squeaked as the door cracked open. I recognized the oval-faced girl peeking out. Her name was Claire, and like Addie, she was a year ahead of me. Unlike Addie, she wasn't pretty. Not in the standard sense, at least. But there was something pleasing about the way her strong features fit together, especially with the electric light casting a halo's glow around her nest of disheveled brown hair.

"Yes?" she said.

My words tumbled out ahead of my thoughts. "Please…Mr. Tyler's head's hurt bad, and Mrs. Tyler, she's…"

Before I could bumble on, Claire lit up with recognition and opened the door wide and called me by name. And there was such a sweetness about her that my tongue tangled and my eyes filled with tears. And I feel no shame in saying that, for it was a moment of true grace.

"Where are they?" she asked. "Can they walk?"

I pointed in the direction of Seventh Street and said I didn't think so. Then Claire told me to drive the truck across the grass and park close to the door.

Once I'd done as she said, she came out of the church with a man and a sturdy woman in a nurse's cap, both of whom climbed inside the truck before I got the engine shut off. I heard the nurse talking in a worried voice, and Joseph saying something about a rifle butt. Then the man went back inside the church and fetched a makeshift stretcher made from a sheet and two mops. Jackrabbit quick, he and Joseph loaded Mr. Tyler onto it and carried him inside.

That surprised me, I'll admit, for I'd been raised in a world where white folks' needs always came first. It shocked the roughneck, too, and he sputtered and coughed around the cloth in his mouth while old Mrs. Tyler watched. Then Claire climbed in and introduced herself, and the roughneck quieted enough for her to take out the handkerchief. And he plastered a false smile across his face and commenced to lying, saying how the Negro boy who'd just carried the old man away had shot him, and how I'd run him over with the truck after that and stepped on his wounded leg to torture him.

Claire looked at me as if to ask was it true. I hung my head and said I'd hit him with the truck all right, but it had been an accident. She didn't inquire about the torture, only told the man there was a doctor inside who could tend to his injuries till morning.

Then the church door opened again and a trim and dapper Negro with rolled-up sleeves stepped out of the church. "He's been shot in the leg, Dr. Butler," Claire said. The doctor climbed into the truck, ignoring the man's curses and slurs. And when he tried to touch the roughneck's leg and the fool commenced to screaming bloody murder, Claire picked up the handkerchief and stuffed it back into his mouth so tight that even his grunts were muffled.

Which was a relief to everyone, most especially Mrs. Tyler. Her eyes sparked to life, and she asked if I wouldn't please take her inside to her husband. I said it would be my pleasure and helped her out of the truck, bending low so she could get her arm across my shoulders for support. We made our way into the church, down a set of stairs, and through a door that swung open when I tapped it with my toe. And it's a good thing I'm built sturdy, elsewise the blur that flew across the room into my chest would have knocked Mrs. Tyler and me down like so many ninepins.

The smell of roller skate grease and the feel of small arms squeezing me tight hit all at once, so that my heartbeat skipped about and the shadow over my soul lifted like a thousand sparrows taking flight. And I reached down with my free arm and lifted Ruby up and hugged her hard.

"Ow, ow, ow!" she squealed. "You're gonna squeeze my guts out, Will Tillman!"

Only I didn't let go.

And neither did she.

Rowan

A spark lit up inside Joe when he mentioned the body, bright enough so I could see it through his wrinkles and the morphine and the pain. I forgot all about being in a nursing home, and the cookies, and even James, and asked him who it was.

"I'm sorry, young lady, but I can't tell you," Joe said.

Which *felt* like the sound a bird makes hitting a window. But short of threatening a dying old man, there wasn't much I could do about it.

James asked him: "You can't or you won't?"

"Both. I swore to my father at his deathbed that I'd carry his secret to my own grave. And there's no breaking a deathbed oath."

Out in the hall, a feeble voice started hollering for Mary to take him home.

Joe sighed. "That's my roommate, Herb. Mary died

five years ago. He forgets. But tell me—what have the two of you learned on your own? I never did promise not to help other folks find the truth for themselves, and maybe I can steer you in the right direction."

Which was better than nothing. So James and I traded off telling Joe about the Polk Directory and the house title and everything else we'd tracked down.

"But how did you find out about my father in the first place?" Joe asked.

"From the receipt," James said.

"Receipt?" Joe brought the back of his bed up higher.

"The Victrola receipt he made out to someone named J. Goodhope. It was in the skeleton's wallet," I said. "Here." I slipped the receipt out of the envelope in my purse and handed it to Joe. "See?"

Joe's fingers trembled as he pulled it close and squinted. "Dammit," he said, fumbling for his reading glasses on the tray. I picked them up for him and held the receipt while he put them on. He mumbled *thank you* and took the receipt again, making a sound that was a sob and a laugh all at once. Then he traced each word and figure with his fingertip, whispering, "I can't believe you found it."

"You knew about it?" I said.

His head nodded on the thin stalk of his neck. "I knew *of* it. It's just not something I ever thought I'd hold in my own hands. You've made an old man very, very happy."

Which wasn't exactly what James and I had set out to do that morning, but it felt good anyway. And when I asked Joe if he knew who J. Goodhope was, he nodded again and said, "Of course. He's my namesake—Joseph."

James and I locked eyes as Joe went back to reading the receipt.

"Joe," James said. "Do you happen to know if Joseph was any relation to Della Goodhope?"

Joe was still running his fingertips over the paper like he couldn't believe it was there.

"She was his mother," he said. "And Ruby was his sister."

James took out his phone and held up the picture of William Tillman for Joe to see.

"And this was your father, William?"

"Yes. Though he went by Daniel after he moved to Kansas City. I've seen this portrait before, on the bookshelf at my grandmother's house. Wherever did you find it?"

"In Central High School's 1921 yearbook," I said. "He was a junior then. But why did he change his name?"

Joe smiled. "Dad dropped out of school and moved to KC after the riot in '21. He wanted a fresh start, and I suppose changing his name was part of that. He did well for himself, too. Sold Victrolas and wax cylinder dictation machines, then radios and hi-fis. Say, you don't happen to have Joseph's picture, do you?"

"From the yearbook?" James asked. "You mean he was still in school, too?"

Joe took a breath to speak, then stopped like he was afraid he was giving too much away. But before long, he got this what-the-hell kind of look and said: "That's right, only he didn't go to Central. Joseph was a senior at Booker T. that year."

Now we were getting somewhere.

"If you were named after him, they must have known each other pretty well," I said.

"They did." Joe folded the receipt back up. "Rowan, would you be so kind as to bring me the photograph in the gilt frame over on the windowsill?"

I picked up the picture he motioned to and saw a younger version of Joe standing next to a wrinkly black woman in sweatpants and a Naughty by Nature T-shirt with the "O.P.P." album cover on it.

"That's Ruby and me back in 2001," Joe said. "June first, to be exact."

I tried to show the picture to James, but he was looking for something on his phone. "Are she and that shirt for real?" I asked.

"Every inch of them." Joe laughed. "Ruby lived out loud like no one else I've ever known."

James was still mumbling to himself. "Let me just . . . here!" He shoved the phone in front of me. The image was of a yellowed page with three photographs in heart-shaped frames. The top and bottom pictures were of girls. In the middle was a serious-looking young black man with chubby cheeks and something written beside him that I had to enlarge the picture to see.

A better soul you'll never meet
No matter where you roam.
His mind is sharp, his manner sweet,
His heart true to his home.

JOSEPH GOODHOPE

"Have you found him?" Joe looked so eager that James handed him the phone and let the picture speak for itself.

"There he is," Joe said softly. "Just like Ruby and Dad described him."

"You mean you've never seen him before?" I asked.

Joe shook his head slowly. "No. Joseph died young. But Ruby lived a good, long life. She was ninety years old in that picture, though you'd never have known it to meet her. She worked as a nurse until they made her retire at seventy-five. After that, she kept busy with volunteer work. She died in her sleep just a few weeks after her ninety-seventh birthday, only a month after she brought me the last pie."

The skin on my forearms prickled. Pie at the Nut-n-Honey Café. Tilda's peach pie at Arvin's funeral.

"Joe, did you say pie?" I asked.

His smile was wistful. "Indeed I did. Ruby made one for us every year on the first of June. In the beginning, she'd take a Midland Valley train up here to Pawhuska and leave them on Granny Kathryn's doorstep. But after Granny died, she brought them to me."

Joe lowered the picture, closed his eyes, and sighed.

"Best peach pie in the whole wide world."

———

Mom was in shorts and a tank top, sitting cross-legged on the back porch swing when I got home. Beaded drops of condensation dotted the untouched glass of iced tea beside her. When I came through the gate, she pointed toward the open back house door.

"Geneva's here," she said. Which wasn't exactly news, since I'd already seen the van. Hammering started up. Mom ignored it.

I sat beside her and asked what was going on, and Mom told me how Geneva had called her at work, asking to be let into the back house to check on something she'd overlooked. Mom had called me, but I'd turned my phone off after deleting the voicemails about Arvin that morning. So she'd come to let Geneva in herself.

"Now," Mom said when she was done explaining, "tell me where you've been all day."

There was no point lying. I told her about Pawhuska.

"You were supposed to be resting," she said. "But I'd probably have done the same thing if I were you."

A man in white painter's coveralls came out of the back house. He laid a floor plank on the grass, saw Mom and me, and gave us an awkward hello before he went back inside.

The hammering started up again.

Board by board, he carried out the subfloor, lining each piece up carefully. Mom's legs stayed tucked underneath her. I slipped off my sandals and pushed us back and forth in the swing. "They're tearing things apart," I said.

Eat your heart out, Captain Obvious.

Mom dipped her finger in the pool of water gathering at the base of her glass. "It seems that way."

We kept swinging, the man kept bringing out planks, and Mom kept not talking. It got so weird that I ended up asking her if I could visit Arvin's aunt Tilda the next day, just to kill the silence.

"You haven't asked my permission for things like that in a long time," Mom said. "Why start now?"

"I don't know," I said. "Maybe it's not so much that I'm asking as that I wanted to tell you."

There was only one rectangle left to go before the floor was completely reassembled on the grass. Mom pinched the middle of her shirt and pulled it away from her belly. We were both sweating like crazy.

"I like that," she said. "It's nice. But there's something

else I want to ask you. You don't have to answer right now. In fact, you should think about it as long as you'd like—at least overnight."

There was nothing to do except say that I would.

"Good," Mom said. "What I want to know is, if you're sure that Jerry Randall used a racial slur and pushed Arvin out of anger instead of self-defense, would you be willing to go speak to the district attorney with me? Maybe even testify about what you saw and heard in court?"

The hammering stopped. The swing stopped. Geneva carried out the last board herself and waved Mom and me over, saying, "I'm glad you're here, Rowan."

"*Think* about it," Mom said. Then she got up, and Geneva told us not to come down off the porch. "You'll have a better view from there," she said, climbing the steps to stand next to us.

She leaned over the rail. The man, who Geneva never did introduce but must have been her gallbladder-less assistant, stood off to one side.

"Sure enough. See that?" Geneva pointed toward a dark stain that covered the board farthest away from us on the left, and parts of the ones around it. "That's where our skeletonized friend bled out. It's a typical spread pattern for exsanguination due to head trauma. But look..." She pointed to a separate stain midway up the opposite side of the reconstructed floor. "That one's from a different victim. Someone who received a significant injury, bled out, then dragged themselves a ways. They never made it all the way across the room, though. See how their blood trail stops two feet short of the other one and spreads again?"

Mom was quiet at my side.

"What does it mean?" I asked.

Geneva rubbed her palms against her cutoffs and shrugged. "It means I should have checked under the floor sooner. But it also means we know more now than we did before. And in my book, that makes it a good day."

WILLIAM

The basement was a big space filled with women and children, all of them frightened and weary, but safe as they could be given the circumstances. A few electric bulbs were strung up overhead, and there were lit oil lamps scattered about. Claire drew two cups of coffee from a fancy silver urn set up on a wooden bench and handed them to Joseph and me. And that was the best thing I ever have tasted in my life, bar none—loaded thick with sugar, and so hot it scalded my tongue.

Then Claire put her arm around Ruby's shoulders, saying, "Won't you introduce me to your friend?" To which Ruby replied that Joseph was her brother, not her friend. And Claire shook his hand and smiled and told Ruby, "I bet these boys would like to sit down. Would you show them to a cot while I fetch Joseph a shirt that's not cut to ribbons?" Her voice was soft and firm all at once, so that Ruby didn't balk. She only said, "Yes'm, Miss Claire," and led us over to an empty cot like the sweetest, most obedient child you ever did meet.

And she sat next to us, chirping on about how she'd set off to find Joseph after I warned her away from the shop. "You sounded for-real scared, Will," she said. "Enough so I knew you weren't just trying to get rid of me." Then she scolded Joseph for not being in any of the places she'd gone looking.

After that, she turned somber and picked at the back of her hands, telling us how she'd hidden behind a shrub at the courthouse while the white people around her got angrier and angrier. And how a single gunshot had turned the crowd into an ugly mob surging towards Greenwood with murder on its mind.

"All except a few of them," she added. "Like the man who snatched me up and carried me off." Then she looked down at her toes, and for the first time ever, I heard something close to shame creep into her voice: "I scratched him pretty good. Bit him, too. But he didn't put me down till we'd got away. Even then he kept hold of my wrist and told me he was taking me somewhere safe, 'cause otherwise I might get killed. He was a good man. That's how I came to be here."

"You mean to say you've been in this church most of the night?" Joseph said.

Ruby made a face like he was stupid. "Course I have,

you big ninny," she said. "Where'd you think I was?" Then Joseph cast a grateful look towards heaven and drank what was left of his coffee in one gulp.

After that, Claire returned with a white, high-collared clergyman's shirt and said there was fresh-baked corn-bread in the kitchen that Ruby should bring down. Joseph and I started to rise as well, but Claire assured us Ruby was up to the task on her own.

When Ruby had trotted off with nary a whisper of backtalk, Joseph asked Claire how on earth she'd managed to charm his sister. Claire smiled and sat down on the cot, saying, "Just lucky, I suppose." Then her face darkened, and she said how my truck couldn't stay where it was. For according to Mr. Geddison, word had gotten out to white rioters that the church was taking in Green-wood refugees.

"Mr. Geddison?" I asked. Claire rolled her eyes and pointed at the ceiling, saying, "Your ever-so-pleasant friend. The one with the hole in his leg."

"You mean the roughneck?" I asked. And Claire nodded, saying, "Yes, though it's a shame calling him that. Plenty of oilfield hands attend this church, and most of them are kind, decent men. Nothing like that ignorant fool." Then she said how there had already been rioters sniffing around the church doors, banging and holler-ing how they'd been sent to gather wayward Negroes and deliver them to the proper authorities.

"We ignored them until they gave up and left," she

said. "Though if Mr. Geddison is to be believed, there's another contingent on the way."

"Which would make having a truck parked outside awfully inconvenient, seeing's how you couldn't very well pretend no one's home," I said with a sigh.

Claire smiled and brushed a bit of grass off my shoulder that must have come from Mrs. Tyler. The tenderness of it caught me off guard.

Joseph bumped his knee against mine. Said, "I don't relish the thought of you going back out there, Will."

"Can't say as I do myself," I replied, "but there's nothing for it. I'll just go straight home and hole up for the night. Come morning, I'll be back for you and Ruby."

Joseph actually smiled then, and stood up and offered his hand and held on even after he'd pulled me to my feet.

"Thank you, William," he said. Only his words sounded stiff and formal to my ears. For after all we'd been through that night, the very least we should have been to each other was friends. And so, not knowing how else to show the way I felt, I got the balance sheet for his Victrola out of my pocket and asked Claire if she might have a pen. She found one, and I asked Joseph to turn around and used his back to mark *PAID* across the bottom.

"You should have had this all along," I said, handing it to him. "What's left is on us."

Joseph accepted the thing without saying it was useless, and took his leather wallet from his back pants pocket and tucked the receipt inside.

334

"Saturday all right for delivery?" I asked.

Joseph said he likely could make that work. Then Ruby was back, toting a big basket of cornbread so hot and fresh that the smell drew a circle of children around her straightaway. But when she saw me and Joseph standing, she set that basket down on the floor and stomped over with her arms locked tight across her chest, asking what was going on.

"Will needs to take his truck home," Joseph replied. "It's not safe leaving it parked outside. The church has to look empty."

"Why?" She pouted. "Can't nobody mess with a church. That'd be a sin!"

Joseph tried to smile, but what he managed was closer to the mash-eyed look you get staring into the sun.

"You're right," I said quick. "But if I don't get Pop's truck home soon, he'll hunt me down and string me up by my thumbs. And I have tender thumbs, Miss Ruby. Very tender thumbs indeed."

Ruby giggled, just as I'd hoped she would. "Besides," I added, "I'm coming back first thing tomorrow morning to fetch you and Joseph home. That sound all right?"

She stopped giggling and nodded.

"Good," I said. "Then go get a good night's sleep and I'll see you when you wake up."

"Promise?" she asked, real quiet.

"Promise," I replied. After which Ruby pointed a finger at me, stern as a schoolmarm, and told me to wait.

And she waded through the ring of hungry children circling the cornbread, plucked a piece out, marched back, wrapped it in her handkerchief, and took my hand in hers, saying: "You best take this now. Won't be any left by morning."

I squeezed her hand and thanked her, and told her she should stick close to her brother.

"Phooey," she said. Then she tugged me towards her like she had a secret to share. I dropped to one knee and leaned close, expecting sass or a raspberry or worse. Only what I got was a peck on the cheek, quick and sweet. "Be careful out there, Will Tillman," she whispered as she hugged me. "And don't you forget to come back."

———

Halfway home, on dark streets wearing their silence like a quilt, I remembered the dead man.

My hand reached back to confirm that the rolled-up tarp was still there, which it was. No one at the church had noticed, and between the Geddison fool cussing and carrying on and Ruby turning up, Joseph and I had forgotten about it altogether.

But there was no forgetting anymore, nor any simple solution to my dilemma. For though dumping the body by the river was the easiest option at hand, the whole reason Joseph and I had picked him up was to see that he was treated proper. The least the dead man deserved was a Christian burial and a person or two to mourn his passing, and I knew Mama would understand if I waited until morning to find his people. Things like that mattered to her, which I suppose was why they mattered to me.

When I pulled into the empty driveway at home, the kitchen lights burned bright. Mama met me on the porch with her arms wide, and there was so much strength in her embrace that if it hadn't been for the evil I'd witnessed that night, I could have almost convinced myself that things were going to turn out all right. When she was done hugging on me, Mama took half a step back and put her cool palms to my cheeks and kissed my forehead, whispering, "Thank the Lord you're home."

In the kitchen, a half-drunk cup of tea sat next to an unfinished game of solitaire on Mama's big butcher block. She poured me a glass of cold buttermilk from the icebox, which I gulped down. And she told me Angelina and her daughter-in-law and grandbabies were still safe in the back house, but there was no word about her son.

"Where's Pop?" I asked.

Mama shrugged, lips tight. Said, "He called from the shop an hour ago, upset you weren't there when he stopped by to check on things. He should be home by sunrise so long as things stay calm on Main Street."

She wanted to elaborate; I could see it in the set of

her body, hear it in her guarded words. But she only told me I should go upstairs and wash, which I did. And once my face and neck were scrubbed and I'd dropped my dusty clothes down the laundry chute, I slipped beneath the clean-smelling softness of my sheets and slept.

Even with a dead man in the back of the truck.

Even with Joseph and Ruby trapped in a roomful of strangers in the basement of a church.

Even with Clete and Vernon Fish and Reggie Gould still loose on the streets.

I slept.

———

Sunshine woke me the next morning. I threw on new clothes, washed the grit from my eyes, and wiggled the stiffness out of my jaw from grinding my teeth as I slept. Downstairs, Mama was sitting on the same stool by the butcher block where I'd left her. There was a haze in the room, and an acrid stink that set my eyes to watering.

"He took them," she said, all dull and quiet. Which I didn't understand until I saw Angelina through the back window, slumped in the doorway of her quarters. And it felt like a punch to the gut, realizing what the man who'd raised me had done.

Pop had taken Angelina's grandbabies away.

Mama mumbled something about breakfast and rose from the chair, holding her body sideways.

"What's wrong?" I asked. She didn't reply. Then my voice came harsh, asking, "What did he *do*?" And Mama shook her head and said, "He came home half an hour ago and found Angelina's family."

Which wasn't what I'd meant.

I caught her up in my arms as she tried to get to the icebox, and felt my insides seize at the sight of the puffy, reddened flesh around her right cheekbone and eye.

Mama stopped my hand as I reached towards the bruise, looking at me with a clarity and resolve I didn't expect. Then she touched my own cheek tenderly and said: "I couldn't keep him from taking them away, but I told him if he put Angelina in that truck, I wouldn't be here when he got back."

I started to speak. Mama pressed her finger to my lips, saying, "Whatever happens between your father and me is mine, William. I'll handle it how I see fit. Right now, there are other matters that need tending to. I want you to tell me what went on last night. Tell me everything."

I pulled my hand back, then sat down and did as she'd asked. The whole story came out, starting with Joseph besting Pop in negotiations for the Victrola, ending with the body in the back of the truck. Nothing changed or got better while I spoke. Still, once I'd finished, Mama smiled a tired smile and told me I'd done right and she was proud.

"I'll fix you breakfast," she said. "Then you go to the church and fetch your friends and take them to Angelina's quarters at the new house. There are only boards in for the floor, but the walls and roof are sound. I'll call the construction foreman and tell him to send his boys to another job for a few days. Those two children should be safe enough holed up there for a while. I only pray they'll have a home to go back to once this is over."

"What do you mean?" I asked.

And Mama turned, loaf of bread in one hand, knife in the other. "Can't you smell it?" she said, her voice far away and sad. "They're burning Greenwood to the ground."

———

Mama called the church while I wolfed down my toast and eggs. Turned out the pastor's wife knit caps for babies, too, and she and Mama were acquainted through a ladies' luncheon group on top of that. By the time I'd mopped up my yolks and put my plate in the sink, Mama was back with the whole plan arranged.

"Joseph and Ruby will wait for you at the same door you used last night," she said. "They're safe for now, but you'll have to be careful; there are gangs of men about town, gathering up Negroes and taking them to McNulty Park and Convention Hall." Her eyes darted to the back window.

"I'll have to smuggle Angelina upstairs," she mur-mured to herself. Then she directed me to fill Pop's and my canteens with water, and loaded our picnic hamper with bread, cheese, and apples, plus a whole Virginia ham she'd bought special for Pop. She put in a carving knife, too, and filled a rucksack with blankets and two pairs of clean skivvies from my dresser drawer.

After that, Mama handed the supplies to me through the side door underneath the porte cochere and I loaded them into the Model T. Lastly, she handed me a drop cloth from the basement.

"They'll have to ride on the floorboards, covered up," she said. "Model Ts weren't made to conceal much."

I said I understood and touched her cheek just below the swelling. She closed her eyes, squeezing them ever so slightly. "Go quickly now," she whispered. "And come home safe."

Then I was off, driving too fast and shifting gears as if I'd been doing it all my life. There were no police about, nor any other people at that early hour, either. Yet someone must have been watching for me at the church, for Claire opened the side door as soon as I arrived, and Joseph and Ruby scurried onto the floor of the Model T's backseat and covered themselves with the drop cloth. Neither said a word. Not even Ruby, who looked like she'd just woke up.

Claire came out, too, and touched my elbow where it rested on the car. "Be careful," she said. Then she favored me with a brave, weary smile so beautiful that the memory of it lodged deep inside me. I told her I would, and drove off fast enough that not five minutes later I had the Model T backed up as close to the new house's servants' quarters as I could get. Joseph and Ruby hopped out and sprinted to the door, dodging stacks of new lumber and bricks. It wasn't until we were inside, breathing the smell of fresh-cut wood and smoke, that Joseph finally spoke.

"They're putting the torch to Greenwood, Will. Shooting anyone who resists and taking whatever they want."

I said I'd heard the same, but that there was no telling truth from rumor just then. Then I tried to change the subject, asking if they'd heard anything about their ma. To which Joseph replied that the best they could hope for was that she'd been taken to McNulty Park or Convention Hall, or possibly the fairgrounds. That's when Ruby chimed in, saying: "Anyone hurts our ma, I'll hunt 'em down and kill 'em myself."

"Hush now," Joseph said softly. Ruby sniffed and scooted backwards against the wall.

"I'll find her for you," I said. "Just promise you'll stay put until me or Mama comes back to give you the all clear."

Joseph frowned. Said, "You really think we're safe here?"

"Safe enough," I replied. "Just stay out of sight and you should be fine." Then I managed to distract Ruby a little, telling her how Mama had put two pairs of my skivvies in the rucksack. "I ain't wearing no boy's unmentionables!" she said, and stuck out her tongue. Which I took as a positive sign.

After that, I told them I'd best be going. Joseph thanked me again, and Ruby looked at me square. "You're a good man, Will Tillman," she said. Which sounded silly and overserious coming from her, but wonderful all the same. And those words buoyed my spirits all the way back to the Model T, until the smoke-filled northern sky and the gravity of the task I'd undertaken pulled them right back down again.

———

Cars were parked chockablock along the southern edge of Greenwood. White men and women milled about in the smoky haze, carrying baskets and sacks filled with stolen treasures from Negro homes: clothes, silver, lamps, china, paintings. Looters picked through the smoldering remains of buildings like vultures after a battle. I left the Model T just south of the worst of it and walked north to Jasper Street, where the Goodhopes' house should have been.

Ash and rubble and a shattered posy dish were all I found. I'd been on a fool's errand from the start, and my heart ached at the prospect of telling Joseph and Ruby their home was gone. Still, I hadn't given up on finding Mrs. Goodhope. So I headed back south, planning to look for her in the detention centers, until hysterical shrieks stopped me short.

It was Eunice, running up the street in a pale green dress too fine and formal to be streetwear. Stolen, no doubt, from some poor Booker T. girl who'd never get to wear it to her prom.

"They shot him, Will! They shot him!" she wailed. I ran towards her then, and when we met up, she clawed at my arm and dragged me towards a crowd of gawkers standing tight in a circle. "Move!" she screamed. And enough did so we could press through to the center. Which is where we found Clete.

At first I only stared, for the sight of the boy I'd grown up with, lying gutshot and bleeding in the street, was the stuff of dime novels and cowboy movies. Then Clete's eyes flickered open, and he whispered something so faint that I dropped to my knees and lifted his head onto my lap.

"It's all right," I told him. "Just you hang in there while someone fetches a doctor."

"You always were a terrible liar, Will," he whispered. Then his lips pulled back in pain and his body shivered in my arms and he spoke again, so soft I had to put my ear to his lips to hear.

"Vernon's gonna kill that brother and sister you got."

He coughed weakly, sending a fine spray of crimson

onto his chin. I told him to hush and save his strength, but he shook his head, saying, "No. Listen. While I was home changing clothes this morning, Mother picked up the telephone and overheard your mama talking to that pastor's wife on the party line. She told me what you were planning to do, and I told Vernon."

A gurgle caught at the back of his throat. He tried to cough, but only succeeded in quickening the flow of blood from his belly.

"Oh, Will... I've done bad things, and now I'm on my way to stand judgment..."

The sound in his throat closed down to a rattling gasp. And before I could lie and tell my friend I knew God would forgive him, he was gone.

The crowd pressed tighter. I set Clete's head down gentle on the street and shouted for them to get away. Only they didn't, so I screamed at them again and again until they'd cleared a space for me to push past them.

Eunice sat on a curb, weeping. When I asked her who'd shot Clete, she started crying harder. I lifted her up and shook her by the shoulders till she screamed how she didn't know, that the bullet had come from one of the houses. And I wanted so much to slap her then that it scared me. But I only pushed her backwards, and she cursed me and looked down and caught sight of my bloody handprints on the shoulders of her stolen dress and loosed a demon's shriek.

I stumbled off, numbed clear through to my soul, until the fact of Clete dying hit me full-on, along with what he'd said about Vernon Fish being out to kill Joseph and Ruby.

Then I ceased my walking altogether.

And ran.

Rowan

I don't believe in psychics or premonitions or fate. Still, something stopped my hand just as I was about to knock on the door.

I'd pleaded with James to call in sick again, but he said a third day in a row would get him busted back to clearing tables. I told him he was my Watson and I needed him. He said bullshit, he was my Sherlock, but that I'd be fine.

I wasn't so sure.

Still, I'd gone ahead and called Tru to tell him I'd be at work on Monday. Then I asked him how to get in touch with Tilda, because I wanted to see if she'd introduce me to her friend Opal. The one with the peach pie recipe. The one Joe Tillman had said was Ruby Goodhope's daughter.

An hour later I was standing on Opal Johnson's front porch.

Now or never, I told myself. *Knock.*
Just knock.

———

Opal Johnson was the jelly bean woman I'd seen using a walker at Arvin's funeral. Inside her house, she left the walker in a corner and steadied herself against furniture.

"Tilda says you're after my gramma's pie recipe," she said, with a dare-me-and-I'll-do-it gleam in her eye that reminded me of the picture of Ruby Goodhope on Joe's windowsill. "She doesn't think I'll give it to you, but wouldn't it just chap her hide if I did!"

I'd spent most of the night before thinking about whether or not I could convince the DA that Jerry Randall hadn't pushed Arvin in self-defense. And about how doing it would mean putting myself out there for every TV reporter, blogger, and racist comment troll to tear down.

When I wasn't obsessing about that, my overactive brain had bounced over to the skeleton and what James and I knew about it. I needed to patch everything together into a story that made sense. The problem was, every time I thought I had, I'd remember some random little detail that didn't fit and my whole theory would fall apart. By the time I actually made it to Opal Johnson's kitchen table, I was too tired and frustrated to worry about being delicate. Besides, Opal wasn't the delicate type.

"It *is* delicious pie," I told her. "But actually, I came here more about your mother than your grandmother's recipe. See, my friend and I visited a man named Joe Tillman in Pawhuska yesterday..."

I paused, hoping to catch some glimmer of recognition in Opal's smart brown eyes.

No such luck.

"Anyway," I went on, "Joe's grandparents built the house my family lives in, and my friend and I went up there to talk with him about what some workmen found underneath the floor of our servants' quarters a few weeks ago."

Opal's face was a mask of calm, but her foot jiggled underneath the table.

"Do you know what I'm talking about?" I asked.

The tapping stopped.

"You know who it is, don't you?"

She nodded.

"We found a receipt from the Victory Victrola Shop in the body's pocket," I said. "And the police anthropologist believes the man who died was young. And black."

Opal blinked slowly.

"Ruby *was* your mother, wasn't she? And Joseph was your uncle?"

"That's right," she said.

"Is it him?" I asked. "Is the skeleton Joseph?"

Opal laced her fingers together and put her hands in her lap.

"I'm sorry, dear," she said. "But I'm afraid my answer is the same one Joe must have given you yesterday: I can't say."

My pulse throbbed in the achy knot at the back of my head.

"Let me guess—you promised your mom on her deathbed," I said.

Opal laughed. "Gracious no, dear. Nothing so dramatic as that. But Mother asked me not to discuss the matter, so I don't."

I stood up quickly, nearly knocking over my chair. The old familiar pinch at the top of my nose was back, and I didn't want to cry in front of a woman I barely knew.

"Thank you for your time." I turned fast enough toward the door that it must have come across as rude. Mom's Mercedes keys were already in my hand.

"Rowan!"

I stopped.

"Yes, ma'am?"

"Do you always give up so easy?"

"I just thought..."

"I know you did. But hasn't anyone ever told you it takes old women like me a while to warm up our engines?"

"I...I'm sorry," I stammered.

She shook her head and sighed.

"Don't apologize, young lady. Just help me to the parlor. And listen."

"There it is," Opal said. "My grandmother's Model 14. But what you're really after is the smaller machine sitting on top."

She pointed to a Victrola cabinet that was as tall as Uncle Chotch's, but not quite as fancy. The thing on top of it was a strange-looking box with a hose and a small horn attached to it.

"What is that?" I asked.

"A Dictaphone."

She let go of my arm, took a cigar box down from the bookshelf beside her, and handed me a key from inside it. "Here you go," she said. "The Dictaphone cylinders are in that locked cupboard over there."

I unlocked the door. The shelves inside were filled with rows of antique cardboard cylinders marked EDISON GOLD MOULDED RECORDS ECHO ALL OVER THE WORLD. Each was numbered in black, starting at one, ending at forty.

My fingertips slid along their curved fronts as I asked Opal what was on them.

"Answers," she said. "To some of your questions, at least. Mother carried the rest of them to her grave. But I never did have children of my own, and it would be nice to pass on what I *do* know before I'm gone. Besides, Tilda said you're the girl Arvin was trying to help when that evil man killed him. I expect the confession on those cylinders won't be your first clue that the world can be a hard place."

351

I took out the cylinder marked #1.

"You're sure you want to know?" she asked.

"I'm sure," I said.

Opal smiled sadly. "Then you'd best settle in and make yourself comfortable, young lady. It's going to be a long afternoon."

WILLIAM

Maple Ridge was still as a grave. No children playing, no gardeners snipping hedges, no workmen
hammering.

But Clete's father's Cadillac was there, parked in front
of a three-story mansion just north of Mama and Pop's
new place. The sight of it froze up every gear inside me
and near stopped my heart.

Vernon had found Ruby and Joseph.

I got out of the Model T, cursing myself for leaving
my Springfield in the truck the night before, and slipped
along the northern wall of our new house. Church bells
tolled ten times in the distance. I peeked around the corner. Saw that the door to the servants' quarters was open.
Caught the wretched stink of a Maduro Robusto min-
gling with the smoke from Greenwood.

Then a gunshot shattered the air into a million jagged pieces, each one sharpened on the high, thin scream that followed. I catapulted across the yard, lurching to a stop in front of the door.

Vernon Fish stood not five feet inside, Maybelle at the end of one arm, Ruby's neck hooked in the crook of the other. Joseph slumped against the wall at the far end of the room, blood seeping from a hole in his left shoulder. And Vernon must not have heard me, for he rubbed his cheek slow across Ruby's, saying: "That's just for starters, boy. I don't aim to let Maybelle have her way with you till I've had mine with your sister."

Joseph said nothing, only heaved forward onto his belly and commenced to dragging himself across the floor towards Vernon. Vernon pressed the gun to Ruby's temple. Joseph stopped.

I raised my hand, hoping Joseph would notice the motion and see me standing there. And though his eyes never shifted and his expression never changed, I knew from the way he held his blink half a second too long that he'd seen me.

Vernon lowered Maybelle and ran the back of his hand down Ruby's blouse. My heart sped up. I bent my knees, dropping down until my fingers wrapped around a brick sitting atop the pile next to the door. I took a careful step forward, making ready to pounce. That's when my foot hit the twig.

Vernon swung around quick as a cat, Ruby hanging from his arm like a broken rag doll. His eyes burned behind the curl of smoke from his cigar. And at the sight of me, he laughed out loud.

"Well, shit twice and fall back in," he spit. "Old Half-breed decided to show up after all!"

I drew myself tall as I could and stepped inside.

Vernon pushed Maybelle's barrel against Ruby's head. Said, "Now, you just put down that brick and don't go getting any wild ideas, boy, or I'll shoot all three of you dead."

I set the brick on the ground and forced myself to smile, saying, "There's no need for that, Mr. Fish. I've come to apologize."

Which I reckon wasn't what he'd expected to hear.

"What do you mean?" he growled.

"I mean I've been to Greenwood and seen what's transpired. I talked to Pop, too, and he explained how he finally saw the light and joined the Klan, and why I need to be a man and do the same. I understand now, Mr. Fish. White folks have let things get out of control and need to set them right again. I may only be half white, but I aim to be part of that, sir. I truly do."

"How?" he asked warily.

I took a step forward. Vernon's arm tightened, lifting Ruby's toes off the ground. "I'll show you," I said, raising both my empty hands. "If you'll just allow me to get something from that boy's pocket."

Vernon shifted sideways, watching close as he let me pass. I went to Joseph and pulled out his wallet. His eyes were downcast.

"Here," I said, showing Vernon the Victrola receipt. "This is what I came for."

I stood up slow, putting the paper and the wallet on the floor in front of him. Then I stepped back, and he dropped Ruby and told her to pick them up. "Do it!" he shouted when she didn't respond. And she did.

"Hold it so I can read it," Vernon barked. Ruby grasped the receipt on either side and raised it high. And then I saw it: a quick little blink my way that told me she was with me.

Vernon scanned the paper. Said, "What are all these figures about?"

"Pop sold this boy a Victrola in a moment of weakness," I told him. "A while later, he came back while Pop was out, claiming he'd forgot his receipt. I believed him, and made one up for him myself. At the time I thought I was doing right, only last night I realized what a fool I've been. Why, all this boy has to do is show that paper around. Then Pop's name could get drug through the mud, and our business right along with it. I couldn't let it stand, Mr. Fish. That's why I brought the boy and his sister here—so I could get the receipt back and make sure neither one of them ever got a chance to ruin my pop."

Vernon's cheek twitched. "And just how did you plan on doing that?" he asked.

I told him I'd aimed to sweet-talk Joseph into giving me the receipt, and once that was done, I'd meant to get my shotgun from the Model T parked out on the street and finish things for good. "There's plenty of places to hide bodies around a construction site," I said. "Places no one would ever look."

Vernon's mouth pulled up in a nasty leer. And he folded the receipt into his wallet and put it in his back pocket, then turned and slapped Ruby so hard that she half stumbled, half flew across the room and onto the floor. Her hand went to her mouth.

"Come here, boy," he said, which I did. And he yanked me closer and laughed as Ruby spit out the tooth he'd knocked free.

"You first," he whispered into my ear.

I stammered that I didn't know what he meant.

"Hell if you don't," he said.

I told him maybe I did, but I wasn't sure how to go about it. He rolled his eyes and pulled at the buttons on his trousers with one hand while the other kept Maybelle trained on Ruby. A feral look came into his eyes as his gaze locked onto her like a wolf's does its prey. He went closer and toed her with his boot.

I looked quick over my shoulder. Saw blood streaked across the boards from where Joseph had quietly dragged himself. Then I felt a tug at my pant leg, and when I looked down, it was him, holding the brick to his chest.

Vernon knelt over Ruby.

Joseph reached for my hand.

Vernon pushed Ruby's knees apart, cursing her for fighting him.

I pulled Joseph up. For just an instant, we looked at the brick together. Then we looked at each other, and we knew.

It happened all at once: the brick caving in Vernon's skull, him collapsing onto Ruby. Then Ruby was kicking and screaming underneath Vernon's twitching body, and Joseph was sinking to his knees. I heaved Vernon's bulk aside and lifted Ruby into my arms and cradled her close, whispering she should look away. Vernon's body jerked and twitched, and blood slicked out across the wood. Forever, it seemed. Only, in the end, it wasn't.

Rowan

I'm running again. Six miles this morning, seven next week. Which means I'll have to wake up even earlier to get to work on time. I don't mind, though. Running makes me feel normal and strong. So does being at the clinic. And those are two things I really, really need right now: to feel normal. And strong.

Mom and Dad got here a few minutes ago. This isn't the courthouse where Sheriff McCullough kept Dick Rowland safe while Greenwood burned—they tore that down a long time ago. This new one is tall and ugly, and at eleven thirty, the three of us will go inside so I can tell the district attorney what really happened the morning Arvin died.

I don't want to testify in court. But since the DA agreed to reconsider bringing charges against Jerry Randall, and since I'm the only eyewitness who can provide evidence that it wasn't just a crime, but a hate crime, too, there's a pretty good chance I'll end up on the stand.

As for Will's story, I've kept that to myself. I know I'll have to tell James eventually, because that's what best friends do.

Opal promised that someday, when she's gone, the wax cylinders, the Victrola, and the Dictaphone will come to me. I told her I didn't deserve them, and that if they were mine, I couldn't keep the stories behind them quiet like she and Joe Tillman had. She said that was exactly why I should have them.

Beside me on the bench, Mom shields her eyes from the sun and looks up at the courthouse. She's ready for battle, but I can tell she's nervous. And for once, Dad doesn't look so sure that everything's going to turn out the way he wants.

"You ready?" Mom asks.

I focus on the Tulsa skyline behind us and think about the stories I've learned this summer—the ones with happy endings, the ones without, and the ones that still need to be told.

"Yes," I say.

"I'm ready."

WILLIAM

It's 1926 now, five years since the Dreamland Theatre and all the rest of Greenwood burned. Some days it feels like a lifetime. Others, no more than a heartbeat.

I've tried to put the worst of it behind me. Problem is, history has a way of sneaking back around. Like last month, when Joseph wrote to say he'd gotten his degree from the University at Buffalo and planned to attend medical school there. And like when Ruby's letter arrived just four days ago, telling me Joseph had drowned trying to save a child who slipped into the river above Niagara Falls.

It's that false sense of distance between the present and the past that set me to thinking how our tale deserves telling. Which is why I've endeavored to record what transpired in my own voice on these wax cylinders. And besides, facts have emerged since that night that no true account of Vernon's death can omit. Facts I learned from Mama when she visited last summer, and which she herself learned from a Georgia lawman who'd come around, making inquiries about Vernon Fish. Only it wasn't me or Joseph he was after. It was Vernon himself.

As the lawman explained things to Mama, Vernon was actually Virgil Fisher out of Decatur, Georgia. A man raised in a sharecropper's shack by a white father who'd taught him to pick cotton and hate Negroes equally well. What that sharecropper failed to tell his son, though, was that Vernon's own mama had been a Negress with skin so fair she passed for white, and that he'd sent her and their newborn second son packing after the babe was born dark-skinned. He'd kept Vernon, though, for he needed help with the crops, and company, too. And Vernon passed for white with ease till he was a grown man, never knowing the truth about his mama. Leastways, not until she died and his brother tracked him down to tell him.

Needless to say, the brother's skin hadn't lightened any since he was born. And, faced with a truth he couldn't bear, Vernon flew into a rage and beat his own brother dead with a shovel.

He'd fled to Oklahoma after that, leaving his brother's body in a dried-up well on his father's plot. But when his father got kicked in the chest by a horse and killed a few years later, the sharecropper who worked the land after him found the body and reported it to the police. Vernon hadn't bothered getting rid of his brother's wallet, so it took the authorities no time to figure out who the dead man was. And at the request of the landowner who'd leased the Fishers their parcel in the first place, Georgia officials were making inquiries as to Vernon's whereabouts.

Now, I can't say as I'm worried overmuch that Vernon's bones will be found. No one knows how many black men were killed during the riot, no one much seems to care. And it's poetic justice of the grimmest sort, I suppose, that for all his hatred and bile, Vernon Fish ended up just another murdered Negro whose death never merited looking into—or even remembering.

Besides, me and Joseph hid the body well, covering it with quicklime from the mason's supply and wrapping it in the tarp from the Model T. After that, we pulled up all the planks Vernon and Joseph had bled on, flipped them so the blood wouldn't show, and set the body on the dirt underneath before putting the planks back in place. When the workmen showed up a few days later, they laid a hardwood floor over top of him, never suspecting they were hammering nails into Vernon Fish's coffin.

As for me, I left Tulsa soon as Mama got settled with her cousin Margaret in Pawhuska. She forgave Pop for taking Angelina's family away that awful morning, but she never could forget. They sold their fine new place to an oilman just a few months after it was complete. Pop stayed in the house I grew up in. I moved north to Kansas City and opened a Victrola shop of my own.

All are welcome on my sales floor, and I'll extend credit to any man or woman who can show evidence of a steady income. I still go by Tillman, though for discretion's sake, I've abandoned the first and middle names given to me at birth. Only my beloved wife, Claire, still calls me Will, and only within the walls of the house we call home.

As for the details of what occurred in Tulsa later that day, June 1, 1921, I can only attest to the few I know. Like the fact that after Pop found the body Joseph and I had picked up on the street, he dumped it onto one of the trucks carrying Negro corpses out of the city and considered the matter closed. And that Angelina's family was held at McNulty Park until Mama got them out, swearing seven ways to Sunday that their mother was our cook. Their father turned up at the fairgrounds detention center two days later, shaken and bruised, but alive.

Up in Greenwood, Booker T. survived the rioters' torches and served as a hospital for the wounded. That's where they treated Joseph, and where he and Ruby were reunited with their mama. And that's where I delivered Joseph's Victrola, along with a stack of records for them and the patients and doctors and nurses at the hospital to listen to. I never did ask Pop for permission to make the delivery, and decided on my own that the records should be a donation from him. I did, however, put two dollars and fifty cents in the register to cover Joseph's finance fee. And every year since then, on June 1, Mama has found a fresh-baked peach pie on her doorstep in Pawhuska, along with a card signed simply, "Love, Ruby."

In the weeks and months following the riot, Tulsa city government refused to accept any of the emergency funds donated by good souls all over the country to help in the aid and care of those left homeless. Greenwood business owners struggled after their insurance companies denied payment on the grounds that the riot was an act of man, not God. But they rebuilt on their own, proud and strong. Even Mount Zion Baptist Church rose again, despite the congregation owing near the full eighty-thousand-dollar mortgage from the new building they'd been forced to watch burn. Proving, I suppose, that while a body can be burned to ash, the spirit inside it cannot.

But pleased as I am that Greenwood rebuilt, I'll always remember it the way I saw it first: lights flickering on over the Dreamland Theatre, families strolling along streets they'd built together. For on that warm spring night, it wasn't just a promise I beheld, but a thing real as bricks and mortar and hope.

AUTHOR'S NOTE

Between the evening of May 31 and the afternoon of June 1, 1921, white rioters looted the thriving African American section of Tulsa known as Greenwood. After taking what they wanted, they burned the rest to the ground. Thirty-five blocks were destroyed. At least 8,000 black men, women, and children lost everything they owned. More than 1,200 homes and businesses were reduced to ash, along with churches. A hospital. A school. It was one of the deadliest race riots in US history.

No one's sure how many people died, but historians put the number at around 300. And though some victims were white, most were not. Tulsans were shot, lynched, burned, and dragged through the streets behind cars that night because their skin was brown. In the aftermath, not a single white man or woman faced charges.

As soon as the smoke cleared, the city started to forget. For more than fifty years, references to the riot were scrubbed from history books, and black and white children alike grew up without hearing a word about it. That's changing now, but not fast enough. I hope you'll want to learn more after reading this book. Online resources, including websites for the Tulsa Historical Society, the *Tulsa World*, and the *New York Times*, are great places to start.*

If you're wondering where fact ends and fiction begins in *Dreamland Burning*, a good guideline is that any characters with dialogue are fictional. I only made up a few places, like the Two-Knock, the Victory Victrola Shop, and Vernon's tobacco store. Speakeasies, brothels, and Jim Crow laws were real. The Ku Klux Klan had just started oozing its way into the state in 1921. In the years following the riot, membership exploded.

The term *Tulsa race riot* is controversial. Some people prefer *black holocaust*, others use *race massacre* or *race war*. I've gone with *race riot* not because I disagree with the accuracy of the other labels, but because it's the most

---

* "1921 Tulsa Race Riot," Tulsa Historical Society & Museum, accessed December 17, 2015, http://tulsahistory.org/learn/online-exhibits/the-tulsa-race-riot.

"The Questions That Remain," *Tulsa World*, accessed December 17, 2015, http://www.tulsaworld.com/app/race-riot/default.html.

"Unearthing a Riot," Brent Staples, *New York Times*, December 19, 1999, http://www.nytimes.com/1999/12/19/magazine/unearthing-a-riot.html.

commonly used historical term. And honestly, I believe *riot* is a fair description of what *white* Tulsans did.

Some characters in the book use derogatory terms for African Americans and Native Americans, though not as freely as they would have in 1921. These words are ugly, offensive, and hateful, but I chose to include them because I felt that blunting the sharp edges of racism in a book about genocide would be a mistake.

The research behind Rowan's, Will's, Joseph's, and Ruby's stories would not have been possible without the University of Tulsa's Department of Special Collections and University Archives at McFarlin Library. Or without resources made available by the Oklahoma Commission to Study the Tulsa Race Riot of 1921, the Tulsa Historical Society & Museum, the Oklahoma Historical Society, the *Tulsa World*, the Osage Nation, the National Museum of the American Indian, and the Tulsa City-County Library. I'm also indebted to reporting in *This Land Press*, the *New York Times*, and *Ebony*, and to the research and writings of Tim Madigan, Dr. Scott Ellsworth, Hannibal B. Johnson, and James S. Hirsch.

Marc Carlson, Dr. Brian Hosmer, Dr. Robert Pickering, Wilson Pipestem, Dr. Robert Allen, Marvin Shirley, Matt Latham, and Jayme Howland all shared their insights and expertise with me so generously—I'm grateful to them all. Huge thanks also go to my eagle-eyed readers Sundee Frazier, Okcate Smith, and Linda Bolin, to my fact checker, Norma Jean Garriton, and to the lady with the hyphens, Christine Ma.

As ever, I'm thankful for Rachel Orr at Prospect Agency, who keeps my chin up and my head straight. Then there's the wonderful team at Little, Brown Books for Young Readers: Marcie Lawrence, Jen Graham, Victoria Stapleton, Jenny Choy, Lisa Moraleda, Stefanie Hoffman, Allegra Green, Jane Lee, Kheryn Callender, and Esther Cajahuaringa. Thank you, all. And thank you to my editors, Pam Garfinkel (who saw the potential), Bethany Strout (who nudged it along), and the very smart and ever-patient Allison Moore (who made it better…and made it happen).

I owe a special debt of gratitude to my friend and reader Dr. Jocelyn Lee Payne, whose work at the John Hope Franklin Center for Reconciliation helped promote racial justice and social unity in Tulsa and beyond. She has been a true touchstone.

Last but most definitely not least, thank you, S, Z, and S, for putting up with Deadline Jen and I-Can't-Right-Now-I'm-Working Mom.

Speaking of which…

Like Rowan's mom, I don't believe that history holds easy answers or simple lessons, because those answers and lessons are stretched out over thousands—millions—of untold stories. But I do believe that if we seek those stories out, and if we listen to them and talk to each other with open hearts and minds, we can start to heal. I believe that good people working together can create meaningful change. And I believe that the Josephs, Rubys, and Wills of this world are stronger than the Vernon Fishes.

Jen Latham
Tulsa, 2017

DISCUSSION GUIDE

1. *Dreamland Burning* opens with Rowan discovering a skeleton in her family's back house. What does that skeleton symbolize, and how does it shape the way a reader will experience the rest of the story?

2. Early in the novel, Rowan quotes Geneva, saying, "The dead always have stories to tell. They just need the living to listen." What does she mean by this?

3. Why do you think the author chose to write about the Tulsa race riot/massacre from both Will's and Rowan's perspectives? And if Rowan had never found the skeleton, how might she have had to grapple with what happened in 1921 in her hometown anyway?

4. When Will approaches Clarence Banks at the Two-Knock, he looks back at Clete and sees "disappointment in his stare. Pity, too, as if I'd failed him and every other white boy in the world" (page 21). Given Will's own mixed racial heritage, what is the significance of this observation? How does Clete's "disappointment" influence Will's behavior?

5. At the end of the novel, we learn that Will recorded his story on wax cylinders five years after the events of 1921. Do you think he would have described what happened the same way if he'd done it immediately after those events occurred? How might Rowan's story differ if she waited five years to tell it?

6. Both Will and Rowan have mixed ethnic heritages, yet Rowan is perceived by those around her as being "black," while Will is generally regarded as "white." How does this influence each character's understanding of the racially charged events occurring to and around them?

7. Will's mother is wealthy, as is Rowan's father. How does the relative financial privilege of each character influence the way they experience and think about racism?

8. At what points in the novel do Will's and Rowan's financial privilege cease to protect them from discrimination?

9. Dr. Woods is surprised that Rowan attends a largely white private school instead of a more diverse public high school. Why do you think Rowan's parents decided to send her there? Do you agree or disagree with their decision? If the choice were left to Rowan,

which school do you think she would choose at the novel's end?

10. In what ways does the physical layout and socioeconomic segregation of contemporary Tulsa seem to be influenced by Greenwood's destruction in 1921?

11. When Rowan and James debate the state of race relations in 1921 versus the state of race relations today, Rowan says, "I'm just glad things are better now" (page 70). James argues back that "the crime's different but the problem's the same" (page 72). What point is each trying to make? Do you agree more strongly with one or the other? Why?

12. The experiences of African Americans and Native Americans in Tulsa in 1921 were in some ways similar but in other ways very different. Are there specific instances in the novel where this stands out? Why do you think this was the case?

13. How do Rowan's experiences working at the Jackson Clinic shape her? How do Will's experiences working at the Victory Victrola Shop shape him?

14. When Will visits Addie to apologize for what happened to Clarence after the incident at the Two-Knock, he says, "I never meant for him to die" (page

155). Addie responds, "But you never meant for him not to." How much blame do you believe Will deserves for Clarence's death? How much blame does Addie deserve? And how much responsibility for Clarence's death was out of their hands?

15. On page 191, Mrs. Chase tells Rowan, "There are things your father will never understand that you and I do. Things he *can't* understand. But he tries, and I love him." Do you think Mrs. Chase would agree that love is enough to overcome the complicated racial issues facing society today? If not, why?

16. When Will tries to warn Ruby away from Vernon Fish on page 203, he tells her, "You don't know what he'd do if he caught you." Ruby replies, "Course I do, Will. Same thing they're gonna try and do to that man in the jailhouse." What does this exchange tell us about how Ruby and Will understand the world they live in?

17. Who were Dick Rowland and Sarah Page? Was the incident between them in the Drexel Building's elevator the true cause of the riot/massacre, or did more deeply rooted social and economic forces lead to Greenwood's destruction? If the latter, what effects did similar forces have in other parts of the United States throughout the twentieth century?

18. What parallels do you see between Arvin's death and the deaths in Greenwood during the riot/massacre?

19. When Joseph contemplates shooting Mr. Geddison, the wounded white rioter, on page 316, Will considers trying to talk him out of it. Ultimately, though, Will decides that "given all we'd seen that night, it didn't seem right, me trying to influence his decision one way or the other. So I rose, silent, and stood at his side." Why do you think Will makes this choice? Is it a decision you agree with?

20. Joseph Tillman and Opal Johnson are living links to history for Rowan and James. What can be done to preserve the experiences, memories, and wisdom of people who live through significant historical events? What other events of the last century do you think are especially important for us to document?

21. Who killed Vernon Fish—Joseph, Will, or the two of them together? In the end, does this distinction matter?

22. How, if at all, did it affect your understanding of Vernon Fish to learn that he was "passing" as white?

23. Many characters in *Dreamland Burning* change over the course of the novel, some for the better, some for

the worse. Which characters do you feel changed the most dramatically? What experiences shaped those changes, and did you end up liking the characters less or more at the novel's end?

24. Not a single white Tulsan faced charges for the murders, looting, and destruction that took place during the riot/massacre. How is this echoed in current events today?

25. On page 191, Rowan's mother tells her, "The lives that ended that night mattered. It was a mistake for this city to try to forget, and it's an even bigger one to pretend everything's fine now. Black men and women are dying today for the same reasons they did in 1921. And we have to call that out, Rowan. Every single time." How much—and how—do Rowan's actions after Arvin's death reflect her understanding of her mother's words?

26. What does Will mean when he says, on page 365, "While a body can be burned to ash, the spirit inside it cannot"? Would Rowan agree?

Turn the page for a preview of

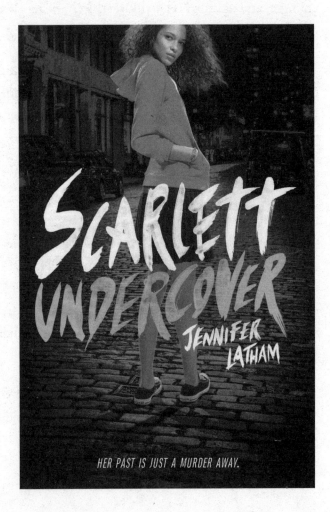

AVAILABLE NOW

1

The kid was cute. Her bare, knobbly legs swung back and forth like pendulums between the chipped legs of my client chair. Plastic safety goggles rested on her forehead, held tight by an elastic band that circled her head and pooched her bobbed brown hair up at the crown. She was thin. Delicate, even. But her eyes were clear and blue and smart.

"I think my brother killed someone."

It was a hell of a thing to say, especially for someone who'd just walked into my office wearing a pale pink jumper only a mother could love. I waited for her to keep talking. She didn't.

"How about you tell me your name before we get into that?" I said.

"Gemma Archer. My brother's Oliver." Her hands twisted the strap of her bag.

"Nice to meet you, Gemma. I'm Scarlett."

She nodded like she already knew that. Which, of course, she did.

"Okay. Now, exactly who do you think your brother killed?"

"His friend Quinn Johnson," she said in a voice flat as truck stop pancakes.

The name sounded familiar, but I couldn't place it.

"He's the boy they pulled out of Las Almas Bay yesterday. The one who jumped off the Baker Street Bridge," she said quietly.

Things clicked into place. I'd just read about Quinn Johnson's death in the paper that morning. The thing was, it hadn't been murder; it'd been a suicide. I looked over at the half-eaten bagel on my desk. My stomach grumbled.

"Well, kid," I said, "I don't think you need me. Two witnesses saw your brother's friend jump off that bridge all on his own. It's an awful mess, and I'm sorry for him and his family and anyone who knew him. But your brother wasn't even there."

"You're wrong," she said. "Oliver might not have been with Quinn when he died, but that doesn't mean he wasn't responsible."

It had happened before—me being wrong, that is. So I shrugged and played along.

"How old's your brother?"

"Fifteen."

"And what makes you think he had anything to do with the Johnson kid's death?"

She chewed her lip, looked around like she wished she could disappear into the walls.

"He's all dark, like a light went out inside him."

I told her she'd have to be a little more specific than that.

"I don't know. He's just…*dark!* And he doesn't talk to me or see me or play his guitar anymore. He cleans his room now, too, and mostly only comes home to eat. Then, when he *is* home, he won't put his phone down. I thought he was on it a lot before, but it's crazy lately."

She got quiet again.

"Look, kid," I said. "I'm not one to turn down a job, but it doesn't sound like there's much I can do for you. Have you talked to your parents about all this?"

Her shoulders slumped, and a soft little hiccup hitched in her throat.

"I tried." She didn't bother to wipe away the tear slipping down her cheek. "They won't listen. No one will."

I dug deep and found my patient voice. "Don't you think your parents would have noticed if your brother was in trouble?"

"My parents don't notice anything," she whispered.

That got me. Right in the gut.

"People change, kid," I said, softening. "And your brother must be pretty messed up after what happened to his friend."

She looked lost. Her mouth trembled. Her head shook back and forth.

"But he's not! Not even a little! That's the problem. Plus I saw him and Quinn together in the courtyard after school last week and..."

Her voice faded to nothing. Her shoulders shook.

"And what? What happened?"

She paused. Gathered herself.

"I was up by the gate and only heard a little. Quinn said, 'We can't let them,' and Oliver said something I couldn't hear. Then Quinn..."

She looked up at me like she wasn't sure she should go on. I gave her my best encouraging smile. She took a deep breath.

"He said, 'Eff you and eff the rest of them, too. You're all crazy.'"

"Only he didn't say *eff*, right? He said the *F* word?"

She nodded.

"What did your brother do then?"

She looked at her hands. Sniffled.

"Gemma?"

"He said, 'Tell us where he is, or we'll kill you and Sam both.'"

"And you don't know who *he* is?"

"No."

"Who's Sam?"

"Quinn's little brother."

"What happened next?"

"Quinn punched him."

"They fought?"

"No." She shook her head. "Oliver just smiled. And even though his mouth was bleeding, he pulled his finger across his throat real slow, like he was threatening to kill Quinn. Then he walked away."

"Where was Oliver when Quinn went to the bridge?"

"At home. But it's like I said, for the last few weeks he's been all dead inside. I know he didn't actually *push* Quinn, but if it weren't for Oliver, I don't think Quinn would have jumped."

I sat back in my chair and laced my fingers together behind my head.

"You know, there's no guarantee I'll find anything if I take the case. And even if I do, you might not like it."

"I've got money." She pulled a wad of cash the size of a melon out of her backpack. "What else am I supposed to spend this on?"

A long list of things came to mind, but I kept them to myself. That's me. Always thinking.

I leaned forward and folded my hands on the desk. "How about I chew on this awhile and get back to you?"

Gemma's lips quivered, but she kept it together.

"I just want my real brother back," she said. Then she gave me her number and walked herself to the door.

"I'll call you," I said.

She didn't stop. Just dropped her chin and kept on walking.

A couple of hours later, my breakfast was long gone, and Gemma was still on my mind. Rain pattered against the window behind me. Tires swished on Carroll Street's wet pavement two stories below. On any given weekday it would have been busy down there, full of people with places to go. But at eleven o'clock on a gray Saturday morning, the only soul out was the General, peeing against a Dumpster in the alley across the street. He was the cheerful kind of neighborhood drunk who'd tip his hat and say, "Thank ye, guv'nor," when people gave him sandwiches or coffee or spare change. He looked up, saw me in the window, and waved with his free hand. I waved back, shifted my focus to the water stain on the ceiling for modesty's sake, and pondered what Gemma had told me.

She was sincere. I'd give her that. And underneath the layer of cute she wore like camouflage, there was a toughness to her—a kind of grit—that I liked. Maybe my first impression had been wrong, and she wasn't just some hysterical kid making up fairy tales. Maybe there actually was something to what she'd said. Besides, who was I to argue when there was cash on the table?

At the very least, I could nose around and see what the brother was up to, figure out what the fight between him and his friend had been about, and give Gemma a better story to tell herself about the whole deal. I could help a sad little girl feel like someone cared.

I drank a glass of water at the sink in the corner and pushed back my hair. It was black, kinky-curled, and stuck out from my head every which way. My hair had a mind of its own, and just then it was asking for a fight.

"Wear the *hijab* like *Ummi* did," Reem would say, "and you'll never have to worry about bad hair days."

But headscarves weren't my thing. Never had been. Not even before cancer swallowed my mother whole.

I dialed Gemma's cell.

"It's Scarlett," I said when she picked up. "I'll take the case."

"Thank you." Her voice was small. Relieved. I asked if it was a good time to come over. She said it was and gave me her address. "I really mean it," she whispered. "Thank you."

"Thank me after I've done something, kid," I said, and hung up.

I grabbed my favorite purple tam from the coat hook and put it on. A raincoat would have been nice, too, but all I had was the fly's eye–green umbrella Mook had given me from the Laundromat's lost and found a few months back.

I put the umbrella in my backpack and gave my Goodwill jeans, white T-shirt, and secondhand men's houndstooth coat a once-over. If I smiled nice and behaved, the outfit would do for a visit to the Archers'. I didn't look like a private detective. I didn't look like an orphan. And that was just the way I liked it.

2

Gemma's apartment was in a strip of converted warehouses off Daly Street, on the north end of Las Almas Bay. They were trendy, expensive, and full of people who never took time to look out their own windows and enjoy the view.

By the time I got there, the morning rain had lifted, and people with cloth shopping bags and expensive baby strollers were out and about. Farther south, Daly was nothing but pawnshops, liquor stores, and grimy little joints that would cash your paycheck for half of what it was worth. This far north, it was all organic grocers and coffee shops.

Ten minutes and six nail salons later, I was standing in front of Gemma's building. The place was flat-roofed and long, boring as a nun's underwear, and full of blank-looking picture windows. Gemma was an Archer. The Archers lived on the top floor. I pressed their intercom button, smiled for the camera, and wondered how many freckled, sixteen-year-old brown girls showed up on their video monitor any given day. The door buzzed. I went in and took the freight-sized elevator up.

Gemma opened the door in her goggles and stepped back to let me in. Her movements were quick. Unhappy.

"Hi," she said.

"Your folks home?"

"They're at work. Dad owns Archer Construction. It's a big deal. Mom does interior design."

"What about Oliver?"

She gave me a somber look. "He's here."

"How about an introduction?"

"Come on," she said, and led me down a hall lined with framed black-and-white photos of skyscrapers. The carpet under our feet was thick enough to lose an ankle in. Spotlights lit the pictures like Rembrandts.

"Those are my dad's." She motioned toward the frames. I gave them a closer look.

"He owns all those buildings?" I asked.

"No. He built them."

I was impressed.

We passed an archway leading to a white-walled room with white leather furniture, floor-length white curtains, and white rugs over bleached hardwoods. Lionfish roamed an enormous saltwater aquarium.

"Fish were Dad's hobby last year," Gemma said when she saw me looking. "They were supposed to help him with stress. Now he just pays a guy to clean the tank."

"Maybe he should have tried goldfish first," I said. She shrugged and kept walking until the hall dead-ended at a closed door.

"Ollllivvvverrrr!" She hammered on the wood with a pale fist. There was shuffling behind the door before it opened.

Oliver was easy on the eyes. Handsome, even, in a boy band kind of way. He looked like he worked out, and the zit fairy had only paid a courtesy call instead of an extended visit.

"What?" He scanned me with his blue eyes like a cashier scans frozen peas.

"Oliver, this is my friend Scarlett. I wanted you to meet her."

"Hello, Scarlett. It's a pleasure to make your acquaintance."

He didn't sound like he meant it.

"The pleasure's all mine."

I didn't sound like I meant it, either.

I stuck out my hand, meaning for it to feel like a challenge. Oliver hesitated, his top lip curling into a sneer before he gave in and took hold of my fingers with a grip three notches too tight. As he did, the sleeve of his rugby shirt pulled back, exposing a line of angry red scabs along the inside of his wrist. He noticed that I noticed, jerked his hand back, jammed his fists into his pockets.

"Aren't you a little...mature to be hanging out with a nine-year-old?" His voice had gone hard.

"It's a Big Sister kind of thing," I said.

He looked at Gemma. Gemma looked worried.

"Funny," he said. "She's hardly underprivileged. And she has a *real* big brother."

"Yet she still came to me...." The sweetness in my voice was anything but.

Oliver scowled. "If you'll excuse me, I've got things to do."

He grabbed the messenger bag leaning against his

bookshelves and pushed past us, slamming the bedroom door as he went. A few seconds later, the front door slammed, too.

Gemma slipped her palm into mine. I wasn't much of a hand-holder, but just then I didn't mind the touch of someone warm and good.

The kid was all right.

Her brother was not.

About the Author

Jennifer Latham is an army brat with a soft spot for babies, books, and poorly behaved dogs. She's the author of *Scarlett Undercover* and *Dreamland Burning* and lives in Tulsa, Oklahoma, with her husband and two daughters.